Death at Dawn

A Crime Novel
By

MOURAD MOURAD

First published by EARTH Pictures in 2023
Copyright © Mourad Mourad
The moral right of the author has been asserted

Photos Credits
EARTH Pictures

British Library Cataloguing-in-Publication Data
A catalogue record for this book is available from the British
Library and the Lebanese National Library
ISBN 978-9953-0-5537-4

Designed and printed by EARTH Pictures

Published by
EARTH Pictures Ltd
Registered in England and Wales
Registration Number: 08581401

Death at Dawn
A Crime Novel

Mourad Mourad

was born in 1978 and raised in Ras Nhach, Batroun
(Lebanon). British – Lebanese Author, Philosopher,
Journalist and Climate Activist who is well travelled
around the world.
He is the Author of *Mesopotamia 681,Our Path To
Eternity, The Polymath* and *On The Cross*.

DEATH AT DAWN

Chapter 1

On an August Friday morning, a Dark green classic Jaguar car was leaving the Stonehenge site at speed going west. Once it got on the A303 road, it had to slow down as the road was crowded by cars, for people usually get away from big cities in a hot summer.

As the car slowed down, arguments inside it became more and more audible. A beautiful red-haired lady in her late 30's was driving, she rolled her eyes in displease as the man sitting next to her was always giving her directions. The man was a super elegant attractive handsome man in his early 60's, with a very well-dressed grey hair and a balanced well designed grey moustache. On the back seat slept Max, a young Golden retriever dog who was raising his right eyebrow as if he wanted to tell them "Shut up and stop that noise of yours".

Col Roger Selway, a retired British army Colonel who turned himself recently into a private detective. And Miss Meghan Dobinson, a former employee of the House of Parliament, whom very recently was appointed by Col Selway as his secretary.

"I am supposed to be your secretary. Not your driver!" Ms Dobinson protested.

"Oh, la la! I didn't force you to drive me today, I asked you if you wished to drive me to my hometown and spend a couple of days in the countryside away from London. And you said Yes, with pleasure" Selway replied.

"Well yes. I didn't expect, you would be so annoying in a car trip".

Selway squeezed his lips showing his surprise to how frank and direct his new employee is. Dobinson stole a glance at him and as if she read his mind, she couldn't hide her smile, then said "Well. What? You want to fire me from the second week. Ok go on. I am an understanding person, we didn't click!".

Selway laughed back and said "No. I want to use you and annoy you more. In fact, I like bold women".

"Are you sure?"

"I won't bother you more right now. Please pay attention and turn left in time into the A350 road, then drive up to Morobury. We are almost there".

The car finally arrived at a house in Morobury located at a road called "Bimport". The house had a private parking, so Dobinson drove in. A man whom Selway hired to look after the house and the garden in his absence showed up immediately with his teenage son.

"Oh! Nice to see you again Colonel Selway after such a long time".

"Thank you, Mr Brown. Nice to see you too".

As the two men shook hands, "Have you finally got married?" Brown asked

Selway waved his hand to the man to lower his voice and said, "No. No. Ms Dobinson is my secretary!"

"Ah! I see".

The Browns picked up the bags and took them into the house. Dobinson looked up at the house of two floors and said, "It's a beautiful cosy looking house with a very nice character".

"Yes indeed! Welcome to the house of the Selway family" Selway said as he showed her in.

Max stretched his muscles and went in too.

The house was full of antiques, luxurious old chairs and items. It was kept super clean and tidy; and that was jaw dropping for Ms Dobinson, "So tidy, so beautiful!" She spoke.

Selway nodded his head confirming what she said, then looked toward Mr Brown and said "Mrs Brown has done great job. Please thank her so much on my behalf".

"Thank you, Sir, It's our duty. However, you will be able to thank my wife personally".

Selway looked at him in a questioning manner. "She will bring your lunch at 1 o'clock" Brown Clarified.

Selway commented with a wide smile "Ah. Great! That's very kind of her".

The Browns left the house and Max accompanied them until they left the garden. Ms Dobinson sat on the sofa, while Selway made himself comfortable on a very luxurious chair in the sitting room.

"This sofa is very comfortable, but the chair you are sitting on looks so heavy and precious".

"It is indeed. It belongs to my great grandfather".

"I see many photos on the walls. How big is your family?"

"Well apart from the two portraits of my brother and my sister, they are all portraits of dead family members".

3

Selway stood up and walked towards the two portraits in the middle of the living room wall, and raising his eagle headed stick he pointed at two portraits, and said "This is my brother George, and this is my sister Theresa".

"Where do they live? Do they still share the family house with you?"

"No. I am the youngest child, but I inherited the family house. Theresa is married, she has children and grandchildren. She lives with her large family in New Zealand. While my brother George and his small family live mainly in Manchester, but they own a house in the French Riviera, in which they spend their summers of course".

"Oh Interesting!"

As the wall clock chimed 13:00, Mrs Brown appeared on the door with a wide smile on her face, "Hello. It's always nice to see you here Col Selway".

"Welcome Mrs Brown. Thank you. You are the most thoughtful and generous woman I have ever met".

The middle-aged lady was carrying a large pan and went straight to the dining room. She put her pan at the middle of the table. Then entered the kitchen, prepared all what was needed for the table, and filled a pet plate for Max with dog food, then returned to the living room.

"Lunch is ready. I prepared the table for you. Will you excuse me? I should return home now as I have to set the table there too"

"Thank you very much Mrs Brown. It was very kind of you. Please don't occupy yourself too much with my presence here. I can definitely manage to cook my own meals".

"I had to make this welcome meal for you. I still remember what kind of food you like. The fridge is full of all the groceries you asked Mark (*her husband*) to buy".

"Wonderful. Mrs Brown. Thank you very much".

"Would you like me to prepare a meal for you tonight?"

"No. No. Thank you. We will dine out".

Mrs Brown left. Dobinson took her seat at the table, while Selway opened the pan, and as his eyes fell on its content, a wide smile covered his face as if he found a treasure. "This Mrs Brown deserves a big kiss. She really knows what I like" he said.

Then he started with serving Ms Dobinson, but as the first spoon revealed the type of meal. The lady said "Oh Broccoli. No. Sorry, but I can't eat it!"

Smile vanished from Selway's face. Then he calmly said "I am sorry that you don't like Broccoli. However, it's made with garlic, yogurt and chicken filet. You definitely eat chicken and yogurt. Don't you?"

"Ok. I think I will manage to avoid the Broccoli".

"Help yourself then!"

Selway was eating as if he hadn't eaten for ages. Dobinson couldn't hide her smile as he finishes his first plate and filled a second.

"I have to admit. This is really delicious" Dobinson commented.

Selway smiled at her nodding his head. Dobinson laughed, then noticed her baggage was still at the bottom of the stairs and asked "I still see that my baggage is still down here. And you haven't showed me my room!"

Selway looked startled when he heard that. Then he said quickly "No my dear. You are not spending your night here".

Dobinson looked surprised and stammered "But, but you. You invited me to spend couple of days in the countryside".

"Yes! That's true, but not in my house my friend". He avoided looking in her eyes, "I have booked you a room in a hotel for a week" he explained.

"What a strange man you are Mr Selway! I think I should be careful with you if our working relationship is to continue".

"I am sorry that you may have misunderstood my proposal".

"Not only that, but I feel like you have used me to drive you here".

At that Selway lost his temper and said loudly "Enough Ms Dobinson. You are accusing me of things that I have not intended at all. I have booked you the best room in the best hotel in the area, because I respect your privacy and freedom. And I hope you respect mine too".

She tried to calm him down "Oh. Please accept my apology Mr Selway. I went a bit too far with my expectations. That's all" she said.

"I quiet understand" he replied.

After coffee, Selway suggested they leave for the hotel. He put Max's collar on, then picking up her bags, he led them out of the house. She headed towards the car, but Selway words stopped her immediately "No my dear, we are walking to the hotel. The Grosvenor Arms is just round the corner".

They left the garden and turned right, then passed by the Town court "The Abbey Court", and then walked through a cemetery. "If you fancy working, I do own an office here" Selway raised his stick and pointed it toward an old Church turned into offices. "Once my business as private detective becomes well established, we will be working here in spring and summer" he added.

They left the church grounds and then walked through a short passage between houses. Then they turned left and immediately the "Grosvenor Arms" Hotel appeared. It was three storied Georgian building.

"You have a room booked under your name Meghan Dobinson".

"Ok thank you. When will we meet again?"

"Tonight, for dinner of course" Selway turned around and pointed his stick towards the corner at the end of the road, and he said, "Shall we meet at King Alfred's Kitchen at 9:30 pm?"

"That will be lovely".

"Good. I look forward to seeing you then".

Meanwhile, in a small house not far from Selway's home, Mustapha Radi, a 33-year-old man of Middle eastern origin was lying face down on his bed, dressed only in his underpants, laughing and talking to someone behind him and waiting for his massage to begin.

By then, Selway had returned home and was spending the rest of the afternoon and early evening checking and setting up his TV, and making sure his internet connection was working in every room, especially in his study.

When the wall clock and the town hall bells announced 9 pm, Selway was filling Max's plate with dog food, and changing his water pot.

For her part, Ms Dobinson enjoyed a quiet stroll around the town before returning to the hotel for a brief rest before getting ready for her dinner with Selway.

She was walking down towards the restaurant when few drops of English summer rain, became heavier. Then she saw Mr Radi walking down from the abbey passage fast, he was pulling his hair in a hysterical manner while shouting at himself. He was surprised by her at the crossroad and as their eyes met, she saw clearly that he was crying hard as if something terrible had happened to him.

As he passed by her and turned right, the rain became heavier. So, the young man seemed to decide to take few steps back and then entered the Restaurant called "King's Alfred Kitchen".

Dobinson's curiosity pushed her into the restaurant too, even if there were some fifteen minutes before Selway's arrival. It was rather a very small restaurant with hardly ten different size tables in it. But that didn't bother Dobinson much. She took a seat on the small table near the window. Radi was sitting on a small table at the wall side, and he was sobbing in an audible manner.

Other than them there was only an old lady on a wheelchair, and her maid or daughter, sitting on a table at the far-left corner of the room near the second window.

As expected, the Restaurant lady arrived soon to her table to ask her what she wished to have. Dobinson replied, "I am here waiting my friend, he booked a table for 9:30".

"And your friend's name is?"

"Mr Selway"

"Col. Selway. He is a regular customer when he stays here. I will come back later then."

As the waitress turned to go away, she noticed Radi sitting in the corner crying. She went over to him remarking how upset he seemed and asking if he wanted anything. He replied "Not yet thank you. I just want a few moments to myself as I have had a very bed shock."

"Don't worry, you just sit there, and I will come back later".

With that she went back to the kitchen. Radi however showed no signs of feeling better and continued to cry and cough like a small child, so much so that Dobinson got up, went over to his table and began to speak to him.

Chapter 2

Radi was surprised by the curiosity of Ms Dobinson, and that made him realise how terrible his state appeared to be. He took a deep breath and tried to appear as normal as possible. "Sorry to disturb you, but you seem in a deep grief, and I said to myself that if you share your problem with me, that could help you a bit to release the depression and the sorrow you are feeling" she said.

Radi looked in her eyes as if he was trying to figure out if she is trustworthy, or maybe he was taking few moments to invent something to say. "Do you speak English?" She asked. He didn't seem to like the question, "Of Course I do" he answered.

"What is the matter? I will quite understand if you don't want to speak to me and I will go back to my table". As she moved her chair a bit, he said "It's just that I love this town, but it seems I am forced to leave it by next month".

"Why? And who is going to force you out?"

He took another deep breath then said "Well, I live in a small house in Bimport, not far from here. And I was just caught with my lover in bed"

"Caught by whom?"

He looked again in Dobinson's eyes and said "Her parents. So now I have one month to leave the place".

"But can they force you to leave?"

"I am afraid they can as I rent the house from them. They own it".

At that moment, Selway entered the restaurant, so Dobinson apologised quickly "My employer has arrived, so will you excuse me? But please don't take it too personally, it's just a cloud and it will pass. They may change their minds before the month ends". Dobinson then stood up and walked over to Selway who stood in the middle of the room waiting for her, then they took their seats on the small table near the window. She sat with her back to Radi, so that Selway was facing him.

Selway waved his finger quickly towards the guy asking his secretary what was going on. Dobinson said "Not a big deal really. He was in tears and agony, and I was curious to know what gave him that huge amount of sorrow".

"And what was that?" Selway wondered.

"He is a tenant, and he was caught in bed with the daughter of the landlord. So, the landlord asked him to move out by next month".

Selway noticed that Radi didn't remove his eyes from him, so he looked back, and the chap smiled at him. Selway continued his conversation "So it's an end of an unfortunate love affair".

"Exactly, and he seems very fond of her".

"Indeed!" Selway replied while wondering to himself why the handsome guy was still staring at him in a rather persistent manner.

The owner of King Alfred's Kitchen was a woman in her 50's and she seemed to have known the former colonel well. Immediately she sang as she saw him "Fifteen men on the Dead Man's Chest Yoo-hoo," then Selway continued "And a bottle of white wine now would do! Drink and the devil had done for the rest yoo-hoo!" They both laughed loudly as it was a line from Robert Louis Stevenson's Novel "Treasure Island", but Selway was used to change the type of bottle from Rum to white wine.

They ordered Fish and chips, as Selway suggested it was the best traditional restaurant in Dorset.

"It's always great to see you Colonel Selway".

"I always miss your delicious dishes, so here I am again".

"I will give the fish my special attention". With that she returned to the kitchen.

While they waited for their food, Selway and Dobinson chatted idly about what they had done that afternoon.

By the time the food arrived, Radi had recovered enough to order his meal. He still stared across at Selway who began to feel that it was all very strange and so paid close attention to his food to avoid making any eye contact with the young man.

When Radi finished his meal, he didn't wait for the bill. He went to the till at the bar and paid there. Then before leaving the restaurant, he came to their table and said to Dobinson "Thank you for your concern" and then he added while looking at Selway "Since I saw you, I am already feeling better". Then he pulled out a card from his pocket, put it on the table and said "These are my contact details. It would be very nice to meet up again if you like. Au revoir"

Dobinson took the card and put it in her handbag. She looked at her employer who simply shrugged his shoulders as if to say it was all nothing to do with him.

Also, in Bimport lived the Claytons. The very wealthy and known physicist Mr John Clayton (65-year-old), his wife the architect Patricia Kelly Clayton (60-year-old) and their son Barry Clayton (26-year-old). They had also an older son and daughter, Patrick (37) and Emma (29) both married. The first lives in Dublin, he is married to one of his cousins (mother's side) and Emma lives in Milan, she is married to an Italian wealthy businessman.

That night was not a normal night for the Claytons. Patricia was in a hysterical mood, her husband made coffee and brought a cup to her trying to calm her down, but as he approached her, she shouted out loud "Don't come anywhere near me!". He put the cup on the table and tried to tap her on the shoulder, but she jumped away warning him "Don't touch me". Then she quickly rushed to her room and locked it on herself, threw herself on the bed and cried like a baby while her hands twisted the duvet expressing her anger and grief.

By this time, Selway had arrived home which was about 100 yards from the Claytons after walking Dobinson back to her hotel and refusing an offer for a late-night brandy. Once in bed, he began to read Derek Jacobi autobiography "As Luck would have it". The latter was one of his favourite actors, so he was interested to get some light into Jacobi's private life. However, it wasn't the most exciting of reads, and he soon fell asleep.

The following day as dawn broke, Radi dressed in training gear, left his house for his usual daily exercise. Normally he went by himself but this time he had arranged to meet up with six of his students from the secondary school at a small memorial garden near his house. Once they were all there, they began to jog up and down Morobury Castle hill, seven times in all. Part of the road was quite exposed with steep boundaries on either side so that it was quite dangerous for people running too fast. Radi had already advised his students to slow down and be careful at this point. However today, though he didn't take his own advice and sprinted along much to the alarm of one of his students, a lad of 16 named Gary who challenged him about it. Radi tried to excuse himself by saying that he had been doing this for over a year and could do it with his eyes shut as he knew every inch of it.

Not far from there, Selway was woken at 6.30 by his mobile. Leaving his bedroom, he was met by Max waiting for his breakfast. Selway fed him, then showered and made a quick breakfast of tea and biscuits. Putting on a tracksuit, he left with Max for his early morning walk. He was usually out by 7.00 before there were too many other people, including other dog walkers, and cars on the road. He was surprised then to see a group of runners including Radi already there. He was relieved to see that they had more or less finished their run, as Radi left them to enter a small house while they carried on down the road.

Selway murmured to himself "Thank G-d, he didn't see me". But he was totally mistaken, for when he passed in front of the garden gate of that house, Radi waited Selway to come up to him, then he said, "Good Morning Colonel!". "Good morning young man" Selway replied. "You look great in sportswear" Radi added while waving his right thumb up. Selway said "Thank you" and kept walking along the road.

Selway started to think about this young man from the Middle East and how odd it was that he seems to be overly interested in him. And as he noticed that Radi lived next door to the Claytons, he immediately realised that they should be the landlords.

Radi meantime had entered his house and had a quick shower. Afterwards he put on just a pair of boxer shorts, walked inside his little house looking at himself in the long mirror he had. Then he turned his laptop on at the kitchen table and surfed on the internet while drinking a cup of milk and eating a sandwich of boiled eggs.

He was looking at the website "Rightmove" to find a new house or apartment to rent because the landlord (Mrs Clayton) warned him that he should leave the place by the first of September. Not many offers in Morobury itself, but he found one interesting place for rent there and also another one in Millingham which was hardly seven minutes of drive by car from where he lived. He emailed the Estate Agents showing his interest and including his contact details.

When the Town hall clock announced 9 am, Mrs Clayton was sitting to a table at the corner next to the door of the Costa Cafe sipping her hot espresso. And at a table behind her Ms Dobinson was having her morning Cappuccino while waiting to hear from Selway. It was hardly a coincidence that people gather at the Costa in the mornings as it was the main cafe in the town located few yards from the Town hall and the bus stop. Also, King Alfred's Kitchen and the Grosvenor Arms hotel were also there in that street known, like in all English towns, as the High Street.

Selway's secretary had never seen Mrs Clayton before, but from her dress she noticed immediately that she was a very wealthy woman. Both of them were busy with their mobile phones. Dobinson was reading a message that has just arrived from Selway.
"Guess who I met this morning while taking Max for a walk?".

"I don't know! Perhaps a Minister or a famous actor or singer?!" she replied, and they went on exchanging messages.

"No! Famous people do not interest me. It's someone whom you met yourself yesterday".

"Me! I don't know anyone here!"

"It's the chap at the restaurant"

"Oh. Mr Radi"

"Yes, he was jogging in the early morning and as I passed by, he saluted me".

"Ok and what's exciting about that!?"

"Nothing actually, I am inviting you for lunch today, I will cook a dish that I used to cook while in the army".

"I hope there is no Broccoli in it"

"No. Don't worry. I am sure it will be tasty".

As soon as she finished her espresso, Mrs Clayton looked into the contact list of her mobile phone and dialled the number of Mrs Jenkins, the wife of the education minister.

"Good morning, Dora"

"Oh! Good morning, Patricia. I haven't heard from you for a while".

"I hope I am not disturbing you in this summer morning".

"Not really a busy morning for me, as you know summer holiday for ministers and MPs is mainly the month of August. So, take your time. What's the matter?"

"I need your help urgently in a private matter which is shaking a bit the serenity and the harmony of my house".

"That sounds serious. How can I help?"

"I don't think it's wise to speak about that on the phone, I prefer to send you an email or a letter. What is best for you?"

"If it's very urgent, then an email is better I suppose".

"Are you still using the old private email address?"

"Yes. As you know it's safer now more than ever to have an email account under a different name. You know how unsafe the internet is these days with all the piracy and hacking stories".

"Yes, especially when it comes to politicians. Hacking them is becoming the norm nowadays. Ok then I will send you a message as soon as I get home. Expect it in the next hour or so".

"Ok dear. Thanks for you call. I hope I will be able to help".

Mrs Clayton looked a bit agitated when talking. And then she left the cafe in a hurry as soon as the conversation ended.

Chapter 3

Radi left his house, passed in front of Selway's, where the former colonel was doing some morning routine exercises to keep his fitness level intact. "Good morning again, can I be of help?" asked the young man. "Good morning. Oh! It's you again! I don't think you can teach an army colonel how to exercise! "Selway replied.

Radi winked at Selway and continued his way on the shortest road cut towards the high street. Once he arrived at the cemetery, he saw Mrs Clayton coming in a hurry. At seeing him she felt like seeing an unpleasant ghost. "Good morning" he said, but her reply was to spit on the grass then hurry back to her home. Selway was still in his garden when he saw her quickly pass his house with a face like thunder.

Clayton arrived home, and at once she called the housemaid Maria Clark, who was a 28-year-old normal looking brunette.

"Yes mam!"

"Go to Tesco and buy me some Ice cream".

"I will go after I finish washing the dishes".

"Now, I said".

"Okay" Clark rolled her eyes in displease mixed with surprise as the lady of the house went to her room. It was a surprising order from her and "why all this urgency in having an ice cream?" the maid was wondering to herself.

Maria took off the kitchen dress quickly, put her jeans on, checked her hair a little bit on the mirror, then as she walked towards the back door to leave, she heard Mrs Clayton calling her.

"Maria. Maria"

"Yes! Coming"

As she approached Clayton's room the latter opened the door and asked her

"Is Barry home?"

"No, he left with Mr Clayton half an hour ago. I heard him saying that he is visiting a friend in Millingham and as Mr Clayton was going to play Golf, he gave him a lift".

"Alright then, off you go"

Mrs Clayton walked quietly behind her maid until she was sure she left the house, then she returned to her room, and dialled a telephone number but no one seemed available at the other end.

Shaking with nerves, she turned to her tablet and wrote an email to Mrs Jenkins. After she pressed the "send" button, she immediately dialled the number of the Minister house.

"Hello Dora".

"Oh! Hi! Good to hear your voice again"

"I have just sent you an email with all the details of the problem I am in, and I look forward to your reply".

"Ok dear. I will look at it at once and I will see what I can do to help".

"Bye".

"Bye".

Mrs Clayton tried once again the number she called previously but again she failed to reach the other side. She was like someone who is sitting on fire. She walked outside and sat in the garden smoking an e-cigarette.

At Tesco Maria met Mr Radi who was also buying groceries for the few remaining days in his current house. They walked back together from there, as the Claytons' house and the annexe rented by Radi were door to door.

"Why do they want you to leave?" asked Maria.

"It's Mrs Clayton you know, she is very angry of me lately and clearly wants to get rid of me as soon as possible".

"But she was okay with you couple of days ago! You must have done something yesterday evening after I left home".

"Maybe I have done something that annoyed her so much, but I am afraid I can't share it with you".

Maria didn't like his answer and pursed her lips in annoyance, then said "Well. I can't see how I can help you then!"

"I think no one on earth could get Mrs Clayton in good term with me again".

The two turned left from high street and took the small passage towards the cemetery, and at that time Ms Dobinson was leaving her hotel taking the same road towards Selway's house, so she walked some twenty yards behind them. She recognised Mr Radi of course, and she assumed that he was accompanied by the girlfriend he was caught in bed with.

When they passed the Abbey court and reached Selway's house, Radi said "I think we better not seen together. Your employer may get mad at you". "Well then, it seems the situation is rather very serious. Ok. Have a nice day". Maria left him there and walked very quickly towards the Claytons house. Ms Dobinson slowed down in her turn and waited until Radi continued his way. While passing, he looked towards Selway's garden, but no one was there, so he kept walking.

Dobinson looked at her watch, it was just 11 am. She told herself "I don't think I would be welcome to pop up early, he is certainly busy cooking". Then she decided to visit the town Museum located some 200 yards away. She passed near "Westminster Memorial Hospital" then turned left toward the Museum.

At noon, Dobinson joined her employer at his home. This time she was less horrified by the dish, and she was rather surprised that the former colonel was really a talented cook.

"The meal tasted great especially with a glass of white wine" She expressed her gratitude.

A wide smile covered Selway's foxy face "Thank you my dear. I am very glad that you liked it".

As they washed their hands in turn, they returned together to the sitting room. Then Selway disappeared again in the kitchen. A couple of minutes later he returned with two ice cream glasses as a cooler, as it had become very hot outside.

"Thank you very much" Dobinson said while taking her glass.

"You are welcome. Tell me how your first morning in Morobury was?"

"I had a little walk, then a cup of Cappuccino at the Costa Cafe, and before coming here I also visited the Museum".

"That's interesting! Not a boring morning then".

"No. I am enjoying my stay actually".

Max interrupted their chat with an amicable bark protesting and demanding his share of the Ice Cream. His master was ready for such demand, and so he cut a big chunk of the vanilla side of his ice cream and placed it in a bowl for him.

"Guess whom I saw earlier today?" Dobinson asked.

"Let me guess. The restaurant lady or maybe the middle eastern guy"

"I saw the unlucky lovers. Yes, the guy of last night and his girlfriend".

"You mean Mr Radi was with a lady?"

"Yes, they were walking few yards ahead of me, then when they approached your place she went along the road, and a minute or two later he followed her. It seems they didn't want her parents to see them together".

"That's Interesting and strange at the same time. I don't know who that girl was, but she is definitely not the Claytons daughter".

"Who are the Claytons?

"They are the wealthy landlords of the annexe rented by Mr Radi".

"Ah I see. And why you are so sure that she is not their daughter, maybe they have only sons?!"

"No. They do have one daughter, but she got married to an Italian businessman three years ago and she lives in Italy".

"Hmm! So, you mean that he lied to me when he told me he was caught with the daughter of the landlord".

"Yes, my dear he did, unless Emma Clayton divorced her husband, or she is here visiting her parents and fell in love with Radi!".

"Yes. I can see now there are many interpretations of that rather strange situation". After a minute of silence, Dobinson said "But you seem to know the family well".

"Naturally my dear, they are old neighbours and Mr John Clayton is a very close friend to my brother George since their childhood".

"Understood; Anyway, it's not our business this entire story of Mr Radi and whoever the lady he is involved with. Don't you think?"

"Yes. But I feel this story has more secrets to it than what we have heard and seen until now".

At that time a black 4X4 car was speeding while climbing its way up from Millingham to Morobury. In it, there were Barry Clayton and his friend Stephen Sumpter.

"Where are we going exactly?" Stephen asked.

"He told me we should be ready in Morobury when he sends us the message, he didn't tell me where we are going to get the presents".

"So we go now to your house, you mean".

"No. I think it's better to park the car at any short time parking until the message comes through".

"Alright then"

As they arrived to the A30, Barry pointed his left hand toward "a one hour" little parking that existed just at the corner of Selway's house, and it was not more than a hundred of yards away from the Claytons house.

Their wait wasn't long, as hardly after five minutes, a message came through social media to Barry's mobile. "After 15 minutes at St Edward's Church" it read.

The Church was nearly seven minutes away by car, so Stephen turned the engine on and drove slowly towards it. As the big car approached the Catholic Church, another message came through "We are inside at Father O'Shea circle. You should put your two hands behind your back, you take by the right, and you pay by the left ".

"What is he saying?"

"They are inside at Father O'Shea circle!"

"Who is Father O'Shea?"

"I have no idea. All what I know is that I need enough presents for the coming week or so".

"I hope you have got enough money for that".

"Don't worry!"

They parked the car at the closest possible empty space to the St Edward's Church. They divided the money between them and walked inside.

"It is a very strange site for give and take. Isn't it?" Stephen whispered.

"It is indeed. However, it's a great choice away from curious eyes".

Once they got in, they saw a priest preaching to a circle of people at the far-right corner of the altar. "He must be Father O'Shea" Stephen said. Barry nodded his head in agreement.

Father O'Shea welcomed them with a big smile as he felt his teaching were getting more and more popular among the young generation. They had a quick look at the faces around them. They took seats next to each other and put their hands behind their backs.

"I believe the west has lost its way completely, they are at odd with our Lord Jesus Christ. Vladimir Putin, even though he is Greek Orthodox in faith, he is a far better leader for the Christians of the middle east than all the western leaders combined". Father O'Shea stated.

Stephen started yawning as the Catholic Father kept going with his political ideas claiming many conspiracies are targeting the Christian faith. Then suddenly a nun entered the church hall and called Father O'Shea. Few seconds later, the two guys felt plastic bags touching their right hands and a voice whispering to them "Don't turn around". They released the money from their left hands. The deal was done in seconds. Shortly afterwards Father O'Shea apologised for the interruption and said "I am sorry. But I have to leave you now, we had enough talk today, see you in the next occasion".

The crowd left their seats. Barry and Stephen turned around but there was no one there. So, they walked outside with what they came for, gained their car and left the scene.

At the Claytons, Maria was serving Mr Clayton at the lunch table after he returned from the Golf club. He asked her about his wife, "She had already her lunch and she is taking a siesta in her room Sir" the maid explained.

"Alright thanks" Mr Clayton was eating his meal, but his mind was far away as if he was in deep trouble, and he had no clue how to get out.

Meanwhile, in her room Mrs Clayton received on her mobile a message from Mrs Jenkins saying "I need to talk to you regarding the problem you want my help with. When can I call you?"

"Okay. Please call me now".

Hardly her mobile rung, Mrs Clayton accepted the call immediately.

"Yes Dora, tell me what it is".

"Dear Patricia, what you are asking me to do is rather difficult, you know. Even though my husband is the Minister of Education he does not have the authority to have teachers removed".

"I know it's not simple, but this is the first time I ask you for help, and I really want to solve this problem I mentioned to you in my detailed email".

"I read carefully your email, and I really don't think it's a disaster if your housemaid fell in love with that teacher. So, I really don't get the reason why you are very angry about their relationship?"

Few seconds of complete silence, then Dora asked "Alo! Are you still there Patricia?"

Mrs Clayton was thinking of a more reasonable excuse to get what she wanted. "Yes, I am here dear. You don't understand really how much keeping Maria is very important to me; she has been working here for three years now. She is very trustworthy and a very good cook. I don't want to lose her".

"Well fine then, let them get married and live in the house he rented!" Dora suggested.

Patricia lost her temper on the phone and exploded in tears "I have other reasons that I can't tell. Please if you don't help me in this matter do not ever call me again and forget our friendship completely" And she ended the call.

Chapter 4

Mrs Jenkins was shocked by how her old friend behaved with her on the phone, but at the same time she understood that Mr Radi was causing her too much pain and sorrow. As she doesn't want to lose her friendship, she decided to press all the possible buttons of the minister in order to get him act on her behalf and move Mr Radi from his current school to a school elsewhere in England, anywhere away from the Southwest.

Meanwhile Radi was a bit relieved to find two positive replies in his email inbox from the real estate agency regarding two rental offers available in Morobury and Millingham. They asked him to come visit the flats next week, and he was looking forward to that, firstly to avoid facing the spitting face of Mrs Clayton and secondly because he loved the area and didn't want to live far away.

In the early evening just before the sunset, Ms Dobinson was walking at the bimport main road and as she passed by his house, she sent her employer a message wishing to explore the office that he owns at the old Abbey building. He agreed and told her to meet him there in quarter an hour, the time to change his outfit. He didn't know that she is already near his house. So, she waited him at the small gate of the garden looking at the faces of the people who at that time of the day take a walk along the hospital and turn into a space preserved for walkers and cyclists. The minutes passed quickly, and as soon as Selway opened the door of his house, Max jumped out quickly towards Dobinson at the garden gate.

"Oh! You are already here" Selway said.

Dobinson was about to reply to him when Mrs Clayton who was walking by, stopped once she saw Mr Selway and said "Oh Colonel Selway; Nice to see you again. You haven't come here in summers for couple of years. Where have you been?"

"Great to see you too Mrs Clayton.; Yes, you are right this is my first visit in three years now. Last summer my brother George invited me to his place at the French Riviera. And how could I refuse such an offer?"

"Indeed. Nice sea views, good swimming, all the real things unlike this boring place".

"You said it".

"I see that you are leaving somewhere, and I don't want to disturb your plan. Who is she? Please tell me you finally decided to get married?"

"No. Sorry I forgot to introduce you to each other. Mrs Clayton my long-time neighbour. Ms Dobinson my secretary".

"Your secretary, from the army you mean?" Clayton wondered.

"No. I have left the army; I am now a former colonel of the Army police turning himself into a Private Detective and Ms Dobinson is my secretary".

"Oh, I see, from an interesting job to a more interesting one. Good to hear your news Mr Selway. Now I have to take my evening walk. See you around sometime".

"See you" Selway replied while nodding his head. His eyes followed the woman until she walked couple of yards further.

Then he looked to Dobinson who whispered, "I saw her today in the morning".

And as the two walked towards the office, Selway asked "Really?! Where?"

"She was at the Costa Cafe".

"I see. That's a bit odd, she usually keeps up appearances and don't show up often in such public places".

"She was busy in, what it seemed, a very important phone call". As the Night lamps turned on automatically, they passed through some of the graves scattered in the yard of the old abbey. Then Selway typed the security codes to open the main gate of the building. Once they heard it ticking, Selway pushed the large wooden gate, and they walked into the historical building that dated back to the 18th century.

They climbed the stairs to the second floor. There was also another code, then the magnetic key for the office door. Ms Dobinson couldn't hold back her admiration for how the new technology was combined with the old building. As they walked inside, it was almost a complete flat "Oh my Oh my! That's far larger and more beautiful than your London office". There was a large bathroom with a shower cabin and a fully equipped kitchen, two rooms one for the secretary and one for Selway's desk, plus a sitting room in case there were visitors.

"This will be our summer desk hopefully from next summer on if we got some cases to solve between now and then" Selway said.

"I think you need an advertisement campaign, so that people would know that you are now a detective, and you are ready to receive their demands".

"You are right my dear. However, I got a promise from my old friend New Scotland Yard Chief Inspector Ronald Smith that he would get me involved with any case that seems to be tough"

"That would help, but don't forget that private detection is not only related to matters of crimes, theft and police. People could hire a private detective for completely private affairs".

"Ok then; you seem very enthusiastic about publishing advertisements".

"Yes, I am"

"Okay. Would you like to come here tomorrow and work on designing some adverts?"

"Yes. I think I would enjoy doing that".

"Very good employee you are" Selway smiled at her, he opened the drawer of his desk and handed her another copy of the magnetic key. He added "The internal door code is the year of my birthday, and the main building code is SP78AZ". She typed that immediately on her mobile phone and said "Thank you. But I need some photos of you".

"What for ?!"

"For the adverts"

"Is it wise for a private detective to spread his photos around since day one?!"

"Probably not, but I think you are a very handsome man, and you look trustworthy, so a photo may attract clients".

"Yes, it will attract all the single old ladies" As she laughed, He then added "No I am afraid I disagree with you on that point. You need to find a way to design an attractive advert without my photo".

"That would be rather challenging" Dobinson admitted.

At that time, Mrs Clayton was sitting on one of the wooden benches situated behind Westminster memorial hospital and looking over the village of St James which was wearing a necklace of lights at the early night. She was staring at the dark horizon thinking of all the troubles that invaded her life in the last twenty-four hours, when her mobile rang in a persistent tone, she pulled it out of her little handbag, and her eyes widened as she saw Dora's number calling.

"Alo"

"Hello Patricia. Sorry about earlier but you know it's not easy for a minister to interfere in such matters".

"Yes, I do understand".

"Well, I have got some good news for you".

"Really?" suddenly the joy and warm returned to Patricia's voice.

"Yes dear. I managed after a long nagging attempt to convince my husband to act towards moving Mr Radi away from Dorset. Well, it wasn't easy, he had to call one of his friends who are a manager of one of Newcastle schools and he asked him if he can demand the service of Mr Radi because he is a very talented sports teacher, and you know that sort of things".

"Great. Newcastle is definitely far enough, and I couldn't have wished for more. Thank you very much my dear".

"You are welcome, even though I really don't understand what is going on between you and that young fellow".

"Maybe one day I will tell you the story, but now can you tell me when he and the school here will get informed of his new appointment?"

"Today is Friday. I would think they should receive a notification any day next week".

"Thank you, thank you very much. I can't thank you enough".

"You are welcome, Patricia. Take care".

Patricia Clayton was a devoted Catholic like many women of her age in her original country: the Republic of Ireland. And as she was relieved by the good news she had just received, she decided to go to the church that evening.

As darkness of the night fell across the town, all the streetlights came on. Mrs Clayton returned towards the Bimport main road then turned right towards the church. It was some twenty minutes' walk, but she wanted to go there unnoticed, and the best way was to go on foot.

As she passed near the Abbey compound, Selway and Dobinson saw her as they were leaving the office.

"Mrs Clayton looks completely weird to me these days! As far I knew, she hardly goes anywhere on foot, so there is certainly some drastic change in her lifestyle".

"Maybe you should have seen her this morning at the cafe. She was talking very nervously on the phone as if she was standing in a trial".

They waved goodbye, as Dobinson walked back towards the hotel, and Selway re-joined Max in his way home which was hardly dozens of yards away.

Selway had strong lit lamps over the walls of his garden, also at the top corners of his house. And as he regained his castle, he fed Max, and made a cup of tea. While filling his cup with hot water over a tea bag, he remembered that he had not checked yet if all the surveillance cameras around the house were still functioning properly.

He took his teacup and mounted the stairs to a small wooden room he called it the "Studio" in which he got screens related to the cameras he has for surveillance around the house. The Seven Cameras he has were kept recording all the time, so he wanted to check if that is still the case. He turned the seven small monitors he has inside the room, and the scenes were moving proving that all cameras were working fine. They were all programmed to record on three weeks basis, that means it held the record of the last 21 days. To explain the mechanism best, the maximum amount of time that the footage is kept in the recorder is 21 days, after that the record would be automatically deleted.

Friday summer nights were usually very busy. Selway enjoyed watching people and cars passing by, while he is sipping his tea. He even spent an hour there without noticing that. He was seeing people whom he hadn't seen for decades; also, he was seeing new faces of all these young generation. So, he enjoyed trying to guess the names, and who could this young girl or that young boy. He didn't pay attention how time passed quickly until he heard the town hall tower announcing ten o'clock.

When he started turning the monitors off, he suddenly saw Mrs Clayton passing on the main road returning home. As she disappeared from the camera lens, he turned the last monitor off. Then he went straight to his bedroom, he threw away that Jacobi biography, and tuned on the TV on ITV to watch a funny comedy series called "Friday Night Dinner".

On her return to the hotel, and before Mrs Dobinson went in, two taxis arrived and from them emerged four stunning looking young ladies. The four were wearing short skirts under tight summer shirts. She paved the way for them to walk in, and she entered after them.

"We have two rooms booked for us" One of them said.

The guy at the reception replied with a big smile "Yes. But I need to see your passports first please".

They started chatting to each other and searching into their luggage for their documents.

From their accent, Dobinson assumed that they were from Eastern Europe. She walked to her room, took off her clothes, and had a quick shower. She put on her bed robe, plugged in the earphones on and turned her mp3 player on some Enya's relaxing songs. It wasn't long before she fell asleep.

At the Claytons, John Clayton was trying for the next consecutive night to join his wife in her room, but she kept the door locked in his face. "Darling there are many things in life that we cannot explain, however I am ready to talk the subject over with you" he said in front of the door. She didn't reply.

After a couple of minutes, he gave up and returned to his room, turned his mobile phone on and sent a message saying, "She is still mad at me, and I don't think she will ever forgive us".

"I am sorry for what happened, but some women are not open minded enough to accept such behaviour" replied the other side.

Not far away, his son Barry along with his friend Stephen was having a crowded party night at the "Legends" night club in Millingham. As the DJ Music was screaming in the tight place, dancers were hitting the floor while the two guys covered each other when sniffing a portion of the presents they got at St Edward church.

Suddenly the door guards paved the way for four hot girls, and the quarter entered the place, the music went louder and louder and Marilyn Manson's song "This is the New Shit" was played. And here are its lyrics:

Everything has been said before
There's nothing left to say anymore
When it's all the same
You can ask for it by name
Babble babble bitch bitch
Rebel rebel party party
Sex sex sex and don't forget the "violence"
Blah blah blah got your lovey-dovey sad-and-lonely
Stick your STUPID SLOGAN in:
Everybody, sing along.
Babble babble bitch bitch
Rebel rebel party party
Sex sex sex and don't forget the "violence"
Blah blah blah got your lovey-dovey sad-and-lonely
Stick your STUPID SLOGAN in:
Everybody, sing along,
Are you motherfuckers ready
For the new shit?
Stand up and admit,
tomorrow is never coming.
This is the new shit.
Stand up and admit.
Do we get it? No.
Do we want it? Yeah.
This is the new shit,
Stand up and admit.
Babble babble bitch bitch
Rebel rebel party party
Sex sex sex and don't forget the "violence"
Blah blah blah got your lovey-dovey sad-and-lonely
Stick your STUPID SLOGAN in:

Mourad Mourad

Everybody, sing along.
Everything has been said before
There's nothing left to say anymore
When it's all the same
You can ask for it by name,
Are you motherfuckers ready
For the new shit?
Stand up and admit,
tomorrow's never coming.
This is the new shit.
Stand up and admit.
Do we get it? No.
Do we want it? Yeah.
This is the new shit,
Stand up and admit.
And now it's "you know who"
I got the "you know what"
I stick it "you know where"
You know why, you don't care.
And now it's "you know who"
I got the "you know what"
I stick it "you know where"
You know why, you don't care.
Babble babble bitch bitch
Rebel rebel party party
Sex sex sex and don't forget the "violence"
Blah blah blah got your lovey-dovey sad-and-lonely
Stick your STUPID SLOGAN in:
Everybody, sing along,
Are you motherfuckers ready
For the new shit?
Stand up and admit,
tomorrow's never coming.
This is the new shit.
Stand up and admit.

Do we get it? No.
Do we want it? Yeah.
This is the new shit,
Stand up and admit.
So,
LET US ENTERTAIN YOU
LET US ENTERTAIN YOU...
Blah blah blah blah everybody, sing along.

Chapter 5

Ms Dobinson woke up on a big noise at the hotel. The early day light was just coming through the window of her room. She checked her watch; it was five minutes after five. She said, "What's the hell?", then she remembered the young foreign ladies "Yes of course, they have just come back from their late night".

She tried to get back to sleep but with no success even though the noise had gone, and the girls sounded to have entered their rooms located next to hers. She decided that there is no point in losing more time on sleep attempts, she walked to the bathroom to take a shower, but as she approached the toilet door which was close to the room door she heard a low laughter and two voices talking, voices of a man and a woman talking at the door of the room next to hers. From the few words she knows in French, she immediately recognised that they were speaking in French, but she couldn't understand what they were talking about. So, she walked into her shower. After it, she dried her hair, and put on a long sleeve summer shirt and trousers.

At seven she left the hotel to the office which was hardly two hundred meters away. The entire building was quiet, and one would expect so, because aside from it was too early in the morning, it was also a Saturday morning. She went through the security doors and found herself finally at the luxurious office of Mr Selway.

At 7:30 Selway left his house for a long walk with Max, and again he midway met Mr Radi and his students, there weren't so many.

"Good morning, Mr Handsome" Radi addressed Selway who was a bit surprised by the description thrown at him by the young man. "Good morning" he replied.

"Beautiful dog" Radi said while petting Max who in his turn was friendly to him.

Selway turned towards the students who were leaving then addressed their teacher "They are less numbered than yesterday".

"Sharp attention to details, yes they are actually".

"May I ask why?"

"As you know schools' days are over since June, but as the school management set a strategy to tackle obesity, they decided to make this summer morning Exercise program which I am of course responsible for".

"Ah I see, very sensible of the Management".

"Yes indeed. However, I am not happy about the level of commitment from the boys and girls. As you have just noticed, some come one day per week, some couple of days, and very few come every morning".

"I think laziness became normality for the youth nowadays. You know with all these smart phones, video games etc. They spend most of their time in front of screens".

"Yes, you are right about that. But I am afraid there are also other reasons for their laziness, and those reasons are far worse than the ones you've just mentioned".

"What do you mean?" Selway barely finished his question when his mobile phone rang, so he said, "Excuse me".

"Take your time. I must be off to my shower now. Talk to you another time" Radi said and waved his hand goodbye.

Selway waved his hand back and answered his phone while walking.

"Alo"

"Good morning. Can I speak to Mr Selway please?"

"Speaking!"

"I know you will be already awake old man. But it seems you didn't recognise my voice".

"But of course, it's you Ronald. How are you doing?"

"I am fine. Where on earth are you right now?"

"Morobury - Dorset. Home sweet home. and yourself?"

"Headsham - Devon. Good to hear that you are in the southwest and close by. I decided to ring you early before you set any plans for tomorrow. I will be glad if you accept my invitation for lunch tomorrow here at my place".

"Not a bad idea. However, I am not here alone. My secretary Ms Dobinson drove me here and she is spending one week, so it won't be very kind of me to leave her and go spend an entire day in Headsham".

"Bring her with you!"

"Are you sure?"

"Of Course, I am. If you are coming by Train just let me know at what time you reach Exeter Central station, and I will pick you from there".

"I will try to persuade her to drive us there by car, so the train will be the last option. Any way I will let you know after I talk to her. Have a nice weekend and thanks for the invitation".

"I look forward to seeing you both".

After a shower, Radi put on his house gown, and sat on his laptop. His mind was fully occupied by the strange behaviours of some of his previously best students. In the last few months some of them became very lazy, short tempered and even their school grades took a huge slide down.

He signed in into the school website. It was a large school that includes Primary and Secondary classes, and pupils were aged from 5 to 18 and few around 19- and 20-year-old.

In his thoughts there was specifically a boy aged 16 called Tom Wright. That guy was the first in his class for years, and then suddenly in the last three months before the end of the previous school year his notes dropped heavily in almost all courses. In the end he only managed to escape through to the final class of the secondary school of next year.

Knowing the guy for almost a year, Radi was certain that something dangerous is affecting the life of the teenager. His father was abroad for months serving in the army, so that could be a reason, "but no I don't think so" Radi murmured to himself, "His father has been for years now in long shifts service at the army while his mother is busy with his youngest brother and sister". So, what was the mystery behind this drastic change? Is he getting access to porn via the internet? Is he being abused physically by someone? The guy used to be super shy, but lately he was behaving very strangely and boldly.

Radi looked at his watch, it was nearly nine. As he did previously with few other pupils, He decided to investigate the case of Tom Wright. He put on a Jeans and a dark blue shirt and left his house towards the house of the Wright family which was a flat located above a pharmacy in the High Street.

There were a Restaurant and a Patisserie in the opposite side of the street. As it was still morning, the patisserie was the better option for the teacher. He went in, ordered a cake and cup of milk and sat on a table which gave him a full sight of the gate of the Wright house.

After his return from Max's walk, Mr Selway took a shower, had a cup of tea and left to the Grosvenor arms hotel. He wanted to see Ms Dobinson to ask her if she liked to accompany him to Devon the next day.

After asking at the hotel, the guy at the reception told him that she left in the early morning. He immediately remembered that she must have gone to the office. He then walked to the Patisserie to buy some nicely handmade cakes. There he saw Mr Radi sitting. "You are here too!" Selway said. Radi unlikely of him replied briefly and quickly said "Yes I am". Then he left his chair and said, "Excuse me". Selway paved the way for him as he left the patisserie quickly with his eyes set on the street.

Selway realised that Radi must be watching someone, he tried to see who that might be, but then the voice of the lady of the patisserie cut his curiosity by asking "How can I help Sir?" Selway then bought what he wanted and left back towards the office; he looked again in the street but there was no longer any sign of Radi.

While Selway joined his secretary in the office, Radi was following Wright from a place to another, but to his disappointment he went to the Tesco Supermarket for some groceries shopping and then returned home.

Dobinson welcomed her boss and told him that she had prepared three different models of adverts so he can pick his favourite. Selway's choice was the simplest one, it read:

Roger Selway

Private Detective

Phone numbers

Email

Website

(Full Discretion guaranteed)

"Well done Ms Dobinson. This one is my favourite".

"Okay. This one is suitable for online advertisements and of course for newspapers. So, what newspapers you wish to advertise at?"

"We should be open to operate in all English-speaking countries and for any individual who speaks English".

"Well. Tell me first what local newspapers you wish to advertise at?" Dobinson asked while typing on her laptop.

"The Times, The Guardian, The Telegraph and The Daily Mail. These are the newspapers in Britain". Selway replied

"And abroad?" She asked.

"I don't think it's necessary to advertise in newspapers in Australia, New Zealand and Canada. We will advertise online. Let us however advertise at the best-known newspapers in the United States of America".

"And those would be?"

"The New York Times and The Washington Post".

"How about Arab Countries? They do speak English and there are plenty of rich businessmen who would hire a private detective".

"Good idea. But I definitely don't know what is the best way to advertise there? However, I believe they all read the British and the American papers".

"Let me do my research regarding this matter, also I need some time to know what online outlets are best for adverts in Australia, Canada and New Zealand".

"Ok. Take your time. But I think we can still go ahead with adverts here and in the States".

"I can start contacting them now".

"Yes, you can, but I prefer if you keep it till Monday. I know most of employees would be lazy in weekends, so they may not give you very accurate and helpful information".

"As you wish!"

"Tell me now: Would you like to come with me to a town in Devon tomorrow? We are invited to spend the day and we return in the evening".

"Invited?! By whom?"

"An old friend of mine, he is a Chief Inspector at the New Scotland Yard, but like us he is spending his summer holiday in his hometown".

"I think it would be good for our business to know him. So, I will come, but I have one condition that should be met".

"Aha! And what is that?"

"I am not driving the car from here to there".

Selway shook his head and said "Okay then, I don't want to force you into something you don't like. You will drive only to the Millingham train station and then we take the train from there to Exeter".

"And how far is that Millingham station from here?"

"Hardly seven minutes".

At that Dobinson smiled and said "Agreed". Immediately Selway called Smith and told him that they will be coming by train, and he will let him knows the train's arrival time once they board it the next morning.

The evening was not a normal one in Dorset, even though it was a Saturday evening when usually people hold parties for fun, love and music. Mr Nicolas Mair (a wealthy young ambitious man in his late 20's) was holding in his house a political activism party for a radical right-wing movement he co-founded in Dorset with other men and women. They called it "The White Cross".

Mair's house was located in the neighbourhood of Westminster Memorial Hospital and geographically it was close to the houses of Selway and Radi, but the access to it, was from a different road.

There was a large space behind the hospital for walking near a Memorial Cross that was raised there for centuries, the party invitees were parking their cars at. The road was crowded with some very luxurious cars which state clearly the amount of money and power the members of that fanatic group had possessed.

Nearby in front of the mirror in his bedroom stood Barry Clayton as his mother was helping him adding the final touches to his suit and tie as he was excited to attend the night of the "White Cross". Suddenly his father opened the room door and said "Well, well, I must say I have never seen you in such elegance before. However, I am repeating my warning to you: please don't go there; this is not the right company for you". Barry looked at his mother who waved her right hand as if she was brushing her husband's words away and said, "Never mind what he is saying".

The father added "And beside it's a party for a group of fanatics, what people of Morobury are going to say if they knew that son of John Clayton, the bright physicist, is joining that extremist movement?".

Barry was about to reply but his mother was quicker to mock her husband by saying "I wonder what Morobury are going to say if they know what John Clayton himself was doing couple of days ago?".

Mr Clayton couldn't hide his anger at the way his wife approached him, but kept his mouth shut. He left the room and slammed the door behind him.

"What was he doing?" Barry asked.

"Never mind dear, go enjoy your night".

Chapter 6

Exceptionally that night, North Dorset police sent twelve officers to Morobury to look after the security of Mair's party. Policemen were all very well-equipped communication wise because there were some very important persons attending the party, including the Russian Ambassador to the United Kingdom and his wife, and many heads of extreme right-wing parties from many European countries and some wealthy white supremacists from the United States.

At the Grosvenor hotel it was a very busy evening too, the young ladies were very well dressed for the occasion and each of them had a man who accompanied her from the hotel towards Mair's house. They passed in front of Selway and Dobinson who were standing near the gate of Selway's house trying to figure out where all these cars and people were flooding to.

"It seems a very large party. Is there any big celebrity from Morobury or resident here?

"I doubt it. Never heard of any, but I have been away for a while, so everything is possible".

"Even those four foreign ladies are invited! Look" Dobinson said as the four ladies passed by with three gentlemen. "It seems rather a global party, because also these girls are Eastern European, I heard one of them talking French at the hotel" She added.

"Really! With whom?"

"To a man who came late to visit them at the hotel, I heard them from behind my door, but I didn't see the man!

"I think I know one of the guys. If I am not mistaken, he is the youngest son of Mr John Clayton".

Suddenly a hand tapped Selway on his left shoulder, and then a voice said, "I heard my name, so here I am".

It was Mr Clayton who smiled at Selway who in his turn said, "I should have wished a million bucks".

"Good to see you, old fellow".

"Good to see you too".

Selway introduced his secretary and his neighbour to each other. And then seriousness appeared again on Clayton's face. As he pointed his finger towards his son who was walking away with his group of friends, John said "You see".

"Yes, I noticed him, and I was telling Ms Dobinson it is your son". Selway replied

"You see what he is attending?"

"No, not really, I have no idea where the party is and what is the occasion!"

"It's a god damn party for white Christian supremacists" Claytons roared angrily.

Selway's jaw dropped in surprise, then he wondered "And who is hosting it?"

"You haven't been here in the last couple of years. That only son of Alexander Mair inherited all the wealth that his father gained from oil business, and two years ago he founded an extreme right wing political movement called - The White Cross" Clayton explained.

"That's not good my friend. And your son shares such beliefs; How come?"

"I don't know if he believes in anything at all! He has been struggling at university for years and couldn't graduate with a Geography diploma yet. But he is so spoiled by his mother, he has nothing from me". John Clayton tried to explain how disappointed he was from his youngest child. Then he looked towards Ms Dobinson, then back to Selway and asked him "Marriage plan at last?"

"No. Ms Dobinson is the secretary of the new Private Detective former colonel Roger Selway". Selway replied with a little smile.

"Good for you. You are a smart man, Roger. If I regret anything in my life lately, it's my marriage".

"Would you like to come in for a cup of tea or a drink?"

"No thanks. I better return home; I am having enough domestic problems to deal with lately. Have a good night".

Mr Clayton left; Selway turned towards Dobinson and said "It's strange how Morobury changed too much in just two years. I had no idea what this party is all about".

"And nothing in such changes to feel proud about, I am afraid".

"True" Selway nodded positively.

"I think I should retire now to my hotel. At what time you want to leave tomorrow?"

"About nine, is that okay?"

"Yes. Alright, I hope you would manage to sleep though, with all the party noise!".

"I will try my best".

"Good night"

"Good night".

When Barry and his friend Stephen and their two foreign companions reached Mair's house, they introduced their invitation automation stamps on a scanner machine held by one of the house guards. It was a luxurious vast house with a stunning garden filled with fountains of all types and sizes.

Their friends seemed to be familiar with such parties, for as soon as they reached the huge ball room in the middle of the house, they went straight to round standing tables with drinks according to numbers given to them in the invitation e-cards. The party was very well organised and to the surprise of no one, Russian dance music was played on as the Russian Ambassador and his wife took to the floor followed by the host Nicolas Mair and his fiancée who was also a Russian lady.

The two ladies who were with Stephen and Barry were a Russian and a Hungarian, therefore they knew very well how to dance on such music, and they forced their men to dance with them. Barry and Stephen tried their best to not embarrass themselves by copying the other male dancers in every move.

Not far from there, Radi was in his small house chatting cam to cam with the head of the school Ms Geraldine Kane. They were discussing the strange behaviour of some of the teenager students recently.

"So, tell me, have you followed Tom Wright today as you told me you would?"

"Yes. But unfortunately, he had only a shopping trip to Tesco, so nothing strange in that".

"Well, I talked to his mother yesterday evening, and she confessed to me that she woke up couple of times at night at him coming back from outside the house. So, he apparently has some secretive encounters at night".

"Very interesting; did she give you the time of his nautical activities?"

"Yes. She said approximately around 1 after midnight".

"So, he seems to be around midnight away of his house".

"Not every night though, because she told me she tried to catch him when he leaves. She tried that for few nights, but he never left".

"I see. That's also interesting. I think I have a duty to watch him every night until we get to the bottom of this issue, even though I prefer to be in bed by 11 pm to wake up as usual for my morning exercise".

"That's very nice of you to do so. The entire school and the town would be very thankful to you if we can manage to solve the secret of this mysterious change in the behaviour of those young lads".

"No need to thank me for anything. This is my duty as a teacher, for Sports include well being too. Let us keep our fingers crossed and hope that he will go out tonight".

Radi looked at his watch and said "It's 10 after 10. I think I should go now to their street and see if he leaves home".

And they ended their Skype conversation with Kane wishing him the best of luck in his coming adventure.

Radi put on his tracksuit and left his house walking quickly towards the high street in which Tom Wright's house was located. He heard all the noise coming out of the Mair's house, and he noticed the streets busier than usual, but his mind was focused only on one thing: the secret of his student's nights out. That area of the high street was almost empty, and to not raise suspicions he sat at the entrance of a Lloyd's bank branch which was a bit looking over the house of the wrights. He sat in a position that allowed him to see the entrance of the building and at the same time he was hidden from the sight of any person who came out of the gate.

When people walked by Radi pretended that he was chatting on his mobile phone. Times passed by but nothing happened. He started yawning and looking in despair to the time.

Quarter to midnight there was no more people in the street, and he started considering ending his shift when the gate of the building that hosted the Wrights apartment was opened. And quietly Tom smuggled himself out of it and turned straight to his left which was in the direction of Radi's hide.

The teacher pulled himself fully into the dark corner and stopped breathing while waiting until Tom passed by. He then waited another minute until Tom became a bit far ahead on the road, then he followed him.

Tom took the small passage between the Costa Cafe and the Oxfam shop just next to the Town hall. At that Radi had to double his speed because the area after the passage was crowded with cars of the large party invitees. So, he knew he should catch up with the teenager before he vanished between the cars.

The light in the area was not strong but Radi was still able to see Tom walking in straight line between the two lines of the cars. He passed by the Abbey Museum and so did Radi. Then Tom stopped suddenly when he approached the memorial Cross, looked around forcing Radi to lower himself behind a car. Then the young lad walked towards the large tree under which there were two wooden benches. But then he stopped before reaching it. Radi looked out and saw a man and a woman sitting on the right bench while the left one was empty. But Tom stood up there and pretended typing on his mobile phone when the couple looked towards him.

Radi was watching that scene from behind a car. The couple didn't seem to know Tom Wright, and the latter didn't take the empty bench next to them, maybe he was shy to disturb them or maybe for some reason he needed the bench they were sitting at.

The second reason seemed more logical to Radi because if the boy was shy, he wouldn't hover over the couple as if he was pushing them to leave. And that eventually happened, a couple of minutes later they left the place, and a sign of relief covered Wright's face.

A minute or two later, Tom sat on the bench as expected. He looked around to see if there is anyone looking, then he pulled out something out of his pocket, and then leaned for a while on his right side at the far-right end of the bench. Radi wasn't able to see what he was doing.

Then the young lad balanced his sitting and blew out a gesture of relief as if he just accomplished a hard task. He looked again around, pulled out his mobile phone and started playing games. Radi had to wait another hour before Tom Wright decided it's time to leave the place. No one came to meet the teenager even though some people were leaving by cars as it was almost 1 o'clock after midnight.

Wright returned on the same road he came from, but Radi was no longer interested in following him, he was more interested about the secret of that bench. He was certain that Wright took something from there or he left something there. Anyway, there was no way to know other than to go and sit on the bench.

At that time nearly quarter of the cars parked there had already left. Radi waited until Wright disappeared from sight, and then he walked in a normal way towards the bench and then occupied it. Knocking on, it was just a wooden and iron bench, and he couldn't see anything suspicious in it. He was puzzled for few moments, and then he focused his exploration skills to the right end of the bench wondering why would Wright lean to the right there? Did he take something left for him there by someone? If so, there was no way to do anything about it.

The light of the streetlamp was coming from behind him, and some branches of tree took some of the light away. And as the colour of the bench was dark brown it was very difficult to see anything unusual on its surface. Is there any secret pouch within it? He wondered. Then he sent his right hand all over the surface back and forth. Then suddenly he felt something slightly different than wood. It was just a tiny bit; he was trying to look normal because the party nearby made the location a bit of hot spot in the middle of the night. So, his fingers tried to measure the length of that thing, and it didn't take him long to realise it was a tiny elastic bond of rubber.

It seemed it was used to hold something and attach it to the bench. "There must be something at the bottom side of the bench" Radi confirmed to himself. He looked around, there was a man and two women standing under the lamp, one of the women was looking towards him. So, he had to pretend he was roping his shoes, and turned the opposite way while sending one of his hands to the bottom side of the bench and there he felt a small plastic bag attached to the bench via the elastic bond. He removed it as gently as he could, once it was entirely in his hand, he coughed a bit loud, and then regained his seat.

Pretending typing on his mobile phone, Radi fingers went quickly through the plastic bag. In it he found five notes of one hundred pound each. He wondered where did the teenager got all this cash from? And why did he leave it there and for whom? Radi's desire to uncover the truth made him forgot to take any precaution after Wright left. And suddenly he felt the danger that the side who was the receiver of the money should have been around at that very moment. And he wasn't mistaken. Someone was watching him already and has been actually there since Wright left the place, but Radi was quicker to reach the bench.

Radi was thinking hard, what step should he take next? Should he leave the money and watch if someone will come to pick it? But what if that someone was already here and he saw that the operation was uncovered, that means he or she would never approach the bench as long as Radi is around. Should he take the money back to the boy's mother and question him at home? Or maybe he should go to the police and leave the entire story in their hands?

He looked at his watch, it was approaching 2:00 am, and he knew that he got very limited amount of time to take a decision about the best way to approach this matter.

Chapter 7

Sunday's morning was unusually calm and completely different of Saturday's noisy night. Exceptionally that morning neither Selway nor Radi had their morning exercise, the first because he was preparing for his trip to Devon, and the second because of his late investigative night.

At 9:00 am Ms Dobinson arrived at the Selway's. Her boss was ready for the trip and Max too. The three of them gained the Jaguar and left Morobury to the neighbouring town Millingham, which had the luxury of a train station.

Dobinson parked the car at the station parking. Selway who had booked online two Millingham - Exeter return tickets, went straight away to one of two ticket machines to collect them. It was a very easy mechanism; he just had to insert his bank card and type the code given to him by the Southwest trains' website.

As usual the train to Exeter had few passengers comparing the one going to London which was always busier. So, bringing Max on board was not an issue for them. Each wagon offered other than the regular seats four spaces with tables in the middle of two seats facing each other. They picked one of those. Once they were seated, Selway typed a message to Smith informing him that they had just left Millingham and the journey takes usually some seventy minutes.

Chief Inspector Smith saw the message instantly for he was expecting it. He replied to his friend and confirmed receiving it. As he moved out of his sofa, immediately his cat Lucy and his dog Lara moved out with him. "Hey, you both, I won't be long, don't mess with the state of the house, we are having visitors" Smith addressed his two pets.

He left his house from the Kitchen door to where his blue Skoda was always parked. Lucy accompanied him to the car because she was able to go out through the cat door in the kitchen, while Lara barked from the inside.

He opened the backyard blue crossed gate, and then gained his car and drove carefully on the tight passage between neighbouring houses until he got to the main road, then drove off to Exeter Central train station.

He parked outside the station and looked up to check the monitor of the Arrivals. He arrived fifteen minutes before the train, so he opened his Times newspaper and went through some headlines with the majority of them linked to the Brexit negotiations in Brussels between the British government and the European Union as both tried to reach a deal on the exit of Britain from the Union.

Minutes went by and Smith soon welcomed his three visitors as they passed through the tickets' gates. The two old men hugged each other, as they haven't seen each other for nearly three years. Then Selway introduced Dobinson and Smith to each other. Max protested with a short bark, but Smith who was obsessed with animals was not late in giving the golden retriever a hug while feeling his warm long tongue on his face.

Few moments later, they gained the Skoda and left Exeter to Smith's house in Headsham, a small town on the river Exe.

At their arrival, Lucy ran towards the car as usual. But this time an unpleasant surprise was waiting for her as soon as she sensed Max presence. She yelled and hissed, her tail became double sized, she roared fiercely before running back towards the house and smuggled herself in through the pet door. Few seconds later, Lara appeared on the kitchen door and started barking loudly as soon as her eyes noticed Max walking towards the house with Smith and his visitors.

With the help of the three humans the battle between the pets didn't last long, even though the unwelcome visitor was alienated by the pair hosts.

It was a beautiful sunny day, so after a short walk inside the house, they decided to sit in the small backyard garden of Smith's detached house. Max followed them outside while Lara and Lucy kept their alliance unmoved and remained outside protecting their castle from outsiders.

"It's very nice to see you after all these years; you look fit and still young. I am the one who is feeling very old these days. I am considering retiring soon as the job duties talking their toll on me" Smith said.

Selway said while putting on his sunglasses "You look good. And I don't believe you will be retiring anytime soon. You say so at the moment, but when you think about it seriously you will realise that you can't sit around doing nothing, unless you are considering joining my firm as a private detective".

The three of them laughed at the thought. As the two went on talking, Dobinson was mute as she looked to the two of them exchanging thoughts and memories. There were plenty of things in common between the two. They were both very handsome, one moustached the second clean shaven. Both are with very witty and jolly good sense of humour. Both single.

Time passed quickly as it always does when people are enjoying each other's company. Then Smith said it's now 12:30 and I should retire to the kitchen to put the last touches on the lunch. Dobinson and Selway offered their help, but Smith suggested they had one of two options, either go into his library room upstairs explore some books or go for a short walk around Headsham until the lunch got ready.

The weather was too good to resist the walk around option. Also, Headsham was a small town which had a variety of houses built differently, so it was a bit colourful to walk in its little roads, especially at the Goat walk on the Exe River. And as expected in summer the water of the river was lower than usual.

"It's definitely calmer than Morobury" Dobinson said.

"Yes, it's calmer but it doesn't have the picturesque stunning views that Morobury offers".

"In this, yes you are right" She admitted.

Few minutes later, Selway's mobile rang. "Yes, we are coming" he said. It was smith of course calling them back as lunch became ready.

They did a U turn and they walked faster on their way back. Few minutes later Lara and Lucy had their lunch in one corner of the kitchen and Max in the opposite. However, that didn't stop them from roaring at each other from time to time.

In the living room, on an ancient wooden table the human trio had their seats. A big smile was drawn immediately at Dobinson's face as soon as she discovered that the main plate was "Stir fry noodles" with very carefully grilled Turkey portions.

"Oh Noodles! Yummy!" she said.

"Mind you no one in the world does it better than Ron".

"I am glad that you are both happy with my choice for lunch today".

While that trio was enjoying their meal in Headsham, Radi in his house in Morobury was very anxious and nervous, as the plan he wanted to execute was completely disabled or at least delayed by the nonresponse he was getting in all his attempts to reach the manager of the school.

When he returned home the previous night, he decided to bring the money home with him, and then call the school manager to decide what to do next, to call the police or to go confront the student in his house with the cash he left at the bench. But his plan was frozen because the mobile phone of the manager was off, also all her internet accounts were. Radi left messages to her in every possible way, but he was yet to hear from her, and it was midday.

They already lost load of time and actually Radi was worried that he was having money, which is not his, also he was assuming that the money was to be given to some bad person, but he can't be sure one hundred per cent about that. What if the potential receivers saw him yesterday and saw that he took the money, what if they planned something to trick him. Plenty of worries and questions were invading his mind. He was attempting to reach Ms Kane at least once every ten minutes.

As he felt he couldn't change anything in the situation until he consulted her, he then decided to prepare his lunch. He wasn't in the mood to cook a real meal, so he went for a quick one. He fetched an Uncle Ben's whole grain rice bag, put it in the microwave for two minutes, then opened a Greek yogurt jar, added 6 large spoons to the rice, mixed them together, turned on the TV on History channel as he liked to watch the "Ancient Aliens" series. He went through his plate as he enjoyed an episode about the Pyramids of Antarctica.

That took his mind away of his worries for nearly half an hour. But when the episode ended, he then reattempted to call Kane but no success. He felt a little dizzy as he didn't sleep all night except for few minutes, as his little adventure fully occupied his mind.

He threw himself on the bed, and tried to get his mind off his anxiety, but after nearly twenty minutes, he couldn't sleep. In the end he turned on his laptop and searched for some white noise sounds that could help him sleep. He picked a storm sound with howling wind joined from time to time by some owls and wolves' howls. Then he managed to sleep after ten minutes or so.

He slept for long hours and did wake up only on his mobile ringing. He jumped like a fool when he heard it, and as expected it was Ms Kane.

"Hello Mustapha. What's going on with you? I opened my mobile just now and founded that you bombarded it with missed calls and voice and text messages".

"Sorry about that but something very important happened last night and we should discuss it together now".

"Oh, it seems you fell on something really important because you sound very worried about it. I am sorry for not being able to reply early, I went to visit my mother in Stokeminster and I left my mobile at home because I wanted to have a day away from all the technology tools".

"No worries. But I believe it's very urgent that we meet this evening. What time is it now?"

"8:15"

"What? I slept nearly seven hours. Good God!".

"Oh, dear it seems you had no sleep last night".

"Can you meet me at King Alfred's Kitchen Restaurant around 9?"

"It sounds very urgent, and yes of course I will. See you there then".

"See you".

Five minutes to nine Radi passed in front of Selway's house as Roger and his secretary had just returned from Devon and they were standing next to the garage.

"Good evening" Radi said as he walked in a hurry.

"Good evening young men" Selway replied with a surprise in his face because the young lad was rather short with him for the second time in a row. He even ignored the warm welcome Max tried to give him.

"He seems very worried and in a big hurry" Dobinson said.

"Yes indeed" Selway confirmed with a head nod.

At nine o'clock, Radi walked in the restaurant, and he was relieved as he saw Ms Kane was already there waiting him on a strategic table on the far-left corner of the restaurant which was crowded that Sunday evening.

Radi told Kane what happened to him the previous night from the moment they ended their Skype chat until the moment he returned home with the five hundred pounds that Tom Wright left behind attached to the bottom side of the memorial bench.

A serious look appeared on Kane's face as she was trying to figure out what service was her young student paying for.

"So, what would you have done in my place?"

"I would have done the same, but you are right the one or more who were supposed to be receiving the money must have been around when you took the money. So, if you left it there, they would have taken it eventually and you couldn't of course stay all time watching there to see who is going to take it".

"Exactly; so, what do you think is the best way to move forward with this? Should we go to the police? Or should we try first to confront Tom with the money and see if he is going to tell us what is going on?"

After few moments of silence, Kane thought hard then said, "I think we should speak to Tom first, because to go to the police right now their involvement may scare him, and he might refuse to talk".

"That exactly what I thought too, should we go to his house now?"

"Tomorrow at school, at the lunch break we will talk to him privately in my office. Speaking to him alone may help in pushing him to come forward with his story".

"You are right. I think this is the best way. Because I don't think his mother has an idea of what is going on, so to confront him in front of her, may offend him too. Talking to him and him alone and in a friendly manner would be the best way to gain his trust and ease his way to share his secret with us".

Kane nodded her head positively. They both felt relaxed at that decision. Then the school manager smiled and said, "What Can I offer you for dinner tonight?"

"I invited you here tonight, so I am the one who is going to ask what I can offer you." Radi protested.

Kane didn't complain. She looked at the menu and said "I don't like to eat heavy things at dinner. So, I will go for the hot cheese and olives sandwiches with a nice cup of Tea".

Radi waved his left thumb up and said, "I would go for the same".

They ordered that, and as it was easy to prepare, they were enjoying the sandwiches and tea in a couple of minutes.

As they finished and were about to leave, Dobinson entered the restaurant as she also discovered those nice sandwiches and she used to fetch one for herself every evening.

Their table was the only free table to be, so Radi waved to Dobinson to get there.

She walked towards them and said "Good evening"

"Good evening. This is Ms Dobinson a friend of my neighbour colonel Selway. This is Ms Kane my boss, the school manager". Radi introduced the two ladies to each other.

The three smiled at each other, and Radi said, "We are leaving, so you can sit here before someone else occupies the table".

"Thank you. Very sensible of you, but I actually take my sandwich with me back to the hotel".

"Oh, I see. I failed to be generous then".

"No. you can count it as if I used the table".

They laughed loud and waved goodbyes.

Chapter 8

At her arrival to her desk in the school Monday morning, Kane received a phone call from the Ministry of Education informing her that one of Newcastle schools wanted the services of Mr Radi, and that the ministry will replace him by another teacher by the coming Friday. She asked the caller to send her a formal letter and an email message about that request.

It was not a good start for her day, and that made her nervous already while she needed all the calmness in the world to deal with the task of speaking to the pupil Tom Wright in the coming couple of hours. It was not a formal day at school, and it was accidentally one of those lonely summer Mondays where some teachers gave some students who performed badly in the last semester of the previous season special classes in order to strengthen them in the fields that they should be relying on at the new class in the coming season.

She left her desk and stared long out of her window. The Ministry demand occupied her mind totally, she then picked up her mobile phone, rang Radi and asked him to come to the school at 9 instead of 10 o'clock.

Radi had a Cappuccino cup at Costa Cafe, then at 10 to 9 walked to the school. And soon he knocked on the manager office door.

"Come in". Kane said

"Good morning"

"Good morning".

"Where is Tom? I thought you called him early to talk to him"

"No, I will talk to him when he arrives for the summer class. But I called you to talk to you about you".

"About me?!" Radi wondered.

"Have you made any contact lately with a school in Newcastle?" Kane asked

"No!"

"Do you know anyone in Newcastle?"

"No. Why? I have never been to Newcastle, not even for a visit".

"That's strange!"

"I don't understand anything. What's going on?"

"I received a call this morning from the ministry of Education saying that a school manager in Newcastle ordered your services specifically for a vacant sport teacher post in his school and that they will send us a replacement for you this weekend".

"But I love my work here, and I don't want to relocate to the Northeast of England".

"Between us it's a very weird request. In my entire career I have never came across of such demand. At first, I thought you might be wishing to relocate to there, but now it's clear you had no idea about it".

Radi looked very concerned then wondered "Can you just refuse the ministry demand, or will it cause a headache for you if you do?"

Kane took a deep breath then said "Look I don't like to use my connections network to influence decisions, but because I like your professionalism and your care for our students, I will call the Prime Minister as I know her personally and I will tell her that the school here needs you and we are not going to allow this move at any cost".

At hearing this, Radi felt some relief.

Kane didn't waste any minute and contacted the Prime Minister immediately. For Radi's luck the two women were close friends since secondary school, but they diverted at University between Politics and General Management. She left a voice message on the PM's private number and asked her to call back when she has few minutes of free time.

At five to ten, Kane used the inter-phone to ring the classroom in which Wright was going to attend. As expected, there was a teacher on the other end.

"Miss Clarke, can you please send me Tom Wright to my desk as soon as he arrives?"

"Yes of course. He has already arrived. I will send him at once".

Kane and Radi took the story of Newcastle out of their minds and focused on the tough task ahead. Wright entered the room with surprise covering his face as he wondered to himself: what was that call about?

"Good morning".

"Good morning" they both replied.

"Please sit down" Kane said. He took seat on the second chair opposite to Radi's in front of her desk. Kane went on "Tom you have been one of the most brilliant students in the history of this school, and I want you to know that you mean so much for us".

"Thank you" Wright shyly replied.

"I hope you won't take any offence of what I am going to say. We are talking to you now as an adult with wise mind, and after one year you will start your university studies, so please listen carefully to what we have to say".

Seriousness mixed with worries appeared on Tom's face.

"We noticed and I am sure you yourself did notice that in the last semester your performance at school and your notes dropped dramatically down for some reason, that we in the school do not now, but we hope to hear it from you" Kane continued.

Wright tried to play down the importance of what was affecting his life in general and school performance specifically. He drew a fake smile and said, "I am just being addicted lately to video games and I believe they are taking so much of my time, that's why I am having lately lower grades".

Kane and Radi looked at each other when they heard that, then Kane asked, "Are you sure?"

"Yes. I am" the student replied.

Kane then gave a signal to Radi who understood what she meant. The teacher pulled out of his pocket the five hundred pounds in the plastic bag and handed them to Wright.

The latter's jaw dropped at the sight, then suddenly he spat at his teacher saying "You. You have been doing this to me!"

The boy went mad as if someone shocked him with electricity, he went hysterical, then left his seat shouting all possible obscenities leaving them stunned and in total shock as he slammed the door behind him.

The shock froze Kane and Radi for few seconds, then when Kane realised what might the student have meant, she ran quickly to the inter-phone and rang the school gate guard to block Wright from leaving the school building and added "I will be thankful if you can bring him back here".

Kane then asked Radi "What does he mean by claiming: You were doing that to him?"

"Was he overreacting in front of us to protect himself? Did he think that I am interfering with his private life? Did he think that I am the one taking his money? I really don't know what he meant".

The inter-phone rang, and the guardian voice came through "I have him here, but he refuses to return to your desk unless---".

"Unless what?" Kane asked.

"Unless you are alone in the room"

"You mean he doesn't want the presence of Mr Radi".

"Exactly"

"Ok then, tell him I will meet him alone and send him over".

Kane then turned to Radi and apologised saying "He doesn't want you to be present. I am sorry but let us do what he wants".

"Ok if that helps" The teacher replied with a low frustrated tone, and then added when leaving the desk "I am at home, and you have my number if you want anything".

Radi sprinted his way back home, and he didn't notice Selway who was looking at the street from the open window of his bedroom

At his arrival home, Mrs Clayton was sitting in her garden. As soon as she saw the gloomy face of her tenant, she spoke out loud to her maid and said "Very beautiful day. Isn't it? But apparently not all people seem to be enjoying it. Maybe they heard some bad news".

Radi entered his place and slammed the door behind him, while a big smile of satisfaction covered Mrs Clayton's face, as she assumed that the Sport teacher has received the news of his removal from his post in Morobury to another in Newcastle. She waited her maid to leave towards the kitchen then picked up her mobile phone and called her friend Mrs Jenkins

"Hello... I can't thank you enough; it seems our plan is going well. They seem to have informed him that he would be moved to Newcastle. I owe you a nice gift for this great help".

The day passed quickly and as Radi didn't hear from Kane. He assumed the worse had happened and couldn't sleep all night, turning to his left side, then to his right side and all dark thoughts crossed his mind. But the most persistent question was "Will he be relocating to Newcastle after all? and what was he going to say to the real estate agency the next day as he had agreed to visit a couple of houses, one in Morobury, the other in Millingham.

To his luck the days scheduled for the students' summer sports program that week were Wednesday, Friday and Saturday, so he didn't have to worry about waking up early the next day.

The tiredness led him to sleep around 6 o'clock in the morning, and before that he set the mobile alarm to 12, as his meeting with the estate agent was scheduled at 2 in the afternoon.

However, he was awakened at 10 to 11 by his telephone ringing. And he was glad to hear finally from Kane.

"I have some good news and some bad news" she said.

"Fire up the good news first then"

"I have just finished talking to the Prime Minister, and she promised that you will continue working here".

"That's great. And now what is the bad news?"

"Tom Wright believes that you are the unknown person who has been blackmailing him for months, and no matter what I tried, he is very convinced that you are the one who is playing dirty games with him".

"Blackmailing him on what?"

"He refuses to tell me what it is. But he is linking your coming to Morobury and the start of his problems with the blackmailer".

"He is entitled of course to his analysis and opinion, but why would I hand him the money back if I was the blackmailer?"

"I asked him that and his answer was maybe you had enough money and you got bored with the game".

"That means the blackmailer had already taken money from him before".

"Yes, it seems the case".

"So, he should be expecting me to pay him what I took, or what does he think now?"

"He sounded a bit afraid that any of this could reach his mother, and it seems to me that he is holding you to account in order to get the money paid back if his mother knew about it".

"I see. And what do you think I should do to erase this unfair judgement from his head?"

"I don't know. And I actually feel guilty for involving you in this mess".

"No offence taken from the boy, as you know my mum is a wealthy woman and I can pay him the money he wants, if that helps him avoiding trouble with his mother and get things back on track when it comes to his performance at school. But the problem would persist if the blackmailer contacted him again".

"You are right. However, if the blackmailer saw you that night taking the money, and if he knows you are the schoolteacher of Tom, he will realise that his trick has been uncovered, so he may hesitate to pursue milking money out of the boy".

"You are right, and the problem I hate in such conclusion that Tom might conclude that I am truly the blackmailer and that's why everything stopped".

"Exactly, this is rather a tricky situation to be in".

"Whatever, I am happy now to remain here in this beautiful town at your service. I will be visiting two properties this afternoon, because as I told you before the landlord here doesn't want to renew my rental contract for another year".

"Good luck then".

Radi turned some music out loud while taking a shower. He dressed the best of what he had in the closet in order to impress the landlords. And once he was sure he was looking very distinguished and elegant and that Mrs Clayton was in her garden, he opened the door and left his place singing and blowing some whistles like a bird. He heard her when he was upset and immediately connected her to the attempt of removing him from the school, so now he wanted to announce to her in an indirect way that her plan had failed.

The happy look of Radi surprised Mrs Clayton and even annoyed her as she felt that something was not right. She got that feeling that something had happened and changed her tenant mood completely. She tried to call the minister's wife, but she got no reply. Then she said to herself angrily "Anyway, we will know eventually".

Radi walked to the high street through the abbey cemetery passage, and then walked up to his left to where the real estate agency office was located just few meters away from the Arts Centre. He walked in exactly at 2:00. There were couple of clients talking to a woman on the desk. Then another woman came out of another room and walked toward him and said, "You must be Mr Radi".

"Yes, I am Mustapha Radi".

"I am Marta, and I am the one who will accompany you to your scheduled visits".

"Nice to meet you"

"Nice to meet you too; Shall we? My car is just outside to the right".

"Alright"

As she opened the car doors with her remote keys, she told him "I suggest we go to the property in Millingham first, and then we return to the one here".

"Sensible idea" Radi agreed.

Chapter 9

Radi decided to rent the house in Morobury even though the one in Millingham had a wider space and cheaper price. He signed the papers with the agent and the landlord, and then Marta drove him to his place.

August was coming to a close and he was to relocate to his new house by next Saturday. So, he was happy to leave behind all his trouble with the previous landlord. But as he was opening the door of his house, the voice that he didn't hear for almost a week, came from behind.

"Good evening my friend. You look happy and I am glad to see that after the ordeal you faced when we last met" Mr Clayton said.

Radi replied with a trembled emotional voice "Good Evening, John. Yes, I am happy because I have just signed a tenancy agreement to stay here in Morobury".

The handsome mature bearded scientist came closer and whispered few words into Radi's right ear.

"Yes sure!" the teacher replied with a wide passionate smile. "In fact, that's why I am staying in this town" he added.

Clayton said in a very low voice "Wish I can come in now, but the bloody woman is here. Take care. See you soon, maybe at your new place".

As soon as Radi closed his door, he heard Mrs Clayton starting a fight with her husband.

"I told you, you must never talk to this guy again".

"We met accidentally as he was returning home".

"Anyway, he won't be here by next week" she said in a very firm tone.

Radi threw her words away of his head, brought his laptop, turned it on and called his adoptive mother on Skype to tell her how things went at school, the story of Tom Wright and the new tenancy agreement.

Anne Watt was a single very wealthy woman (by inheritance from her mother side) in her late 60's, a former diplomat. She used to work at the Foreign Office. And at a period of time in the 1980's she worked at the British embassy in Lebanon. While working there the Israeli invasion of Beirut and the late years of the Lebanese civil war were taking place, and she had several friends at the Palestinian refugees' camps in Lebanon. Two of her friends called Zaki Radi and his wife Leila were killed in a massacre committed in 1985 by armed militias supported by the Syrian army, and they left behind their only child Mustapha who was only 6 months old. In the chaos and the uncertainty of the other Palestinian families, Watt found herself facing the huge responsibility of looking after the child, and to make things easier for her legally, she decided to adopt the child and take care of him as if he was her own.

Watt was happy to see her adopted son smiling again after a week in which he was delivering to her almost a daily report of bad news. She promised him that she will come to Morobury on Friday evening to see the new house and watch the relocation process. And he was delighted to hear that from her.

While happiness invaded Radi's place, just few yards away Mrs Clayton was living a nightmare as the news reached her that Radi will be staying at the school after all. Nothing was able to ease her anger, and maybe it was the first time in her life she didn't get what she wanted. And that put her in a hysterical state.

Her maid didn't know what was going on, but she was shocked and rather frightened as she saw her screaming in her room like a mentally ill person. She also smashed the glass of water she brought to her while shouting "I don't want anything. I just want to die or at least fall into a coma".

The disturbed maid then walked to the laboratory of Mr Clayton bringing him a cup of tea. She put the cup at the desk in front of him. But she didn't leave, so he looked up at her "What is the matter?"

"Mrs Clayton is in a very bad mood".

"A premiere!!" he said with a mocking smile.

"I mean this time; it looks very serious. She is saying: she wants to die".

"Oh well. Don't worry, she will calm down eventually". He puts back his glasses and carried on continuing what he was doing as the maid left the laboratory and returned to the kitchen.

The days of that week passed quickly; Dobinson returned to London leaving Selway alone in the company of Max. Anne Watt arrived to Morobury midweek accompanied by her sister Ruth and a friend. However, the Thursday morning wasn't a pleasant one for her.

While Radi was having his after-exercise morning shower, the Watt sisters were in their way from the Grosvenor Arms hotel to his place bringing him a very nice breakfast. As soon as they entered his little garden space, Mrs Clayton shouted out loud at them "Miss Watt, I need to talk to you now urgently".

Anne nodded positively and said "Alright, I will be with you in a couple of minutes Mrs Clayton".

The sisters prepared the table, and shortly Radi joined them, but Anne apologised for not being able to eat with them.

"Why?" asked her son.

"Because Mrs Clayton wants to talk to her now" Ruth said.

Radi shook his head, while his adoptive mother left the place and joined Mrs Clayton in her garden.

The story that Mrs Clayton told to Anne was not a surprise for the latter, however she knew she couldn't escape the woman without promising that she will do all what she can to keep her son away from the Claytons once he moved to his new address.

At that Mrs Clayton felt some relief, but that didn't last long as her husband saw her from the window of his office talking to Miss Watt.

When Watt withdrew to her son's, Mrs Clayton entered her house too. But as soon as she walked in, Mr Clayton exploded his anger on her

"You didn't tell that woman what happened. Did you?"

"Of course, I did, because this unnatural business has to end and forever".

"Why involving the honourable lady in the affair of two adults? Why are you doing this?"

"Because I believe this is my right as your wife to stop your insanity".

"You are my wife, but that doesn't mean you own me".

"Well, the church says so: until death separated us apart".

"I don't care what your church said. My freedom as an individual comes first and you must respect it if we are to continue our life together. You have been always the only woman in my life, and I think this should satisfy you".

"Enough of your satanic manners" and tears flooded in her cheeks like all other women when they feel defenceless.

Their son Barry heard the argument from start to finish then he joined his mother as she ran towards her room.

What did upset Mrs Clayton most was the sign she got from her husband that he had no intention of changing his ways. And her anger and frustration pushed her to tell her son everything, without realising how grave was what she told him.

The shock was too much for Barry's consciousness. After his mind digested rather slowly the information he had just heard, he went banana. He jumped like a crazy man shouting, "I swear to Jesus, I will kill him". He then hurried toward his father room but found no one there, hurried towards his study but also, he wasn't there. Then he left the house like a wild beast and knocked heavily by his feet on Radi's door, but the latter had left already with the Watts to continue furnishing his new home.

Mr Clayton was at the local Sports Club pub, having a drink hoping for anything that can calm him down. Few minutes after his arrival to the pub, a man he helped signing for the club walked in. It was the trainer of the Rugby club, Pascal Marchandise, a very muscular big man in his late forties. Clayton who was involved with the management of the club called him immediately to join him on his table.

"Oh! Hello, how is our great professor and scientist doing?" Marchandise said.

"Bad. I am afraid. Very bad"

"Oh dear, it seems you are really facing a big problem. Can I help?"

"No one can help I am afraid. It's a very private matter that's rocking the foundation of my house at the moment".

"The foundation of your house! Hmm. Let me guess". "You were caught red-handed by your wife, sexting someone or something?"

"Something of the sort but far worse than sexting"

"What? Did she catch you naked on a cyber-camera?"

"No. Why should I tell you anyway?"

"Sorry, but I was just trying to help you out if I could".

"No worries, but definitely you cannot, because my wife saw me in the act"

"Oh dear! How on earth could that happen? Did you bring someone to your house?"

"No, she surprised us in another house"!

"That's really a strange story unless your wife is watching you all the time".

"I don't know. Perhaps she does. As you said it was a strange occurrence, and I couldn't manage to discuss it with her further".

"Well, it happened to me once in France, but it was someone who informed my girlfriend that I am with another girl at a specific address at a specific time. In the end I discovered it was the girl I was dating, she wanted to break my relationship in order to replace my girlfriend".

At hearing this, Mr Clayton sent his tongue from one corner of his mouth to another and raised his left eyebrow thinking of such possibility. Mr Marchandise looked at his watch and said "I think I should go home to prepare for the afternoon game. It was nice to see you, and I wish you all the luck of the world to get your issue sorted out".

"Thank you. And I am happy with the team results lately. Keep up the good work" Clayton replied before Marchandise left the pub.

Meanwhile nothing had taken away the dark cloud that invaded Barry's head other than a phone call from his friend Stephen asking him to wait him on the road, for he had received an important message from the drugs supplier.

Few minutes later the black 4x4 car arrived to Bimport, and quickly Barry jumped into the front seat. Stephen wasn't late to notice his friend gloomy state, and he asked "What's the matter? You do look shaky today!".

"Nothing that concerns you" replied Barry.

"Hear, hear. Barry is holding secrets from me! Are you falling in love suddenly or what?"

Barry didn't reply, he was busy sniffing a cocaine shot.

"Don't consume too much, what if we didn't get supplies tonight".

"But you told me he contacted you"

"Yes, he did, but he didn't mention supplying us with more staff".

"Oh well. He always does when he initiates the contact".

"Whatever! No harm in being prudent regarding what we have".

"As you say, anyway where are we going now? Did he give you a place and a time?"

"No not yet. He said he will be in touch during the night, and he will give us the instructions in due course".

"And where are you taking us now?"

"To the cinema, there is a new horror film of Stephen King ET and those scary clowns".

"Ok I will watch if I remained awake".

At sunset, there were signs of very dark grey clouds gathering in the sky, and wind started to strengthen its speed. All the ingredients of a huge storm were building up. The sky mood was a bit similar to the mood of Mrs Clayton after she recognised that she will not be able to remove Radi from town, and also, she was worried about her son reaction to his father's affair. She was sitting on her bed fighting her anger and anguish when her husband knocked several times on her door, but she refused to answer.

"What a difficult creature!" Mr Clayton murmured to himself. He wanted to ask her some questions that became persisting in his head after what he heard from the Rugby coach.

After he gave up and withdrew to the living room and turned on the TV. His wife put on her long dress with a black coat and a hat, and smuggled herself silently to the main door, but when she opened it, a huge lightening appeared in the sky followed by a scary thunder sound, then the rain started falling heavily.

As she realised, she couldn't go out. She returned quickly to her room, pulled out her mobile and called a Taxi. Usually, Taxis do not answer calls for such a short distance from Bimport to the Catholic Church, but when the call comes from the very wealthy Mrs Clayton, any taxi driver would have known immediately that the payment for their service would be handsome.

Hardly seven minutes later, a message on her mobile phone stated that the taxi is waiting her outside. Mr Clayton saw the light of a car outside, he stood and looked out of the window, when his wife opened the door and ran towards the car. He recognised it was a Taxi, but wondered where she would go in such terrible weather conditions.

At that time, Radi was with the sisters Watt at Anne's hotel room. After they had their dinner together, he wanted to return home to sleep around 10 pm as he had to wake up for his early morning exercise. Anne saw how terrible the weather was and she insisted that he should take a taxi.

"But it's hardly 300 yards away. And as you know, I exercise normally under such weather".

"I know you do. But you are not wearing exercise suit, and it's not an exercise right now".

He couldn't break her word. And few minutes later, a new taxi light appeared in the garden of the Claytons. Mr Clayton thought his wife returned quickly, but to his surprise Radi emerged from the car and walked home.

Radi was spending the last weekend at that address, and he was moving out on Monday morning. When he opened his laptop, Skype showed him a message from the school manager. And couple of minutes later he was chatting with her when he heard a knock on his door

"One moment please. Someone on the door" he said.

He opened the door, and it was Mr Clayton getting almost wet under the heavy rain. Radi paved the way for him with a smile, but to his surprise when the old man came in, he looked rather angry and strange.

"I want to know something from you, and I hope you will be frank with me?"

"Yes. Go ahead".

"Did you tell her?"

"Tell Whom and what?"

"My wife, did you tell her?"

"About?"

"Us. And left the door open for her to catch us in the act?"

"Oh my god! How can you even think about this?"

"Why should I believe you?"

"I can't believe it"

"And I don't believe you"

After shouting out loud his accusations to his lover, Mr Clayton left the place in total anger.

Chapter 10

The storm was unprecedented in Morobury since decades. The wind battered the roofs, many trees fell down, and there were some electricity cuts during the night.

The weather didn't calm down before 7 O'clock that Friday morning. Emma Kavanagh was fighting herself out of bed, as her work at the hospital starts at 8:30 am. She looked at her watch; it was five minutes after 7. She jumped quickly to her closet, pulled out her tracksuit and fed her Dalmatian dog "Pop". She smuggled her feet into two long rubber boots, and then took the dog for 20 minutes' walk at the footpath close by. Hardly five minutes into their walk, Pop barked out loud and jumped hysterically near a small rock at the far-right side of the footpath that goes round the bottom of Castle Hill. "What's the matter? Come here now. We don't have much time!" But the dog stood there and kept barking nonstop. He also looked several times in the direction of his owner and then to the rock, as if he was calling her to come and see.

Emma gave up and walked towards Pop to see what alerted him that much. And she was stunned like someone had hit her in the head when she saw a man on the ground with his head covered in blood, and a small Swiss knife dropped close to his right hand. She lost her reasoning for few moments, before her nursing duties came to the fore, she held the man's left wrist, and she knew immediately that he was dead.

She didn't have her mobile phone on her; she looked around at the spacious area where people usually come in the morning for jogging or dog walking, but as the weather was horrible there was no one there yet. She had to make up her mind, she either had to run to the hospital where she works, she would inform them, or she can return home and call the police from there to inform them.

As her house was slightly closer than the hospital to the scene, she took the second option.

She sprinted her way home with the dog running behind her. And as soon as she arrived there, she dialled the police station number, and told them what she had just discovered, and described to them the exact area where to find the body. They took her name and address, mobile number and asked her if she recognised the man, she denied knowing who he has, even though she might have seen him before in Morobury, but she didn't know his name or his address.

She looked at her watch; it was already 10 minutes to 8. She took her clothes off and then took a quick shower in preparation for her work shift at the Westminster memorial hospital.

It took the police some twenty minutes to reach the site, and there were already dozens of men and women and dogs gathering near the rock. There was also the Catholic Priest Father O'Shea in his black dress on his knees saying a prayer next to the body.

Chief Constable James Owen waited the priest to finish his prayer, and then ordered everybody to leave the site and his men started cordoning the area. As the priest turned his back to leave, Owen asked him "Do you know the dead man?"

"I don't know him personally, no. But I know where he lived. He was a tenant of the Claytons Annexe. I know his details because Mrs Patricia Clayton is a regular church goer, and I saw him in their garden once".

"Thank you for this information".

The priest left the designated area as police officers hurried everyone out of it. Owen got busy with informing the Claytons on the phone, and he asked Mrs Clayton about Mustapha Radi family members.

Around 8 o'clock, Roger Selway was taking Max for his daily morning walk, when he saw police and ambulance cars speeding towards and from the footpath where he walked every morning. So, he hurried up quickly to see what was going on.

Even though the rain had stopped, wind was still howling and hitting people faces with some very cold slaps. He saw some men started to gather at the top of the hill which situated at the higher half of the path. he ran quickly towards there, and as he was approaching the crowded area there was a man dressed fully in black drawing a thanksgiving cross sign towards the heaven unaware that someone was coming from behind. As soon as Selway saw the cross on his chest, he recognised him as one of the priests of the Catholic Church.

Selway reached the cliff where three other men stood, and down there saw the police men installing a ribbon around a body. He didn't wait a second; he ran quickly followed by Max around the path until he reached the lower half and joined the police officers there.

Chief Constable Owen recognised him immediately "Hello Colonel, this morning doesn't seem to be a good one".

Selway looked at the body and covered his face in shock. It was heart breaking for him to see his young new neighbour Mustapha Radi lying there dead and his head covered with blood. It took him couple of minutes to regain his control over his emotion as he sobbed quietly.

Meanwhile, once she opened her door to go out, the first thing Emma Kavanagh saw was the police boots, as two officers were about to knock on her door.

"Ms Emma Kavanagh".

"Yes. It's me".

"The chief Constable is at the scene, and he needs to talk to you right now".

"No problem, I will come with you, but first let me call the hospital to tell them that I will be late because of what is happening".

She called the hospital and told them briefly what happened in the last hour or so, and then she gained the police car.

Even if the scene was close by, the car was able to reach a further point closer to the scene where the public were not allowed.

As the forensic team was taking photos of the body and the surroundings, Selway and another man casually dressed were the only two standing with Constable Owen as he questioned Ms Kavanagh,

"Ms Kavanagh, please tell me exactly and in every detail, what happened this morning and how did you discover the body?"

"I am a nurse and I work at the memorial hospital. There are two days every week Sundays and Thursdays in which I have long shifts of 12 hours, from 8:30 am till 8:30 pm. So, I have exceptionally to wake up a bit earlier in the morning to walk my dog before I go to work, because in the evening it would be already night. So, I left home with Pop around ten minutes after 7; and once we reached the little wooden bridge there" she waved her finger towards the bridge behind them. Pop ran quickly towards here and started barking persistently in a hysterical manner, and when I came to see why he was behaving oddly, I discovered the body. My mobile phone wasn't with me, so I had to return home in order to call you".

"Do you know the dead man?"

"No. However, I must have seen him around couple of times, but I do not know his name or any details".

"Can you please have a look at the body again and tell us if you notice something you didn't notice before, because there is a gap of nearly half an hour between the time of your return home and the time of our arrival".

Emma hovered over Radi's body for few moments and said, "No there is nothing unusual, it is still in the same state as I left it".

"Ok. Can you" before the constable finished his stance, Emma interrupted him by saying while looking again at the body "Wait a second, there is something missing. I saw earlier something near his right hand, but now it's no longer there!", then she asked, "Have you picked anything from the scene?"

"No. Not yet" answered Owen. "What did you see earlier?" he asked

"I saw a red little Swiss knife. You know these little packed knives with the white cross on them"

Selway's ears listened carefully to such detail.

"Tell me where was it?" demanded Owen.

Emma bowed down as she waved her right-hand finger in a circle around the area where she saw the knife. Then Owen asked her "Please re-look again carefully in case you missed something else".

Emma looked again for a few minutes and then said, "I can't see anything missing other than the knife".

"We thank you very much for all what you have done this morning" Owen said as he signalled by his head to one of the officers to drive Ms Kavanagh to the hospital where she worked.

Selway spoke at the scene for the first time since his arrival and asked the constable "So what do you think we have here? An accident, a crime or what?

Before answering, the constable looked at the two men surrounding him and said "Let me first introduce you to each other. Mr Roger Selway former army colonel, now he is private detective. Mr Omar Al-Douri, high rank officer from MI5.

They shook hands. Then the constable said, "It looked like a terrible accident to me until Ms Kavanagh mentioned that knife".

The three of them looked up towards the top of the hill. Selway then said, "You mean that you think he fell from there while jogging and then his head hit the rock here".

"Yes".

"It's very possible, an accident could indeed happen during such a violent storm like the one of last night. But what on earth was he doing exercising in such terrible weather conditions, and at what time does he exercise?" Al-Douri wondered.

"He exercises every day at dawn" Selway replied.

"Do you know him?"

"Yes, I do. It's really a very tragic shock for me, because I used to meet him returning from his exercises when I go out to walk Max".

Selway's dog was sitting near the body and his face expressions were full of sorrow.

Owen approached the body and looked carefully at it again, then he said "The fall from above is a very logical explanation especially when we take in account the monstrous wind, the not so lighten time at dawn and the slippery ground. But what twisted my mind is that knife story. If there was a knife here who would have picked it, and why?"

As he stood back, he added "The injuries in his head are certainly from hitting the rock. No knife on earth would have caused that".

"You are right. It's a very strange story, the knife one" Selway admitted while squeezing his mind to find an explanation which could link the knife disappearance to what it looked like an accidental death.

Radi was wearing his dark blue tracksuit, and the three investigators were staring at his body for the last time in place. Then Al-Douri noticed something that put them into more mysterious state regarding the death of Mr Radi. The MI5 agent sank to his knees next to the body and said "look there is something on the right sleeve. I think it's liquid, it could be blood".

"Impossible, how the blood would reach his right hand if he fell, head hit hard on the rock, he should be dead instantly or maybe not. I am really getting confused".

"You are considering it impossible because you are assuming the death was accidental. But the knife story and now blood on the outside of his right arm make me really smell something fishy about this death".

After spraying around the body, Owen asked The forensic team to pick it up gently, take it to the morgue and examine it in order to establish the cause of the death, and also to examine the liquid on the sleeve because the red blood when absorbed by a dark blue suit it's hard to notice if one doesn't look very carefully to the smallest details.

After the forensics left with the body, Owen ordered his men to use the metal detecting machines they had and search the area surrounding the body very carefully. Maybe for some reason the knife was displaced but still around.

After nearly half an hour of very careful search, they found nothing. Then Al-Douri suggested that the knife could have been in Radi's hand or pocket and when he fell it dropped out near the body. But the question persisted "who picked it and why?"

The three walked up at the path that Radi would have passed through all the way down. They looked at the herbs, but they couldn't find anything that would suggest that someone else were present there. And the wet herbs made things even more difficult to establish anything, so they couldn't get any useful evidence from the larger circle surrounding the body location, because it was a public footpath where many people walk and run every day.

Selway turned his new mobile phone on and took photos and videos of every corner that he felt might shed light on what really happened that morning. He was eager to spend time studying them when he returned home.

Suddenly Constable Owen came up with a very odd but possible explanation to the knife disappearance. "Could it be that the lady's dog had swallowed the knife for some reason known only to dogs?" he said.

"There were up to 30 minutes time between the discovery of the body and your arrival, so the people who have gathered gradually here, and other dogs too, one of them could have picked it. So, G-d only knows how it did vanish" Selway said.

"Are there some cameras on the streets leading to this path, maybe by checking them we could see who did come here at those 20 or 30 minutes" Al-Douri suggested.

"Sensible idea; but there are at least six entrances to this passage, and I am afraid there could be only cameras on three or four entrances, because the other ones are not entrances from main streets" Owen explained.

"They are still better than nothing. I think you should have a look at them" Selway proclaimed

"Indeed, colonel indeed" Owen agreed. "Anyway, let us hope the experts at the morgue would give us better clues and the definite real cause of the death".

"Have you informed his next of kin?" Selway wondered.

"Not yet. But I called the Claytons and Mrs Clayton informed me that Anne Watt his adopting mother is staying at the Grosvenor Arms hotel, and I will pass there now myself to take her to the morgue to confirm the identity of the dead man. Such moments are the worse in policing career". Owen replied

"Can I go with you?" Selway wondered.

"Yes sure" Owen said, as the three left the area guarded by six police officers forming a triangle around it.

Chapter 11

When the police car parked in front of the hotel, the sisters Watt were leaving the building in their way to have their scheduled breakfast with Mr Radi. The ladies left without paying attention to the police who also didn't know who the ladies were.

After Owen asked at the hotel reception, they told him the Watts were the two ladies who had just left the building. Immediately Al-Douri ran behind them and couple of minutes later he returned with them. They couldn't have told them in the street what happened, so they had to sit at the hotel lounge, and the Chief Constable had to fulfil one of the ugliest parts of his duty.

"We are sorry to interrupt your plans, but unfortunately the reason for that is very grave, very grave indeed".

"What is it?" Anne asked while looked shocked and frightened as she merged her hands with her sister's hands.

"We believe that Mr Mustapha Radi is your adopted son. Correct?"

"Yes. What happened? Did he break the law?"

"I am afraid the situation is far worse than that".

"What is it? Did he kill someone?"

"Your son seemed to have slipped while jogging this morning and he fell on a rock and died".

A disbelief covered Anne's face, then she fainted. Al-Douri was already prepared for such possibility, and he had informed the ambulance crew who were ready in a car outside. They moved her to her room at the hotel, and after a small injection she regained her conscience. Once she opened her eyes, she looked at the faces around her, then threw her head on her sister's chest "Please tell me this is just a nightmare, please tell me this is not real", and they both exploded in tears.

Selway who had also tears all over his cheeks, gave his colleagues a signal to leave them alone for few minutes to digest the horrific news. They left the room and Owen said to the sisters "We will be outside; once you feel ready, we can go to the morgue so you can see the body and confirm his identity".

The younger Watt nodded her head positively, while Anne's cry went louder and louder as the door closed. Arguing among their flooded tears, Anne blamed herself

"I told him to not run in such a terrible weather, but he never listened when it comes to any of his daily routines. But I should have found a way. I am a bad mother".

"Stop blaming yourself please. This is life and regardless of how much we describe it as beautiful, death always reminds us that it's not so. Our mortal existence is so cruel" Ruth said.

Outside, a second police car arrived to pick the sisters up to the morgue. The driver joined the constable, the detective and the Intelligence agent in the hotel lounge.

Then a taxi driver entered the hotel, and he asked the receptionist about the four ladies he came to pick to Millingham train station. The receptionist called one of the rooms. Couple of minutes later, four young ladies came down with their travel bags and left with the taxi driver. Selway explored them in almost every detail; three of them seemed looking forward to leave while the fourth looked like a sleepwalker.

The detective remembered that Ms Dobinson told him about those ladies when they first checked in, so they spent two entire weeks in Morobury. Also, he was suspicious he saw some of them somewhere, and then he remembered that one of them was in the company of Barry Clayton during that White Christian supremacist party a week ago.

The former colonel wondered to himself "Was it a coincidence that those foreign girls are leaving the town couple of hours after the incident that could end up as a homicide case? Radi was a Muslim with Mediterranean skin colour, and if they hold extremist anti migrant ideology, he might be classified by them as a hit target. He thought of alerting the chief constable, but then the police can't go on questioning the entire Morobury population about what happened.

Also, Selway didn't like to appear like an amateur in investigations, as it was actually the first crime that happened under his nose since he announced himself as a Private Detective. Although his name has been advertised for nearly a week now in all the main newspapers and websites.

Next to him, Owen was recalling all what happened that day. He received a call from Emma Kavanagh who informed them about the body. They drove up from Millingham to the footpath where the body was found and there, they found dozens of people, among them the Catholic priest Father O'Shea who told him that the dead man is a tenant of the annexe belonged to the Clayton family. He then called the Claytons and Mrs Clayton received the call and she told him the full name of the man and where he can find his next of kin.

Back to the Clayton house, what happened when Mrs Clayton received the call about Radi's death, she was delighted; she felt like as if she was freed from all the burdens of the world. Her husband was still asleep. Then she smuggled herself into her son bedroom, he was asleep too. She looked at him, as the room was well heated, he was sleeping half naked. She noticed immediately a very fresh deep scar on the right side of his stomach just above his hip. Suddenly she went hysterical, she woke him up and said "Barry, I will fill your bank account with money, but now you remember your wish to go with Stephen and spend a long holiday in Athens. Please go, don't worry about the money I will transfer enough money to you, but you have to leave today. I will book you both first class tickets on the first plane to Athens".

She didn't give him a chance to speak, but as he appreciated the idea too much, he said "Alright! What a great way to wake up on such news". While he was getting dressed, she opened a travel bag, and filled it with several shirts, trousers, socks, underwear, and everything he might need.

The frightened mother ordered her son to drive immediately to Heathrow, and she told him she will call him and send him the flight time and number and all the details once she booked it. She then called the airport, and after chatting with the British airways' tickets desk, she was informed that to Athens the earliest next flight is around noon, and the earliest flight inside Europe is to Rome around 10:30. So she booked two tickets for

Barry and Stephen to Rome because two hours make big difference in such circumstances. After receiving the receipt and booking details, she forwarded by text all the information to her son who had already joined Barry in the latter car and off they left for Heathrow.

Finally, the long wait at the hotel ended as the Watt sisters managed to get their stirred emotions under control. The two cars drove off to the morgue. There the coroner and other members of the forensic experts were waiting as they have already finished their job in determining the cause and the time of death. The staff paved the way for the Watt sisters, the coroner, the chief inspector and the detective as they went into the chamber where Radi's body was covered.

The coroner uncovered the body's head, and Anne Watt instantly fainted again. It was too much of a shock for her to lose the orphan that he spent almost all the last three decades with her. And the moment he was grown up and started his own path in life death took him away as if he never existed.

While the medical staff looked after her, Selway was listening attentively to what the coroner had to say to the police about the cause of the death.

"We studied the body very well and we did several scans, and I can confirm that the cause of the death is an internal haemorrhage caused by a very strong hit on the right side of the skull. Also, we believe that death was instantaneous, I mean just few seconds after the hit" The coroner said.

"And what time the death happened?" asked Constable Owen.

"We can't give the exact minute of the death, but I can confirm it took place between 5:30 and 6 this morning".

Anne Watt regained her strength, bowed and kissed Radi's on the head front, then hugged the body for few minutes while crying her heart out for her huge loss. Selway couldn't fight his tears too, as he had been in almost regular contact with the lad before this disaster.

Then the coroner told them that the visit to the morgue should end shortly, and he asked Ms Watt about the burial. Ruth explained that they will get in touch with him later in the evening after they make a decision on where and how the body will be buried.

At that time John Clayton was doing a cardio exercise, he took a shower and as he walked outside the bathroom putting on his bath robe, he heard a strange man voice coming out of the living room. "This is not Barry's voice" he murmured to himself. He approached the room door on the tips of his toes, and he heard his wife saying

"I don't know. I don't know, any way good riddance and well done".

Then a man saying "You know I had to act after our conversation last night. But as you said: good riddance".

"I can't tell you how relieved I feel. However, there is still one worry".

"Well, I heard the police saying it was an accident, and regardless of that, it was a good idea that you sent him away".

Mr Clayton was eager to know about what they are talking, as their voices sounded very serious, so he coughed loudly before appearing on the door.

"Hello Father" he said.

"Oh! Hello Mr Clayton. I hope you are well" replied the Catholic priest

"I heard you talking about an accident or something of the sort?"

"Yes. Didn't you know?" the father looked at Mrs Clayton for few seconds.

"No, I did not. What happened?"

"They found your tenant dead down the hill at the footpath. It seems he fell while jogging in the early morning when the storm was still raging on".

Mr Clayton held his head in shock and disbelief, and then said "Oh my G-d. What a tragic news?" then he withdrew towards his room.

His wife couldn't hide her smile, and so was the priest who smiled back at her. Then after a wink, he said "I think I better off. Keep the story between us and everything should be okay".

Owen drove the Watt sisters back to their hotels. During the very short trip, Ruth asked him "So in your opinion Mustapha's death was accidental?"

"The coroner report and the majority of things at the site, the storm and almost all facts hint in that direction. However."

"However, what?" Anne interrupted him

"However, there was something odd at the scene, we are trying to figure it out. It might not prove important in the end".

"You mean you will open an investigation about it".

"Formally I am not sure yet. I need to discuss it with my bosses in London. However, I will be glad to talk to you later today when you feel you are ready for few questions and answers".

The car arrived at the hotel. The sisters entered the building and went up straight to Anne's room on the first floor. Once they were inside, knowing her sister, Ruth suggested that she should say a prayer to relax her nerves and sleep a little bit before they make a decision on where to bury Mr Radi.

"What do you think of what the Constable told us? Could it be a murder?" Anne wondered.

"We can't teach the police their job. He said they are almost certain it was an accident. However, we will see when he comes here this evening".

"But you know as I told you before that Mustapha had been bullied several times because of his Muslim background after terrorist attacks happened in the country".

"Yes, I remember you told me that. Now please let us say a prayer together and take some rest, we will be having a tough evening".

They held each other hands and recited a prayer for the soul of Mustapha. "O God, whose mercies cannot be numbered: Accept our prayers on behalf of thy servant *Mustapha Radi and* grant *him* an entrance into the land of light and joy, in the fellowship of thy saints; through Jesus Christ our Lord, who lived and reigned with thee and the Holy Spirit, one God, now and forever. Amen

As Anne lied in bed, Ruth signed into the internet on her mobile phone. It was a Friday and most of burial services were off during weekends, so basically, they couldn't do anything until the next week, but she wanted to have an idea about procedures of transporting the body from an area to another, and if there is an   Islamic   burial   site   or   not.

After half an hour of research and saving some websites, she felt pain in her back and her eyes started hurting. She put her phone aside, closed her eyes and relaxed herself a bit on a chair while putting her legs on another. She had a nap of half an hour, and when she looked towards the bed, she felt good to see that her older sister was asleep.

Chapter 12

Selway returned home with Max after he learned that the result of the DNA test of the blood samples found on Radi's sleeve will not be revealed before next week.

Max barked in consistent manner; the dog was hungry of course as they spent the entire day outside. Selway filled his pet plate with some can dog food. But he had no appetite to prepare anything for himself. He rather found himself crying quietly about the sudden death of that young man whom he had just known for couple of weeks.

Then he remembered that Ms Dobinson had met Radi first in the restaurant. Therefore, he thought she has every right to be informed of that tragedy. He asked her for a Skype chat in a half an hour time for an urgent matter.

He didn't feel hungry, but he knew he needed to eat something. He then inserted a rice pack in the microwave for couple of minutes, then mixed it with a can of soup, and sat down eating while his mind was busy retrying to rearrange the events of that day.

He then turned on his laptop, plugged his mobile phone in and transferred the photos he took of the scene. As he was about to open the first image, Ms Dobinson appeared online on Skype and initiated a video call.

"Hello"

"Hi"

"You look gloomy. What is the matter?"

"Mustapha Radi died today at dawn" Selway replied with tears sparkling in his eyes.

Sorrow and shock suddenly invaded Dobinson's face. "How?" she asked loudly.

"His body was found at the bottom of the Castle Hill where he used to run every dawn. He seemed to have slipped because of the heavy rain and the strong wind that was hitting the area last night. And he fell heavily on a big rock down under and died instantly according to the coroner".

Tears started making lines on Dobinson's face as she was hearing the tragic news. Then she said, "So it was an unfortunate accidental death".

"Everything indicates such conclusion, but."

"But what?!"

"The woman who found his body insists that there was a small knife next to his right hand when she found the body. But when she went back home to call the police, and after the time taken by police to arrive to the scene, the knife had mysteriously disappeared".

"That's really a strange story".

"Very strange indeed; because the cause of the death seems to be the hit of his head on the rock. So logically and scientifically the knife had nothing to do with it".

"But who took it, and why it was there?"

"I am still thinking of this point over and over. I think there is one of three possibilities, and I find the first of them the most logical. First the body was first discovered by another person and that person accidentally dropped the knife at the scene, then he discovered later that he or she lost it there, so he or she returned and picked it up after the woman left the area. This is for me the most logical explanation. The second one was suggested by an intelligence agent, he said that the knife could have been in Radi's hand or pocket and was dropped off when he fell, but that scenario doesn't explain how it vanished. The third: Radi was killed by the knife owner who dropped it accidentally next to the body then he recovered it later.

"The first and the third possibilities sound more logical, and as you said the first one looks the more credible if all facts point towards an accidental death".

"If you want to attend the funeral, I think it could take place tomorrow or after tomorrow, because if he is to be buried according to the Muslim traditions, they usually bury their dead as soon as possible. However, his next of kin hasn't decided yet on when and where the funeral will take place".

"I will take the first train to Millingham tomorrow morning, you never know we might investigate that accident in the coming days, and I think you would need me".

Back to the Grosvenor Arms hotel, The Watt sisters were trying to make decision about the funeral. "It's Friday, a day off in Islamic Centres around the country. And there is no Islamic centre near here to ask for their services, however I managed to collect some numbers from the internet, but you have to decide whether to bury him here or in London". Ruth said

"I will contact the North Dorset Council to see if we can buy a burial space for him here. Even though this terrible accident had happened here, but he loved this town passionately" Anne suggested.

While looking from the window as the sunset colours shaped the sky, Ruth asked "The sun is already gone, do you want me to call the constable for a chat as he suggested earlier?"

"I think you better call the coroner first. He is expecting an answer from us tonight. Tell him that because it's Friday we couldn't get in touch with religious and local authorities yet, but we are sure that the body will remain only this night at the morgue, and he can be sure that it will be buried tomorrow during the day".

Ruth called the coroner and delivered the information to him. Then she looked back at her sister, and asked "Should I invite the constable now? Or do you wish to leave it until after the funeral?"

"What do you think? Was it really an accident? And why the police constable didn't tell us of the odd thing related to the finding of the body?"

"I don't know. But frankly speaking it was crazy from Mustapha to go exercising under such horrendous weather. If the storm was not that bad, I would have thought of a homicide, but knowing how strong the wind was, the logic says it was a fateful accident".

"And what the constable was talking about?"

"I have no idea".

"Ah by the way, there is a private detective here in Morobury, and he seems to be important because his firm is advertised on a half-page of the Sunday Times". She handed the newspaper to her sister and said, "So if we feel that police may not deliver all the answers, we can still pay for this man to establish all the facts".

"That looks interesting; especially that he has an office here" Ruth replied as she looked at the advert Anne discovered earlier in the Newspaper.

"Whatever my personal opinion is regarding how serious the police investigation is, it may take days, weeks or months before they give us all the details of what happened, and we can't remain here all the time, you should return to your work mid-September, so I think we better hire a professional to follow the investigation step by step".

"That makes a lot of sense indeed".

"Ok call the detective first, and then call the Constable later. So, when the latter arrives, he would deal with the detective from tomorrow onwards".

Ruth tried the London office number first, but got no answer, then tried the Morobury office number, also no answer. Finally, she tried a mobile number, and she got Ms Dobinson on the other end.

"Hello, can I speak to Detective Roger Selway please?"

"His secretary speaking, how can I help?"

"We are in Morobury and we think of hiring him to investigate a death incident".

"He actually in Morobury right now, I will send you his private mobile number in a message and you can get in touch with him directly".

Few seconds after ending the call, Selway's number landed into Ruth's phone inbox. She then wrote it down on the paper, then dialled it carefully on her phone keypad and called him.

"Mr Selway".

"Speaking"

"This is Ruth Watt. I have got your mobile number via your secretary, as I called her earlier asking for your services to investigate a death incident".

"Thanks for your call and for putting your trust in me, and I accept respectfully your request".

"I learned that you are now in Morobury, so I wonder if you can visit us at."

Selway didn't want her to finish her sentence; he continued it "The Grosvenor Arms hotel".

"Yes. How did you know that?"

"I will be with you shortly and you would immediately know how I knew that".

As Ruth turned her phone off, her sister noticed that surprise on her face. She asked, "What happened, did he accept to investigate?"

"Yes".

"Is he coming?"

"Yes. But how did he know that we are here in this hotel?"

"Dear we are not in London, he certainly learned about the accident, and I think many people in the town know that we are here".

"Sound plausible".

After nearly half an hour, the room inter-phone rang. It was the reception informing them that Mr Selway had arrived and that he was waiting them at the lounge. Ruth told the receptionist to ask the detective what he likes to drink and serve him until they arrive. She also ordered two coffees for them.

The two sisters now dressed all in black with black hats, walked down the stairs and then into the lounge. Once they saw who Roger Selway was, they recognised him immediately as he was with the police all time during the day.

"Ah. It is you!" Anne said

"Yes, this is me" Selway replied.

"I thought you were one of the police officers" Ruth said. Then she added "Now that explains how you knew where we are staying".

Two cups of coffees and one cup of tea were served with a little plate of Mcvitties' biscuits. Then Selway opened the discussion saying, "I am at your service".

"I have the impression that Constable Owen is assuming already that Mustapha's death was accidental. However, he told us that he is investigating what he called an odd finding near the body, and once he got that sorted out, he would confirm whether the death was accidental or not. He didn't tell us what that odd thing, claiming that it may not be proved important after all" Anne said. After sipping a coffee shot, she went on saying "I don't know why he wouldn't tell us exactly what that thing was. And as Mustapha was all my life, I don't want to economise any effort that could help establishing all the facts surrounding his tragic death. And if the investigation went longer than two weeks, which would likely be the case if there was a foul play, I can't remain here to remain at top of every detail and all advance investigators make. That's why I decided to hire a professional like you who could investigate the facts himself while keeping me updated with the advancements that the police make".

Selway was about to speak, but Anne continued "And don't worry about the money, I will pay you handsomely if you can give me peace of mind regarding what happened".

"Thank you for your trust in asking for my services" Selway said. He then added "I want you to know that I am concerned about what happened as much as you do, and I am very sad for your loss. So let me make it clear that I won't accept money from you in this case, because I am taking it to investigate the death of one of my neighbours and my friends".

The sisters looked at each other expressing their total surprise. Then Ruth asked, "Did you know Mustapha?"

"To some extent I can say yes. In the last two weeks I used to see him almost every morning when he returns from his long exercise while I am walking my dog. So, we had short conversations from time to time, and I am really very shocked and sad about his death. I only learned his adoption story from the chief constable this morning before we came here to take you to the morgue ".

Moments of silence invaded the lounge as tears shined in the six eyes under the light of the lamps, as if they suddenly remembered their huge loss. Then Selway said "I hope you will help me in every detail you can remember in order to get a fast start in our investigation".

"Of course, we will" Ruth confirmed.

"Can you please tell me if you know anything about the odd finding that the constable mentioned to us?" Anne asked.

"Yes".

Suddenly the sisters' eyes widened as they heard the answer they did not expect. They turned very attentive with full curiosity and looked at the detective as if they were saying "Fire it away".

"The woman who discovered the body saw a small Swiss knife near Mustapha's hand and the police are puzzled about where does this knife come from?"

A sad look mixed with disappointment appeared on Anne's face. She covered her face as she exploded into tears for couple of minutes. Ruth tried to calm her down while Selway was left wondering what triggered her reaction.

Anne then looked at him through her tears and said "Sorry about that! But what you have just said seems to have confirmed to me that the death was for sure an accident".

"Why are you assuming this?" Selway asked.

"Because the knife is Mustapha's, so if the police think it was left there accidentally or deliberately by someone else, there is no need for them to investigate further".

What she said fell like a bomb in Selway's ears because it evaporated all the theories, he was trying to build about what happened. "The MI5 agent was right after all" he murmured to himself.

Then as the three looked at each other, Selway said "Even though Mustapha's ownership of the knife took several possibilities out of the equation, there is still something odd and even very strange".

"What is that?" Ruth wondered.

"When the police arrived at the scene and the lady returned with them, the knife was no longer there. So, who picked it up and why?"

Chapter 13

Attention regained Anne's face as she heard the strange story of the knife disappearance. And Ruth agreed "This is really very strange". She then wondered while waving her hands in a puzzled manner "Who would pick a knife from a death scene? And for what reason?"

"It's strange indeed. I was building different theories such as the body was discovered first by an unknown person who dropped the knife accidentally near the body, and then he returned to pick it up. Another possibility I was thinking of was that if someone deliberately killed Mustapha by pushing him down towards the rock, he could have dropped accidentally the knife on the scene then he picked it later. But all these theories are now destroyed when you revealed that the knife is Mustapha's. This fact is really making things far more puzzling".

"He bought the knife after he received some racist abuses. I advised him against carrying it. He said it's just for defence purposes only".

"That's rather significant information, but it won't give some meaning to the knife disappearance. I think you should call the

Constable immediately and inform him about the threats that your adopted son might have received".

Anne looked at her sister who understood immediately, picked up her mobile and rang the police.

"Good evening. Can I speak to Chief Constable Owen please?"

"He is not here. He is home but if it's something important we can call him".

"Yes. It's related to today's death; please tell him that that Watt sisters are waiting him at the hotel".

After Ruth ended the call, Selway asked them "I knew from Mustapha that he was moving to a new house, did he move any of his belongings to there?"

"Yes, he moved some furniture and clothes. He was scheduled to sleep there from tomorrow night onwards" Anne replied before her tears beaten her again. Then Ruth suggested "We haven't contacted the new landlord yet, of course we have to remove Mustapha belongings from the house, so it will be very helpful if you know a charity that could take them"

"Yes. Do not worry about that. I will take care of his belonging, and I can put them in my house until a charity, I know, send a van to take them".

Selway then pulled his mobile from the internal pocket of his jacket, apologised from the ladies and walked outside the hotel to ring his friend Chief inspector Ronald Smith.

"Good evening, Ron"

"Oh! Hi. Good evening, Roger; How are you doing?"

"Getting busy here at Morobury, if you heard about a death incident today"

"Yes, if you mean that young teacher, I saw the news on BBC Southwest in the afternoon".

"I am sitting now with his adoptive mother, and she wants my service to establish all facts about his death".

"But the news said it looks rather accidental".

"We have some little details that can put the accident theory in doubt".

"Ok then how can I help you? Who is on the case there?"

"Chief constable Owen".

"I don't know him; Anyone else?"

"Well, there is a man who is not a police officer, an MI5 agent".

"What's his name?"

"He has a strange name. Al-Douri I think".

"Oh Yes. I know him very well; he is the rising star of the intelligence".

"Really!?"

"Yes. I don't know why he was present there, unless he is on a very important case".

"He could have come for that White supremacist party that took place here last weekend".

"Probably; anyway, if he is staying in this investigation then cooperate with him, because he is reliable and very intelligent".

"And good looking too! Quite frankly he came up with the right answer about a knife seen near the body, but it later disappeared"

"So that's why you are saying the death may not be accidental".

"Yes. However, it's very strange though that the knife had vanished. Al-Douri suggested it could belong to the dead man and it was dropped from his hand or pocket when he fell. And he was right because the mother of the deceased has just confirmed to me the knife belongs to her adopted son. But who took it and why?"

"I am puzzled right now with what you are saying. You are saying that the knife was seen near the body, but then you are saying it's not there? How and who saw it?"

"The woman who discovered the body saw the body and a small Swiss knife next to it. Then she went back home to ring the police. Later when the police returned with her, the knife was no longer there!"

"It's really a strange story. Anyway, what was the reason of your call?

"Yes, I almost forgot. Since I am now hired officially by the family of the dead, I hope you would be able to do this request for me".

"What is it?"

"I want the Royal Mail to deviate all the letters coming to the address of the dead man to my house address. And I will ask his mother now to give me the right to access all his belonging mainly his laptop and mobile phone. She said he was targeted from time to time by racial abuses. So, I want to know everything related to him. Maybe he was receiving hate email or letters".

"Ok consider it done, but please send me a message with both your addresses, his and yours".

They ended the call and Selway typed to Smith quickly his full address and the address of Radi's annexe which was rented from the Claytons.

As he finished his contact with his old friend, a car parked in front of the hotel. It was Constable Owen who as soon as he saw Selway asked him "Good evening. What are you doing here?"

"My job" with a pale mile Selway replied.

They went in, and as soon as they joined the Watt sisters in the lounge, the waiter asked the police officer what he would like for a drink. He apologised saying "Nothing. Thanks".

As the waiter left, Owen said "So you are ready now for a couple of questions and answers".

The sisters nodded positively. And Selway said "I think they have something important information related to the mysterious knife".

Owen didn't like Selway's quick interference, and said "Can I please talk to them?"

At that Anne said, "Mr Selway is now officially at the case on my request, so in every future matter related to Mustapha's death you would deal with him as our representative".

Owen didn't look happy about that, he looked to Selway and said "Sorry" in a hardly audible voice.

Then Anne went on "Now please ask whatever questions you have because tomorrow we have to organise the funeral and I hope to have couple of days of peace to mourn peacefully my son".

"Ok. Let us start then. It seems that Mr Selway had already told you about the knife seen at the scene. So, what important information related to it can you tell me?

"This knife was Mustapha's and he kept it always with him since his second month here in Morobury, because in his first month there were terror attacks in Europe, and some young guys here threw at him some racial and hate slurs. So, he decided to keep the little knife for protection purposes in case someone attacked him".

"Interesting information from which we can conclude that Mustapha was feeling threatened, and the knife was his".

"Exactly" said Selway

"Actually, I sent an officer in casual costume to watch over the Clayton property until things get clarified. However, after the information we have now about the knife, we will need as you said to put our hand on Mustapha's belongings to see if he received any threats. And what could motivate someone to kill him, that of course if the death was not accidental. But let us get some more information from the ladies first".

Owen then looked towards Anne and asked

"Does your son have any biological cousins here in the UK?"

"No. Or at least not to my knowledge" She answered

"Does he have any inheritance or property in the middle east?"

"None; all what he has is here through me and through his work income".

"You lived together near London. Why he decided to move and live alone in Morobury?"

"He used to teach sports at a private primary school in London's Muswell Hill, and his contract with them ended two years ago, and they didn't renew it because they were about to change the school from a mixed one to a girl only school, and they preferred to hire a female sport teacher. After that he applied to several schools around the country. And after he visited several places, he decided that Morobury would do it for him".

"He told you that he faced some racist abuses. Did he give any name? Did he receive such abuses in his workplace, I mean at the school for example?"

"No, he never mentioned any problem at the school. Also, he never gave me names, but the abuses occurred during his running exercises. He used to do his jogging during normal day times or before sunset, but it seems the abusers pushed him to prefer going out exercising at dawn. Also, he told me that his religious beliefs state that dawn is the best time for humans to breathe fresh air, and he found it rewarding to sleep early and wake up early".

Owen looked at Selway and said, "Now with the knife story and abusers targeting him during exercises, it seems that getting pushed to his death rather a possible scenario".

Selway nodded positively.

Then Owen continued his questioning "Do you visit him regularly or was there a special occasion that brought you here?"

"Well yes to some extent. I come here a weekend per month or so. But this time we came to see him relocating from his current house to another house here in Morobury. He was due to move tomorrow actually to his new home when all of this tragedy happened". Anne then exploded in tears and her sister took her on her chest trying to comfort her.

"Was there any reason for his relocation?"

Anne looked toward Ruth, and then the latter said, "The contract ended at the end of august which is today, and the landlord didn't wish to renew it, so they give him a month notice to find a new home".

"Did he move any of his belongings to the new house?"

"He moved the TV, wardrobe, carpets, tables, chairs and clothes, but the bed and other belongings were to be moved tomorrow before handing his keys back to the landlord at noon".

"And the new landlord is aware of what happened?"

"We haven't talked to them yet, but I think the entire town knew about the accident, and we have just asked Mr Selway to move the belongings to his house in order to send them later to a charity".

"Have you decided where the burial will be and when?"

"The burial will certainly take place tomorrow during the day but where, we haven't decided yet, because it was difficult to get hold of religious authorities and council staff on a Friday afternoon. But tomorrow morning we will do all the necessary contacts to get things arranged".

"We will collect all your son very personal belongings and mainly his mobile phone and computer. I think you wouldn't mind that. Do you?"

Anne went into tears again. Then Ruth answered "They are all yours. Mustapha is gone and nothing would bring him back".

Selway said "I think you heard enough from them", then he told the sisters "Please go up to your rooms and relax, for tomorrow will be a very tough day for you. May God be with you".

Owen also said "He is right. And thank you very much for your time, please accept my sincere condolences, and I promise to do all what we can to establish all facts related to this tragic death".

Chapter 14

The Watt sisters went upstairs, while Owen called Mr John Clayton informing him that they will be shortly at his address and asked him to prepare the keys of the annexe which was rented by Mr Radi.

Selway and Owen then regained the latter's car and drove off to Bimport where the Claytons and Radi's address were located. They parked the car in front of Selway's house, and then walked some hundred yards from there. As soon as they entered the Claytons' main garden the automatic lights came on, then Mr Clayton appeared in front of his door welcoming them.

The chief constable waved to the host as he walked straight towards the annexe, and Selway followed him. It was clear that the police officer didn't want to go to the Claytons house that night, and his business was exclusively focused on the annexe.

Mr Clayton joined them and opened the door of the annexe. Owen immediately asked, "Has anyone entered this place after Mr Radi's death?"

"No one of us come here if Mr Radi is not home, this is the spare key. So, I can't see anyone did come here at all, I didn't see my wife coming here today even though she heard the bad news before me".

They were shortly joined by the disguised officer whose duty was to watch over the house since noon. He also confirmed that he didn't see anyone going inside the place or coming out of it.

"May I ask why you decided not to renew the contract of your tenant?" Owen asked.

"It was my wife's wish actually. She doesn't want to rent the place any longer" Clayton replied.

"You are wealthy enough, so why renting this place at all?"

"Actually, it was my idea in order to get monthly addition to our contributions to charities. All the money of the rental goes to charities, we don't pocket any penny from it".

"Hmm. Very sensible".

It was a small annexe, a sitting room opened to a small kitchenette, and from it a corridor that leads to a bedroom and a bathroom. So, in couple of minutes Owen and his assistant checked the entire place, which was actually almost empty apart from the bed, few clothes on a chair, toilet towel and shaving tools, a mobile phone and a laptop.

The police picked up everything, then Owen said, "We will keep this key with us, and we trust that no one have another key apart from the one we found with the deceased".

"Yes, there are only two keys".

"Ok. We will keep this key with us so this place must not be used for a while until we finish our investigation".

Mr Clayton wondered "You are saying there is an investigation, but I learned from the Catholic priest this morning that it was considered an accidental death".

"It looks accidental, but there are some strange happenings related to it, that we are still trying to clarify" Owen clarified

"You mean he could have been murdered?" wondered Clayton

"We don't rule out yet any possibility, we are still looking into it". Owen replied. Then he added "Thanks for your time and for the key, we will be in touch in due course. Have a peaceful night".

"Have a good night" replied Mr Clayton as he walked back to his house while the three visitors left the place.

As they approached the car, Owen ordered his man to keep watching the place. And he promised him that he will send him a replacement for the night shift.

Selway asked Owen to come into his house, but the latter apologised saying that the next day will be a very busy one and that he better goes to bed as soon as possible.

Selway didn't bother about Owen, all what he wanted was to try and get Radi's mobile and laptop for his own investigation. He looked a bit worried as he felt those items should have rather been in his possession. He looked at his watch, it's almost 11 o'clock and he felt hungry, and so were Max who has been locked inside the house for the entire evening.

After he made a quick meal for himself and the dog, Selway went through the photos of the accident scene that he took that morning. He was looking again to the position of the body and wondering if the blood on the right sleeve has come from Radi's head after he fell heavily on the rock. He was trying to imagine how the fall happened and in what position his friend was falling down, on his back, on his side or on his front. He spent nearly half an hour thinking deeply of that, then he told himself "Whatever happened we have to wait the DNA test result of the blood trace, which should be available sometime next week".

A message landed in his mobile. It was from Mrs Dobinson saying that she would arrive at Millingham station around 9:30 am. He immediately called a Taxi firm in the town and booked her a taxi, then sent her a reply that a taxi will be waiting her at the station.

Selway went upstairs to the bedroom, changed his clothes and went under the duvet. He tried to sleep but he couldn't as his mind was revisiting all what he had seen during that dark day. After giving up of falling asleep quickly, he decided to revisit all his memories about Mustapha Radi since he first saw him in the restaurant when he was in a terrible emotional state.

He started talking to himself: The guy was kind and very well built. He stopped at that point, this reduces a bit the possibility of a free fall, even if the storm was so strong, a man with such strong physic running on a track that he has been running on almost every day for a year, he surely could memorise all its details and risks. But then accidents happened. Who knows?

And what about that story of his relationship with a girl in the Claytons house. There are no girls there. And why he looked very upset that day I saw him returning home from the town?

Selway had always the feeling that Radi's involvement with him had rather a physical attraction, but Mrs Dobinson saw him once in a company of a girl, so when she comes tomorrow, she has many things to remember. Also, the smallest details of her first conversation with Mr Radi seem very important now.

The Watt sisters woke up early and prepared themselves for the toughest day of their lives. As soon as the town hall bells announced the 9 o'clock in the morning, Ruth started calling the council and religious authorities who are responsible for burial services.

They have decided that a burial in Morobury or Millingham at any cost would be better than transporting the body all the way to North London. And after several calls and negotiations, Ruth managed to buy a burial plot very close to them at the King Edward's Cemetery which was less than one hundred yards away from the hotel. It was very costly, nearly 10 000 pounds, but they were wealthy enough to seal the deal.

The second communication mission for Ruth was to find an Islamic cleric to lead the funeral ceremony, and that was not easy for the nearby towns and small cities didn't have a mosque or an Islamic centre. After looking on the map and making several calls, she managed to find a cleric in Exeter city who was ready to do the ceremony in mid-afternoon which is the time of the third Islamic daily prayer. Anne then in her turn called the morgue and informed them that the body will be buried in the mid-afternoon.

Meanwhile Selway was having his breakfast in the garden when a Taxi arrived and on board was Mrs Dobinson.

She looked exhausted as she said "Good morning and Bon Appetit" as she threw herself on a chair close by.

"Good morning. You look exhausted. Let me guess, you didn't sleep well".

"Right. Hardly an hour".

"That means Radi's death took its toll on you as much as it did to me".

"Yes. I can't stop thinking about it. It's very sad for a young man to depart so soon".

"Come on, join me for a sandwich. Help yourself".

"Thanks. I had already a croissant and orange juice in the train". The she asked, "At what time is the funeral?"

"I don't know yet, but the parents will call me as soon as they get it arranged".

"And why they should call you?"

"Oh yes I haven't told you yet. We are officially hired by them for the case".

"Good. So how are you going to begin your investigation?"

"In couple of days we should have the result of the DNA test of the blood on Radi's sleeve. And I will start officially from there. However, I think I should talk to everybody who had known him. And I can start now by asking you few questions".

"Well. Go ahead then".

"I suggest you better go inside and take a nap because you really look wore out and there is a long day ahead of us. You can go into the guests' room and try to sleep. There is a nice bed there and it would help. I also keep an audio player in which you can play some natural sounds, a forest, a storm, birds, and many other sounds".

"That sounds an irresistible offer!"

A van arrived at the gate and disturbed their conversation. A man walked inside and asked, "Can I speak to Mr Selway?"

"Speaking"

"We are checking that you are ready to receive the furniture you called us about".

"Is the landlord there at the address?"

"Yes, and he is waiting"

"Well ok then please remove everything and bring it all here".

The man regained his van and left

Dobinson immediately asked, "What furniture?"

"We are just removing the furniture of Mr Radi from the new home which he was supposed to occupy from today on".

"Oh, how sad".

"Yes, it's so sad really. Now go upstairs, shut the door and get some sleep. Hurry up".

Dobinson went upstairs, opened the guests' room, she picked a snowstorm with wind sound. As she was totally exhausted, it took her only couple of minutes to fall asleep.

Less than half an hour later, the van returned with the furniture. Selway rushed straight away to the gate and asked them not to unload anything. The driver then opened the door of the van for him. Selway went inside and checked the items, opened every drawer and emptied all clothes into bags, then told the driver to go down to Millingham to a charity which he had already called to take the furniture.

Selway took the clothes inside his house. Soon after, he received a call from the Watt sisters informing him that the funeral was arranged to take place at 3 o'clock in the afternoon at King Edward's cemetery.

He looked at his watch, it was 11 30. He was about to turn his laptop on when letters were pushed through the door box by the postman. They were some wine offers and a booklet of the month of October from the Morobury art centre; however, that booklet was not addressed to him, but to Mustapha Radi. He understood immediately that his friend the chief inspector Smith had already stood by his promise and contacted the Royal Mail to divert Radi's address letters to his.

At 2 o'clock Selway prepared lunch and woke his secretary up. She took a quick shower, dressed up. They had their lunch and then drove the car off to the Morgue. There in a specified room, The Watt sisters and the head of the school were mourning Radi. His head was totally cleaned of blood, and he looked just sleeping. Selway and Dobinson couldn't fight their tears at the sight.

Dobinson looked again and again at the third woman; she has seen her before, but where? And after few minutes of twisting her memory, she remembered seeing her with Radi at the restaurant the night before she left off to London. Dobinson murmured to herself "Yes. She is the School Manager".

Suddenly a man showed up at the door. It was Mr John Clayton. He approached the body with shaky steps. Then he stood next to Radi's head with tearful eyes, he then said "I am sorry. I am so sorry. I didn't mean it. Please forgive me". After a minute he left the place in a highly emotional state.

Quarter to 3, the police showed up and after them the Islamic cleric with four well-built men of his assistants. The time is up and soon the funeral ceremony will start. Anne Watt threw herself one last time over her adopted son exploding in tears and crying "How I wish it was me instead".

Chapter 15

The Muslim cleric covered Radi's face. Then his men moved the body into a wooden coffin and carried it all the way to the designated cemetery. The cars carrying the others reached the cemetery before them.

Hardly ten minutes later the men arrived, they put the coffin at the edge of the grave after asking people to stay away for a minute or two, then they spread a fabric sheet over the grave and they smuggled the naked body into its last destination, and fixed above it couple of wooden tablets they brought with them, then started pulling soil over it. Anne approached and threw a bouquet of flowers into the grave, before it became all covered up.

The cleric recited few prayers in Arabic and English. And the ceremony was over.

There were dozens of people there, mainly teachers and students who had known Radi through his work at the school. As people started withdrawing from the cemetery, the School Manager was standing between the Watt sisters comforting them. Selway whispered to Dobinson "I wonder, who is this lady?"

"It's the head of the school. I saw her with Radi at the restaurant the night before I returned to London" She replied

"Ah ok".

Suddenly the mobile phone of chief constable Owen rang consistently, he then pulled it out of his jacket and replied "Yes. Speaking"

He nodded his head as serious expression covered his face features. "Ok understood". "Absolutely"... "We need that to establish the facts of the incident, so even if it takes time, it's very important for the investigation". "Ok we are fine with that, and we will wait the results".

As Owen finished off the call, he saw curiosity in the eyes of Selway, and he couldn't hide a little smile as their eyes met. He said "I know you wonder what that call was. It's from the DNA Laboratory in Bournemouth and they said it's difficult for them to get the blood sample out of the clothes properly, and they don't have the necessary equipment for that, they are suggesting it should be sent to London to a laboratory where they could properly study the DNA of the blood on the clothes and give a definite result. However, they said it may take a week to get this done. And I told them no matter how long it takes as long as it gives a definitive result.

"Have you looked through the laptop and the mobile?"

"Not into many details. No not yet. As you see we have been busy today with the funeral and so on".

As they spoke, they were joined by Al-Douri whom this time had a big smile as he shook warmly Selway's hand. The latter immediately understood that Chief Inspector Smith had already stressed to the MI5 man to fully cooperate with him.

Al-Douri then pulled out a letter out of his pocket and handed it to Owen, who once opened it, he looked surprised. He then looked at Al-Douri then at Selway and said, "Well I guess the two electronic devices would be now yours to explore and keep as long as your investigation going".

Al-Douri said "Thank you", while Selway looked puzzled as he didn't understand what was going on.

Owen and Al-Douri noticed that, and then Owen said, "we will explain to you on our way to my office".

Selway waved his hand to Dobinson who joined him as they expressed their deepest condolences to the Watt sisters, then the detective asked his secretary to make herself comfortable at the hotel or at the office until he finished his work at the police station.

As soon as they got into Owen's car, the constable said "The letter sent from the general police administration hands the case to Agent Al-Douri and his team who are investigating a larger case and they will take the accident as potentially linked to it. So, from now on I am off the case, so all things related to this case will be handed to Al-Douri".

Al-Douri on his turn said, "And I will be honoured if Mr Selway joined me in this investigation".

Selway replied seriously "Thank you, I would certainly do my best, at least for the part related to Mr Radi's death".

At their arrival Owen reported to the police administration in England and Wales that the case had been handed fully to Al-Douri's team as requested by the formal letter. Police officers then filled Al-Douri's bag with all the electronic materials of Mr Radi and all the photos and papers related to the investigation including the interviews Owen made with the lady who found the body, Mr Clayton and the Watts sisters.

Couple of minutes later a car arrived outside and waited for Al-Douri who then asked Selway if he wanted a lift.
"Of course," the former colonel agreed instantly. They waved

goodbye to Owen who took a sigh of relief as the case was taken off his shoulders.

In the car, Al-Douri introduced Selway to the driver who had a full white hair, yet he looked stiff and younger which gave him the age of the 50yish years old.

"This is Mr Gareth Hughes my assistant. This is Private detective former colonel Roger Selway".

The two men nodded their heads to each other and laughed as the words "Nice to meet you" came out of their mouths at the same moment.

"Chief Inspector Smith told me about your long friendship and he insisted that we should work together on this case if there is one related to Mr Radi's death". Al-Douri addressed Selway.

"You seem to know him well. Yes, I had him on the phone last night and he explained to me how intelligent and professional you are" Selway said.

"I am his student and I trust blindly what he says, so I am sure we would make good teammates".

"I hope so, but don't forget this is my first ever case. By the way I hope you would allow me to look at Radi's laptop and mobile phone sometime when you finish with them".

"Don't worry about that, I remember you told me you have known him for couple of weeks and that makes you even more helpful for the investigation. Therefore, I promise we can go through them together if you can come tonight to the remote hotel we are staying in".

"Where is that?"

"Faraday Abbas at an old cottage, very calm area to work and think".

"Not a bad idea, but my assistant Mrs Dobinson is also in Morobury today and I wonder if she can join us too".

"Yes, that wouldn't be a problem".

"Could I know what type of investigation you are leading, and Radi's death might be linked to it?"

"We will talk about that when we meet later".

The car arrived in front of Selway's house. Al-Douri wrote quickly the hotel address on a paper and handed it to Selway as the latter left the car. "Shall we see you at 8 pm tonight?" asked Al-Douri. "Yes, indeed and thanks for the invitation" Selway replied.

As Selway walked through his house door, Max showered him with barks. The dog was hungry indeed, so his owner filled quickly his plate. Then he checked what the postman threw to him through the door box, and there was nothing significant. But also, there was a pizza advertisement, he picked it and said, "This would do!"

He wasn't in the mood of cooking and also, he thought about Dobinson, so he ordered two pizzas to be delivered to his office address, and he walked out and joined his secretary there.

The pizza delivery was so quick, as it was delivered couple of minutes after his arrival. As the two went through their late lunch, they discussed the coming hours.

"Be prepared, for we will join another team on the case".

"What you mean by another team?"

"I mean Owen is taken off the case. It's delegated to a mixed team of intelligence and police, as intelligence seems to have been on a case related somehow to Mr Radi".

Dobinson played with her hair while saying "What type of investigation as it might shed a complete new light on his death?"

"You are absolutely right" replied Selway. "But I still have no idea what that larger investigation is about. But as long as the intelligence is involved it could have some connection to crime networks such as drug dealing, terrorism, money laundering or something of that type".

"But I think things should move quicker, hardly anyone have been questioned yet. So where do you think we should start?"

"We have an important meeting tonight; we are invited to Al-Douri's hotel in order to set out a plan and to get more information regarding what the intelligence services are after".

Later on, Selway sent a message to the Watts promising to meet them the next day and told them to not hesitate to call him if they needed anything.

At 7:40 pm Selway and Dobinson were in the Jaguar studying the road map they printed from the internet to get to the hotel which was located in a pretty rural isolated area. Dobinson drove the car as usual. She had to slow too much down at some points because the road was very tight, and it was dark and no road lights at all in the area.

Luckily enough it was close, hardly took them fifteen minutes to get there. Dobinson parked the car in the little park of that old two floors large cottage turned into a family house on the ground floor while the first floor was occupied by hotel guests.

As soon as they left the car, Al-Douri showed up at a very small gate which almost covered by plants and trees. He turned the light of a flashlight on and off, and they noticed him immediately.

"Good evening"

"Welcome to our quiet place".

"It's beautiful and calm".

"Yes. It's very nice for thinking and meditation".

At the end of a very tight passage and by the end of almost a tunnel of large trees a big light appeared shining through the main door of the cottage which was called "The Old Forge".

The door was shut but not locked; Al-Douri pushed it gently and paved the way for his guests. As soon as they got in, the hotel owner and his wife welcomed them with smiles and told Al-Douri that they can use the lounge to sit down and talk. The MI5 refused gently their offer and said "Thank you. We will be fine in my room".

They climbed the stairs and there was Mr Hughes waiting, he welcomed them warmly as they entered Al-Douri's room. It was a tiny room with one bed and two chairs. Al-Douri said "I apologise, the room is not big enough, but we will be fine sitting on the bed while you occupy the chairs".

Once the four took their seats, Selway asked immediately "First of all I want to know what big case you are on if Radi's death might have connection with".

"Well, you don't seem willing to lose any second. And you are quite right because if the case was proven to be a murder every minute passes could give the murderer more chance to hide any traces that could lead us to him or her or them" Al-Douri replied.

He then added "I came here mid-august after the Dorset police notified us of several cases of drug dealing and Internet criminal activities taking place here in the area. And such activities appeared suddenly on the police records out of nowhere, which by the investigations dictionary indicates that these crimes have to be related to some individuals or network members that have relocated recently to the region".

"Interesting" Dobinson said, while Selway's mind was recording every word that came out of Al-Douri's mouth.

"After looking at the councils' official records, we had list of dozens of individuals who relocated to North Dorset in the last year or two. Mustapha Radi was one of those names, and we were about to start to get an eye on him when his death occurred".

"Hmm. And do you have in his civil record any criminal activity of any kind?"

"No. His record is fully clean, and when I said his name was on the list, I didn't mean that he was necessarily suspicious, but he was one of those individuals who moved recently to live here. And that's why we had to check his recent activities out".

"Ok got it. Have you found anything suspicious linked to such activities on his laptop or mobile phone?"

"I have gone through them for hours before your arrival, he doesn't have any password on the two electronic devices and that gave me access to almost all corners and applications he had on them but found absolutely nothing that could be related to internet blackmailing or drugs trafficking".

"Found anything that could shed some light on his death?"

"Nothing caught my eye. Most of the pictures he stored are his own photographs and selfies; also, his Facebook account doesn't show many friends. Same can be said about his Skype and mobile contacts list. The last calls of the last couple of months are mainly with his mother and the school manager".

"Alright then; How do you think we should start investigating this death?"

"I think you would know that better than me, you had been in direct contact with Mr Radi in the weeks prior to his death. And maybe you know some information about his private life, which something I hardly found anything related to in his belongings, even though we live at the high peak of the digital age".

A quick smile appeared on Selway's face, he then said enthusiastically "Does that mean you are giving me the upper hand to set a plan for the investigation and you go along with it?"

"Actually, to some extent I can say yes. Because we will be looking mainly to continue our own investigations regarding the ring or individuals who could be pursuing the criminal activities I mentioned earlier. So, investigating Mr Radi's death wouldn't be our first priority. I trust Chief Inspector Smith who pushed the buttons at the highest level to get us on the case, because he told me he believes in your talent and that you would certainly get to the bottom of the Radi case".

Selway looked energised after he heard Al-Douri's words. He looked to Mrs Dobinson and said "Ok. And I promise you that you can trust us. I will certainly establish all the facts surrounding the death of Mustapha Radi".

"Glad to hear that and see how enthusiastic you are. And we will fully cooperate with you, and even lead the questioning procedures together, but while your focus will be just on Radi's death, our investigation will keep the bigger case as the top priority".

"Ok, agreed then. Can I take Radi's laptop and mobile phone with me now?"

Al-Douri nodded his head positively; he then waved to Mr Hughes who immediately understood the signal. He stood up, pulled the electronic items of Radi from the drawer and handed them to Selway.

"Thank you. How do you like us to proceed with the questioning?" asked Selway.

"As I told you I trust your planning abilities. So, you set a schedule for the people you are going to question, and I will try my best be join you in each and every questioning session, with some focus of course on the people who might have information that could help us in hunting the criminals".

"Alright; expect an email from me later tonight or early tomorrow morning with this week schedule of the people I want to talk to. And after I arrange an exact time with them, I will inform you of the questioning sessions one by one".

Chapter 16

After having a quick look at the contents of Radi's electronic devices, Selway made himself a cup of tea, then sat in his bed writing down a schedule for the people he deemed important to talk to, regarding the incident.

He spoke to himself "I believe the Clayton family members should be the first to be questioned because Radi seemed to have had tough times with them in the last couple of weeks. So, I will schedule them for tomorrow which is Sunday".

Selway then decided to interview on Monday the School manager and other teachers who co-worked with Mr Radi.

He took a deep thought of who else could have known Radi closely, maybe some students. He then remembered something very important that was off his mind during the very busy previous 48 hours. He said to himself "We should check what the streets cameras recorded in the night and the morning of the accident, that could help us reduce the circle of suspects", but then he remembered that Constable Owen said that not all roads that lead to the public footpath where the accident took place were covered by CCTV cameras. And that means no one can be certain that the knife picker or the criminal, if there is one, would have appeared on the recordings of one of those cameras. However, this matter was to be dealt with immediately.

At that thought, he looked at his watch; it was nearly half an hour to midnight. He picked his handy landline phone and called Al-Douri who answered immediately.

"Good evening. Sorry for disturbing. Selway here"

"Please Colonel Selway, can I call you Roger?"

"Yes of course"

"Please Roger stop using all these respectful words, in the police world there is no disturbance, you just pick your phone at any time and speak".

"Ok no worries, I will be bolder next time".

They both laughed, Al-Douri then asked: "Tell me what is it?"

"I wanted to turn your attention to the streets cameras, their recordings might hold important information regarding the accident, maybe they can help us find who could have killed Radi if it was a murder, or at least who picked the knife".

"Do not worry, I certainly didn't forget about that, and we made contact with the local council today and they promised to deliver to us all the required recordings with their timelines by tomorrow noon".

"Ok great then. Regarding the questioning procedure, I decided that we should talk tomorrow to the Claytons; and after tomorrow to the school manager and some teachers if possible. These are the only sides that I believe Radi was almost in daily contact with during the last year or so. I will let my secretary ring them in the morning and fix an hour to visit them. Once I get everything scheduled I will text you".

"Alright"

"Thanks for taking the call. Have a good night".

"Good night".

Selway opened his old notebook, in which all the phone numbers of the neighbours were written, then sent an urgent text message to Dobinson asking her to call the Claytons in the morning and arrange the time for questioning them regarding Radi's death.

The following day, Selway took his morning shower, fed the dog, prepared his porridge breakfast, got dressed and waited for news from either the Watts or Dobinson.

At 10 he received a call from his office. "The Claytons can receive us at 3 pm this afternoon" Dobinson said.

"OK good, that gives me enough time to pass by the hotel and speak to the Watts in case they needed anything".

He called Al-Douri and informed him to be ready for the 3 pm meeting.

The weather was nice for a walk. So, half an hour later Selway walked with the Watts sister at the path close to the museum.

The detective looked to Radi's adopter and said, "You told me earlier that Mustapha received some threats." But before finishing his stance, the mobile phone of the younger Watt rung suddenly, so she apologised and withdrew to talk on the phone.

"Sorry about that" her sister said. "Please go on" she added.

"Your son was receiving threats because of his origin or religious belief only?" Selway wondered.

Watt got closer to the detective as if she was about to reveal a top secret to him, she whispered in an audible voice "Mustapha was also homosexual but in the closet to some extent, and he was attracted only to."; before she finished her words, Selway completed them and said, "mature men". The woman opened her mouth in surprise then she asked, "How did you know that?"

"Well. As you know I have known him for couple of weeks before his tragic death, and every time I encountered him his eyes told me loads, but I wasn't one hundred per cent sure until now. Now can you please tell me if he had ever received threats because of his sexual orientation?"

"He never told me so, as I explained to you earlier, he wasn't very openly gay, and he kept that only to the closest in his friends circle" She replied.

Anne then turned her head towards Ruth who was talking on the phone on the side of the road two yards away from them. Anne waved to her youngest sister asking whom she is talking to all that long. Ruth replied mutely by moving her lips twice. It was someone called "Andrew". Anne then turned back to Mr Selway while saying in an irritated way "Ah that man again".

Selway then asked her curiously "Who is Andrew?"

"Andrew Johnson. A man she fell in love with, but I don't think he is the right man for her".

"Why? Maybe they truly love each other".

"You know women when they get older and single, they could fall for anyone. I warned her several times about keeping their relationship going but she ignored my requests".

"And why are you suspicious about him?"

"Because since he showed interest in Ruth, I have investigated his past through several channels. And they all concluded that he is addicted gambler, divorced twice, have four children from his two marriages and never looked after them. He just left them to their mothers to struggle with them on their own".

"And you told her that, and yet she insisted to keep their relationship going?" Selway wondered.

"Yes. She is in love because he is one handsome beast. However, I think he is after her money, he would rely on her to feed his addiction for gambling and all those sorts of abominable activities of his".

This new information took some kind of twist inside Selway's head.

As he went deep into his thoughts, he didn't realise that Ruth re-joined them and that the two ladies were trying to re-communicate with him.

"Are you alright Mr Selway?" Anne asked while touching his shoulder slightly. "Yes, I am fine. Sorry but I got away with some thoughts". He smiled to them as they smiled at him back.

Then suddenly a big noise of men shouting with loud voices invaded the peaceful sight, and the eyes of Selway and the two ladies fell on a group of very well built men running in a specific rhythm behind what looked to be their trainer, and then they saw some young people who were walking around hurrying towards the group to take selfies and photos with the group. As they passed by, there were some shirts with a rugby ball drawn on them, so it was clearly the Rugby team of the town going through some long heavy exercise.

They stole the attention of almost all the walkers in the area as they went through the tight passage that led towards the high street.

Selway used that chance of the players catching the attention of the Watt sisters to observe the younger Watt with big attention to details. There was a cloud of new thoughts invading his mind, yet he had to settle down with the schedule he had already planned for the rest of the day.

As they reached the memorial cross near the hospital, Selway's house was hardly two hundreds of yards away, so he asked them to join him for lunch, but the two sisters apologised, "We are so sorry, we can't accept your invitation because we have already ordered our lunch to be delivered at the hotel at 2 pm". Anne explained. Then the two of them shook the detective's hand and walked back towards the hotel while he charged home.

As he approached the garden gate, his mobile rang. It was Al-Douri.

"Hello Roger"

"Yes Hello".

"I hope you haven't had your lunch yet".

"About to cook it. Why?"

"Then stop. I and Hughes are coming and bringing some tasty Lebanese dishes from a Lebanese restaurant. I hope Ms Dobinson can join us too".

"Well thank you very much. We will wait you here".

Selway invited Dobinson. She arrived after ten minutes, almost at the same time when Hughes parked the car next to the gate. The two men came in with all the food delights. Even Max was eager to have his portion of the tasty mixture of meat which had a very inviting odour like no other.

While eating, they had a little chat. "Lebanese food is super delicious" Selway said. Dobinson and Hughes nodded their heads positively, while Al-Douri raised his right thumb up.

Then Selway asked him "We know that there are variety of good foreign restaurants around, why the Lebanese? Are you originally from there?"

"Originally I am half Lebanese half Iraqi. My mother is Lebanese, and my father is Iraqi".

"Interesting and how you ended living here?"

"It's a long story, but briefly we left Iraq in early 2003, just before the invasion was launched against the regime".

"Oh dear! Glad you made it unharmed. But how do you see what happened there? Were you happy of the fall of Saddam Hussein?"

"No, not at all; even with all his negatives, the regime really built a strong economy. Half of the women were educated and employed. Look at the state Iraq is in right now. Bloodshed, sectarian and ethnic violence"

"You are right. I have never trusted the government report that led to the invasion".

"I love the United Kingdom and that's why I was upset to see its army involving in such unjustified war. I still think that this country can and should clean its past from the stains left by the lies and deceit of that report".

"I am with you all the way. Justice must always prevail. But tell me, are you happy with your current job with the Intelligence services?"

"To be honest, the first couple of years were very difficult as I wasn't sure where I am standing. But later as I got involved first hand in some big operations and experienced how much our job protect the society from evil, I fell in love with it".

"Good. Very good"

After the lunch ended, Selway guided his new friends to the toilet room to wash their hands, while Dobinson cleaned the table and returned the empty dishes to the kitchen. She then prepared four cups of green tea as they sat down and discussed their coming visit to the Clayton family.

"What happened to the CCTV streets recordings?" Selway asked.

"I have just collected them before coming here" Hughes replied.

"Great. Do you need to look at them or can I take them now?"

"As we agreed earlier, we are on the case for the drugs and internet crimes, and these recordings are related to the case of Mr Radi which is yours to solve. So, you can have them right away" Al-Douri replied, and he waived his hand to Hughes who immediately walked outside to the car and brought the recordings which were saved into a small but super memory card device, and he handed it to the detective.

"That's all then?" Selway wondered.

Hughes smiled and said "Yes. You see what technology can do nowadays; each street camera is named separately with the video recorded on it for the 24 hours up to the police arrival at the scene".

"That's good. Thank you very much, I will check the content as soon as we finish our visit to the Claytons" Selway replied.

The four of them got ready in front of the mirror one after the other. And they left the house some five minutes prior to the meeting time, as the Claytons house was hardly one hundred yards away from the Selway's.

Chapter 17

Selway had already informed his companions of how he wished to proceed with the questioning procedure. And the plan was that while he, Al-Douri and Hughes questioned Mr and Mrs Clayton, Dobinson had to go to the kitchen in order to question the servant.

On time, Selway led the group and pressed the bell button of the Claytons door, few seconds later Mr Clayton showed up with a little smile and welcomed them in. As they approached the sitting room, Mrs Clayton welcomed them and guided them in.

They took their seats in a strategic way leaving Selway to be the closest to the hosts who took their seats to his right side.

Mr Clayton started the conversation "Where is the Chief Constable Owen. Is he late?" he asked.

Selway coughed a little, massaged his moustache with his left hand, "I am now leading the investigation regarding the death of Mr Radi" he replied.

"But you don't work for the police. Do you?" his neighbour wondered.

Al-Douri interfered, "Yes he is officially on the case which is also related to a bigger investigation we the intelligence services are leading. So, I hope you will take his questions very seriously. The more you cooperate by giving us as much details as you could, the more we can get done with Radi's case. I believe you would rather see the end of it as soon as possible, instead of being questioned about it every then and now", he said.

The eyes of Mrs Clayton widened "Why should we believe you? Constable Owen is not here, and we heard that the police counted it an accidental death, so I really don't know why we have to answer your questions!" she protested.

Al-Douri stood up and approached the hosts. He pulled out his intelligence ID card and the letter he received from the police services which states that he was handed the investigation. He handed those documents to the couple, who took couple of minutes checking them.

Mrs Clayton looked very irritated as her husband handed the documents back to Al-Douri. Mr Clayton regained his seat and he said "Alright! How can we help you?"

Al-Douri pointed his finger towards Selway and said "You have to cooperate with him. Mr Selway is officially recognised as a professional private detective, and both we and Mustapha Radi's mother are hiring him to investigate her son's death".

"Dear John, Look I know we know each other for a long time, and we are neighbours, but from now on and until the end of the investigation you have to deal with me in a professional manner. Please let our friendship be a blessing for the investigation process instead of undermining it" Selway said.

"Ok. Alright!"

As soon as Mr Clayton finished his words, the servant entered the room with some cup of coffees. Selway immediately winked to Dobinson, and he asked his neighbours "Your maid?"

"Yes" Mr Clayton answered promptly.

As soon as the servant distributed the coffee, Dobinson stood up and told her "We need to chat a little bit in the kitchen please". She looked at Mrs Clayton as if she was waiting her permission.

"Yes, it's alright" Mrs Clayton answered while shaking her head, showing her irritation.

After the two ladies left to the kitchen, Hughes turned on a small camera device that could catch the entire room and record the conversation. "Now we are all on the record. This conversation will be recorded for the investigation purposes. Once the case gets officially closed, this record will be destroyed".

Mrs Clayton rolled her eyes in disbelief but forced herself to swallow some protesting words she wished to say.

"Will your son join us anytime soon? For we need to talk to him too" Selway asked.

"I haven't seen him for a while" replied Mr Clayton, then he turned toward his wife who said, "He is not here I am afraid, so definitely he won't be part of this investigation".

"No problem I can arrange to talk to him another time".

"I am not sure it is necessary unless you will need more than a month to solve the case if there is one".

"What does that mean? Can you please explain?"

"My son is abroad with his friends so I can't see how he would be of interest in what's going on!"

"But I saw him couple of days ago. So, when did he travel?"

"The night before the accident"

"Where to?"

Mrs Clayton took a deep breath then answered, "Actually they are going to do a tour in Europe, all what I understood from him that Greece is on their scheduled trip, but how and when and the details of the voyage are something I don't know".

"Why didn't he inform me?" her husband interrupted her.

"He wanted to do so but you weren't home, and his friends were waiting him, they only told him in the last minute, so I gave him my permission".

"I hope they are not those nuts of the White Cross group". Her husband said

Selway then re-asked "Have you got any proof that he left the country or at least Dorset before the accident?"

"I don't know what you mean by proof. Nowadays it's very easy to book a plane seat or a train seat online instantly, so I really don't know what type of proof I can show you! However, you just heard his father saying that he didn't see him for a while, so if he was here today or yesterday, he would have noticed that".

Mrs Clayton then lit up her cigarette and looked relaxed as she felt her words sounded convincing to the investigating trio.

Selway went on "We heard that you ended the tenancy of Mr Radi prematurely after giving him one month notice. What kind of trouble you had with him that might have triggered such decision?"

A sign of discomfort appeared on Mr Clayton's face, he then looked towards his wife for a rescue. However, he pushed an answer forward and said, "You can ask her because she decides everything related to the rental of the annexe".

Mrs Clayton sucked deeply her cigarette as if she was taking her time to give an answer. "It wasn't what I would call trouble, but I took the decision to end the agreement because the tenant was chaotic when it comes to the recycling procedures and the bins. As you know there is one bin for recycling, another for food waste and the main bin. He mixed up things several times, and we received warnings from the council about that. I explained things to him, and I gave him several warnings about it, yet he kept going as he pleased. So, I got fed up with it and I decided that we should depart ways with him".

Selway looked deeply to her eyes as she finished her story. When their eyes met, she turned hers away in a sign of discomfort. However, the detective didn't insist on that point for reasons known to him. Then he addressed the husband "When I came last time with Chief Constable Owen to the Annexe, you told us that you give the money of the rent to charities".

"Yes correct" replied Mr Clayton.

"And you said also that your wife decided to no longer be having tenants, Is that true Mrs Clayton?"

"Yes".

"Why? Have the Charities got enough money! Or the bin problem was very much annoying to you?"

The woman didn't like the tone of Selway's questions as she felt the detective is trying to outsmart her in the conversation. She had a short cough and said "Excuse me. Maybe it was a decision made at the heat of the moment. However, as you can see here that is what we are getting out of having strangers sharing our space. Death, investigation, questions. That's a good reason to no longer have tenants here".

"You told us last time that the annexe has only two keys one you gave to us; and the one which was with Mr Radi". Selway addressed again Mr Clayton who nodded positively reconfirming what he informed them previously.

"So basically, every tenant who lived in the annexe had a copy of the keys and they returned it at the end of their tenancy".

"Correct".

"Have you changed the padlocks for any reason during a tenancy or between two tenancies".

The couple looked at each other, and then Mrs Clayton said "No, it still the same door lock for almost a decade now".

"I suppose you do keep copies of tenancy agreements".

"Yes of course we do".

"Can I have a look at them if it's not a bother? If it will take time to find them, you can send them to my office later".

"They are in a file in the library room. I will bring them immediately".

Mrs Clayton left the room, brought the file and returned. She opened the file to check the content then handed it to Selway "Here are the five tenancy agreements, the newest at the top and the oldest at the bottom" she said.

"Thank you" replied Selway as he checked quickly the names. He then asked "Do you have any kind of friendship with any one of those tenants? I mean were they known for you prior to their tenancies?"

"No. All of them came through the rental agency".

"Has your daughter lived with you here recently? Let us say during the last couple of months?"

"No. Why asking? You know very well that she is married and lives in Italy".

"So, she is still abroad and still married, no divorce?"

"I don't know why you are asking. But She is fine with her husbands and children!"

"So, you are sure that no one of them visited you in the summer".

"Yes. The last time they visited us was the Christmas 2015. And last year we spent the summer in Italy together".

"And when did you employ your housemaid?"

"It's her fourth year in a row now".

"Do you have any travel plans in the coming three or four weeks?"

The couple looked at each other, and they replied at the same time "No".

Selway then winked at Al-Douri as a sign that he finished his questions with them. So, the latter came forward with his questions. "I heard you Mr Clayton when you said you hope that your son is not with his friends from the White Cross group. Is he a member of that group?"

"I don't know if he is a member or not, but he was invited to that big party they held last week".

"Have you any idea for how long he has been in connection with them?"

The father shook his head in denial, but the mother said, "Fairly recently as far I understood from him".

"Why he picked such a group? Does he have such strong white supremacist views?"

"Maybe out of curiosity, I don't know" she replied.

"He is still young; he will discover one day that it's not the right place for him. Life is a good teacher" Mr Clayton expressed his view on his son's choice.

"What does he do for a living? Is he working?"

"No. He is still a university student".

"What field and what university?"

"He is studying Geography at Bournemouth University".

Dobinson had finished a long chat with the servant and re-joined them in the room, she had everything recorded, but from the look at her reddened face, Selway felt that she has got some useful information out of her interviewee.

Hughes asked his colleagues if anyone wants to ask more questions as he stood ready to turn the camera off. Selway said "I have one more question regarding your previous tenants. Do you have their new addresses?"

"I don't think so" replied Mr Clayton while looking towards his wife.

"But sometime letters may arrive after a tenant left the address and my experience tells me that in most of cases the tenant leaves behind an address for those late letters to be sent to him later by the landlord".

"True. But I am not sure if the addresses of the old tenants are useful or still available. They may have relocated to different addresses". Mrs Clayton explained

"I understand that, but I trust you may still have the address for example of the former tenant, the last one before Mr Radi".

"Probably, but that needs checking in my diary of last year and it may take some time to find through its pages. Can you wait as long as it takes, or it is better to text it to your mobile phone later".

"Yes please, the second option would be better".

Selway and Al-Douri left their visit cards to the couples on the table. Hughes turned off the camera. They thanked the Claytons for their time and left the house walking back to Selway's.

Chapter 18

Al-Douri and Hughes gained their car near Selway's' house and returned to their base in the Campton Abbass area; while Dobinson returned with Selway to his home, where they were greeted warmly by Max as usual.

Selway was very excited to hear the questioning of Maria Clark the servant of the Claytons. To do so he wanted a space isolated completely from any kind of noise. There was no place better than his wooden cosy desk room upstairs. Dobinson joined him; they emptied the recorded audio from the recorder to the computer system. Then Selway turned the file on, and the conversation begun.

"I will try if I can help".

"Have you known Mr Radi before he lived here?"

"No. The first time I met him was here".

"Were you friends or just a rare type of contact?"

"We were friends".

"How have you developed your contact into a friendship, have you been cooking for him also?"

"No. I only work for the Clayton family".

"How have you managed then to build a friendship when you don't usually be in the same house?"

"He was a very kind chap. Several times when I was sent to the Supermarket we met there or on the road or accidentally sometimes we met here at the main gate going to the town centre when I am leaving home. I mean our meetings were occasional but frequent".

"Hmm. And was it just a friendship or maybe a love relationship?"

"Frankly I wish it went that direction, I was attracted to him, but he was dealing with me as a friend and sometime as a sister. So, nothing really happened between us".

"Never! Not even a kiss?"

"Never"

Mourad Mourad

"Have you ever been alone with him in his place?"

"No. Never"

"One can't say I am friend of someone if they just met walking to and from the supermarket. Right?"

"Well whenever we met, we were very much open to share our stories, worries, seeking advice from each other. And of course, sometimes we sat on a public seat or had a coffee or beer together in a pub".

"Ok. That sounds more convincing. So, you can say that you know a big deal of his lifestyle, his problems and ambitions etc.."

"To be honest, I don't know how much I know about him really, because sometimes I felt him hiding some issues from me, but I always failed to unveil them".

"What kind of issues? Did he suffer of any problem in particular?"

"For example, I tried several times to get into his private life, to know about his love affairs, you know that kind of thing. But he was never open about that. Whenever I try to push him into telling me what kind of girl he likes to have in his life. He always managed to change the topic. So, I can't tell you anything really about his love life".

"Understood; so, what kind of problems you were talking about?"

"He is a good cook by the way. We had some interesting conversation about dishes. And we were thinking of launching a channel on YouTube where we can cook a dish once or twice a week. Also, he spoke about his dream of becoming a big football coach one day, and the rest of our conversation focused on the problems we were facing in our daily work, me in my work here and him in the school".

"I see. So, what kind of problems was he facing at the school? He seemed to have a very good relationship with the school manager. I saw them once dining together at the King Alfred's Kitchen restaurant".

"Mustapha was a very sensitive guy. The problems in school weren't related to him personally, but to his pupils, he cared too much about their well beings, and lately there were some of them going through a sudden and deep change in their general behaviour and their performance in school. Their notes were dropping sharply in almost all fields. Mustapha was eager to know the reason behind what was happening in order to preserve the future of those kids".

"Interesting; did he tell you about his findings or suspicions?"

"No, not really; all what I know is that he will be trying to cooperate with the school manager and the parents in order to get to the bottom of this matter".

"And what about his relationship with your employer, I mean with the Clayton family in general. Why did they end prematurely his tenancy agreement?"

"Everything was good for almost a year, until very recently a couple of weeks ago Mrs Clayton suddenly became very anti - Mustapha for some reason which I tried several times to know from Mustapha, but he refused to tell me anything about that".

"And what about Mr Clayton?"

"You mean the father or the son?"

"Well, both of them".

"Well Barry was just in formalities, I rarely saw them speaking to each other. But Mr (John) Clayton was in a very good friendship with Mustapha. They used to sit and talk on different topics; they even attended events in the area together".

"So do you think they have known each other before Mustapha rented the annexe?"

"I really don't know. Such thought never occurred to my mind".

"Did Mustapha have any friends? Have you seen people visiting him?"

"I don't know how large his circle of friends was, but from the amount of time we spent together and his determination to always avoiding speaking about his private life; I have always wondered if he had any friends at all. I have never seen anyone visiting him apart from Mr Clayton. The only people I saw in his company outside, I mean in town or at the footpath were his students when they exercised together".

"Did he ever mention to you that he was threatened by someone regarding his origin, skin colour or whatever reason?"

"No. Not really. The only thing that seemed to have annoyed him lately was the row he had with Mrs Clayton and her decision to end his tenancy".

"Have you heard Mrs Clayton at any time speaking about Mr Radi or with Mr Radi?"

"She never spoke with him in front of me. If she spoke about him, I frankly can't remember, nothing came to my memory".

"If you ever remember anything related to Mr Radi, would you please call us or even pay us a visit, we are at the old abbey offices just around the corner".

At that moment Ms Dobinson handed Maria their visit card.

"Definitely I would if I remembered anything of significance".

The record ended there.

Dobinson and Selway stared at each other. She was hoping for feedback but didn't get one. So, she had to initiate the chat regarding Maria's information.

"You said that the Claytons' only daughter is married and live abroad. And Maria has just told me that she had no affair with Mr Radi. That means the latter lied to me when I first met him in that restaurant. Correct?"

"Perhaps"

"Or maybe Maria is hiding their affair from me?"

"Perhaps"

Silence fell down for over a minute. And that enervated Dobinson who then complained "That's all what you have to say: Perhaps".

"Perhaps" he said for the third time, and he smiled a yellow smile to his assistant who rolled her eyes in desperation.

He then added "I think I should meet this lady because I have different questions for her".

"Are you implying that my questions were stupid and not useful for the investigation?"

"No. I didn't mean that at all. The questions were good".

"Hmm. Why then you want to ask her other questions?"

"You did ask her the right questions, but what I want to ask her now is related to the answers given to us by her employers. I want to compare them".

"Ah now I understand what you mean" Dobinson replied with a sigh of relief.

"So can you arrange that now?"

"What you mean by now?"

"I mean I would prefer to talk to her as soon as possible. Have you taken her mobile number".

"Sure, I did".

"Well call her then, or even better text her. Text is better than turning the attention of the Claytons".

"You seem having something in your mind. I think the best way is to text her first then ring her and hung up before she replies. This way we would be certain that she read the message".

Selway raised his thump up for that good idea.

Dobinson asked him "What do you want me to say?"

The detective straightened his moustache "Tell her. We would like to talk to you this evening after you finishes your work. At what time should we wait you at our office? And please don't say anything about that to your employers".

In less than a minute the message was sent to Maria's phone. Dobinson then rang her and once she replied she hung up on her.

Few minutes later Dobinson received a reply saying at 8 pm, Maria will join them in the office.

They waited her at the office and in time she rang the doorbell. Dobinson welcomed her in, and after the formal introduction she took a seat on the chair to the left of Selway's desk.

"I heard on the record your earlier conversation with Ms Dobinson, and I appreciated that you were in good terms friendship with Mr Radi".

"Yes, we were good friends".

"I do have more questions for you if you don't mind. Do you have any engagement or totally free tonight?"

"I have just finished my job. I called my mother that I will be a bit late. So, you can take your time".

"Good and thank you. Would you tell me please, do you have any boyfriend or an ex-lover?"

"Currently no; I do have an ex of course but he no longer lives here".

"Is he British? And where does he live now? Are you still in touch?"

"Yes, he is English. He lives and works in Canada since 2015. He is in my friends list on Facebook, but we rarely message each other".

"And why did your love relationship end? Who ended it? You or him?"

"His relocation abroad was definitely the main reason behind ending our relationship". Maria looked a bit agitated, and she blushed as she elaborated "I tried to convince him that I can also relocate to Canada and find a job there, but his opinion was, that we should put an end to our love story and remain just friends".

"Sorry to hear that. Have Mrs Clayton questioned you about the interview you had with Ms Dobinson?"

"Yes, she did. And I told her in general what the questions were about".

"Alright. Now I want you to tell me when did Barry Clayton travel abroad?"

Maria squeezed her bottom lip, as if she was trying to concentrate her memory "Frankly speaking, I didn't know that he is abroad until today".

"And when was the last time you saw him?"

Maria moved her eyes ups and downs as if she was trying to remember than a surprised look mixed with fear covered her face, as if she had just remembered something very important. "The last time I saw him was the day before Mustapha's death".

Selway read the change and the worries that suddenly appeared on Maria's face, "At what time of the day?" he asked.

"Morning, not early morning but around 11; because he usually doesn't wake up early"

"And what was he doing? Packing his clothes or something?"

A strange look reappeared in Maria's face, she looked to the left and to the right, and then she pushed herself forward and said in a low but audible voice "He was in a very angry state".

"Can you please elaborate? What did you exactly see or hear?"

"I heard him shouting inside the house, and when I opened the kitchen door to see what was going on, I saw him storming out of his mother's room. And he looked in a crazy mood. I have never seen him with such an angry temper. He was certainly full of rage at that moment, and his mother was trying to calm him down".

"Yes, continue please, they must have said something".

"Yes, they did, but I am trying to remember what was said".

"Remember every word please. They could prove to be very important".

Maria closed her eyes as if she was reliving the moment, then she opened her eyes and said "Mrs Clayton was blaming herself that she shouldn't have informed him about something. Because it seems what she told him made him mad, and he left the house shouting -I swear I will kill him- as he slammed aggressively the main door behind him".

Selway eyes widen up and so did Dobinson's as they shared a glance at each other.

Selway then asked, "And you are sure that he left the house angry at that time and he didn't carry travel bags or whatever?"

"No, he was empty handed, he just left the house in angry mood, if he had luggage, I would have notice that he was travelling".

"Very interesting. And are you sure that was the last time you saw him. Are you sure he didn't return home before you left in the evening?"

"I am positive, it was the last time I saw him. He could have returned later that day after my work ended; I don't know".

Chapter 19

Monday morning Al-Douri and Hughes rejoined Selway and Dobinson at the town school for the next interviewees in the investigation. This time they had to divide themselves thinly in order to talk to the school manager and as many as possible of the teachers who were the closest colleagues of Mustapha Radi.

The four of them were very well equipped with recorders. The school questioning procedure was very important for the big case that Al-Douri and Hughes were handling, and that's why they were expecting to spend a long day there hiding behind Radi's death while in reality they were trying to find any link related to the drugs and internet crimes that have rocked the region in the last few months.

Selway had to interview Geraldine Kane the head of school manager who seemed by many accounts very close to Mr Radi during the year he spent at the school under her reign.

At her administrative desk they sat on the sofa, Selway put down the recorder on the small table after he refused to drink anything offered by the attendant. He wanted to be in full concentration because the task ahead was also very important, and it could be crucial for the crime file which was under investigation by Al-Douri team.

"You have known Mr Radi for almost a year. What can you tell me of him both as a teacher and as a person?".

"Mustapha was a shy fit man. He looks a bit distant and cold but when you get to know him well you find that he is very soft hearted and very sensitive person. He cares about people around him, and he notices quickly if someone is having bad time. He is generous and would take risks in order to make others happy. That's him as a person. As a teacher, he is a very good one, he is very close to his pupils and masters well all possible physical activities. His pupils are very important to him, and he takes them as friends. He is also very cooperative with other teachers; we had never had any complaint about his behaviour, attitude or professionalism during the short time he spent in our school".

"Thank you for this summary. How did he get his job here?"

"Well, our previous sport teacher signed an interesting deal with an English school in the Arab Gulf with good money, so the post was vacant. Radi applied among 10 other teachers, and we decided to hire him because he seemed very approachable, very fit, yet very soft looking man. Also, he had great University grades and showed huge interest in living in the countryside. With all this enthusiasm it didn't take us much time to hire him for the job". She sipped a bit of water from a glass on the table then added with sadness in her eyes "I am very sorry that he lost his life here, he is gone soon, too soon".

"Yes, but there are many countryside places in England other than North Dorset; so why do you think did he pick here? Have you got any idea about that?"

"I would say it is difficult maybe for teachers from foreign origin to find a job in a town school, because you know schools in such remote places away from big cities prefer to hire local grown teachers. However, he had a strong bond to Morobury, and that was clearly proven when a school in the outskirts of Newcastle asked for him by name and proposed him a good job there, he refused totally, and he was upset to some extant because the ministry of education was behind the move. I found it a strange demand myself, yet as I was very happy from his first year here, I managed to use my links with the government in order to keep him here. And he was super delighted when the decision was made for him to remain here for the coming year".

Selway's eyes widened as he smelled something strange and suspicious of what he had just heard "Can you please repeat that again please? You are saying that the ministry of education wanted to appoint him in Newcastle?" he asked.

"Yes. And frankly speaking I found it a very strange demand, I have been in schooling managerial job for more than four decades, and it was the first time I had ever received such a strange call".

"And when did this happen, please?"

"Just some three or four weeks ago, during our short summer schedule".

"Very strange indeed; let us now talk a bit about your connection with Mr Radi. My colleague saw you once dining together at a restaurant. So that indicates to me that your connection was not exclusively a relation between a manager and an employee".

"You are right. We were friends to some extent. And what drove us to develop this friendship was our concern for the wellbeing of some of our young students who have for some reason changed their behaviours in the last quarter of the last school year".

"What kind of change? Can you please explain that with as much details as possible?"

"Some of our most brilliant students started suddenly to behave in an unusual manner. They seemed depressed; their notes dropped. So, I can't say one specific change, they were totally transformed into a new type of beings, from happy smart lads to over worried lazy students".

Selway knew that he did hit the nail by getting into this topic, *"For sure this information will be very important to Al-Douri"* he convinced himself.

"And have you found any clue about what happened to those students, have you spoken to them?" The detective asked.

"We don't know exactly what is going on. Yes, we spoke to almost all of them, and they all managed to act normally in the interviews, they tried their best to convince us that nothing really going on and it was just a period of time they tended to be lazy at. But Mustapha was not convinced, and we decided to investigate things further; and to do so we picked few students that Mustapha decided to watch their daily movements outside school".

She stopped talking for few seconds as she reads some suspense on Selway's face. Then she added "And after several attempts he managed to make some breakthrough with one of them". Again, she stopped and looked to see the impact her words were having on the detective who said impatiently "Yes go on please".

"During that big political party which took place at the Mair villa.".

"You mean the celebration of the -White Cross- movement" Selway interrupted.

"Yes. That's how Mustapha narrated to me what happened that night. Late at night our pupil Tom Wright left his house and went through the tight passage next to the Oxfam shop and came across the Museum. There were plenty of cars parked there; they belonged of course to the party attendees. So, Mustapha followed him step by step. The student then sat on one of the two benches located under the main tree behind the memorial cross. He waited there some half an hour during which he typed on his mobile phone and also Mustapha saw him kneeling under the bench. Then he returned home later. Mustapha decided that he should try and inspect the bench. He sat on it and started touching its corners with his fingers, until he touched a little plastic bag attached at the bottom right side of the bench. He pulled it out and in it he found five hundreds of pounds cash. He then thought should he put them back and keep watching the site to see who might come and pick them up, but then he said maybe it was too late and that the other side of that potential deal might have seen him already, so he or she may not show up at all. So, in the end he decided to bring the money to the school and confront the pupil with it".

"Interesting; and I thought I am the only detective around! Yes, go ahead. What happened next?"

"After he came to school the next day and told me the story from A to Z, we both came to the conclusion that someone is blackmailing our students or selling them something".

Selway nodded his head approving their conclusion.

"First Mustapha didn't want to be present during the confrontation with the student, but he was then forced to do so because the student when talking to me alone denied having any links to the cash money. So, when Mustapha told him about every move he made that night, suddenly the pupil went mad and furious. He accused Mustapha of being behind what he has been through. Mustapha as a very sensitive man felt very offended and he left here almost destroyed by the accusation, and I couldn't reconnect with him until few days later".

"Interesting story; and I guess I saw Mr Radi returning home that day, because I noticed how upset he was. So, tell me, do you think is it probable that Radi really was behind the blackmailing?"

"Oh God no! I don't think he could do harm to anyone; He was a very kind soul".

"I personally agree with you but in police business one has to keep his personal feelings aside, so we can't rule out any possibility. And I think talking to your pupil will be very helpful if not crucial for the investigation".

"You mean Mustapha's death could be a murder related to those activities?"

"There is something in there, but it's not yet clear. However, I am thinking about the reaction of the pupil when you confronted him with the truth. The way you described it to me shows that either the pupil really doesn't know who he was dealing with and that's highly likely because it seems he was asked to leave the money under that bench, and that indicates there is no face-to-face deals with the blackmailers or drug dealers. And there is a less likely scenario but it still possible that the teenager knew all the way that his teacher was dealing with him, and maybe they both arranged to pull that acting scene in front of you to drive eyes away from them".

"Ah no! That would mean that I am a complete idiot in getting to know people, but I am good at that. Mustapha was no liar. Also, you are saying drug dealers. I don't think it's a drug deal, because the pupil yes is showing change in behaviour lately, but drugs would leave some traces for us to see, and that is not there".

Selway balanced his moustache with both hands, nodded his head showing his agreement of what she said, but as he explained earlier; a detective should never rule out any possibility regardless of how small it might be.

"Can you please give me the pupil's full name and address?" he asked.

"Yes, here you are..." She wrote Tom Wright details on a paper and handed it to him. "But please we promised him that we keep the story hidden from his mother, can you arrange to interview him here?" She asked.

"Yes, it's possible, don't worry we won't go to his house, but to know where he lives is important formally for our files".

"Ok thank you for this. You know when dealing with a teenager we prefer not to break our promises to them because that would make them lose trust in people when they become adults".

"Very sensible; now let us return to Mr Radi. You said you managed to reconnect with him. When was that? And have you spoken again about that pupil?"

"Yes. I managed to have a video chat with him on Skype the night before his death". She then tried to stop tears from going down on her cheeks.

She took her time to recover, went to the private toilet in the corner, washed her face and regained her seat. She said "As usual he was full of life, and he told me he forgave the student even if he got hurt by the accusation. And we talked in a very friendly manner, and it was business as usual, when suddenly someone knocked on his door".

"Can you please remember at what time was that?"

"I can't say exactly, but when I return home this evening, I can look on my Skype's history record for the exact hour, however it must have been after 10 pm. And I asked if he was expecting someone because it was an unusual time for a visit, and he said no. Then he opened the door, and the camera was still on, and I could see the back of Mustapha when he opened the door".

She sipped a bit of water, while Selway looked very excited to hear the rest.

"He seemed to have known the late visitor, because I heard him saying "Ah you". But then things seemed to have not gone smoothly between them as I heard them arguing about something, the man who came in was accusing Mustapha that he informed someone about something, and Mustapha was denying it, then the visitor left and I quickly turned off the camera, then I left a message to Mustapha that I better go to bed early wishing him a good night".

"Have you seen the face of the visitor?"

"No, only his clothes"

"What was he wearing?"

"Beige trousers and some brown and beige blazer I guess".

"These are very important information. I only wish you had continued the conversation with Mustapha later, he could have maybe told you some very important information".

"I felt like spying on them through that camera, so as soon as the other man left, I decided it was more respectful to end the session".

"Thank you very much for all the answers and information. You have provided us with very important details indeed, and we might meet again soon".

"You are welcome any time".

<u>Chapter 20</u>

When the four of them gathered for lunch, they all had some new information to share. However, Selway's were the most important, especially for the investigation that Al-Douri was leading.

It was maybe the longest lunch each one of them had ever had, as each one gave a briefing of what he heard from the witnesses he interviewed.

The other three heard suspicions about some students lately, but what Selway heard from the school manager stunned Al-Douri and Hughes as they felt the pupil called "Tom Wright" will definitely give them a line which would allow them to make a big breakthrough into the illegal activities that spread around the area in the last year or so.

"We should arrange to meet this student as soon as possible" Al-Douri said.

"I promised the school head to not question him in his house, so we have to arrange that in the school. Therefore, we can't, but wait at least till tomorrow" Selway said.

The detective then rang Ms Kane and told her that they should talk to the student at the earliest opportunity "tomorrow morning". She promised to get that arranged as soon as the student arrived at school around 8 am.

After they shared their recorded files between their smart phones, each two of them returned to their bases analysing and absorbing all what they heard.

Selway asked Dobinson to unload all the files on their office main computer, and then he left his house where he had to feed the dog.

On the road his mobile rang, and it was Ms Watt.

"I hope I am not disturbing you".

"That's alright".

"I am just calling to inform you that my sister is leaving tomorrow afternoon, so if you still need to talk to her or something, you can do so tonight or tomorrow morning".

"Tonight, and tomorrow morning I am very busy with the investigation. How about you both come to lunch at my house tomorrow before her departure?"

After a short chat with her sister, Anne said "Yes, that would do. Thanks for the invitation".

"You are welcome".

Selway then swiped through his house, fed the dog. And then rang a cake maker and ordered two packs of donuts and other slices to be delivered to his office. After that he went upstairs collected the electronic devices on which the CCTV streets cameras footage was recorded and left back to his office.

On his arrival the bakery was already delivering what he ordered. He thanked the delivery boy and joined his secretary. After dividing the sweeties between them, he ordered her to go to her desk room and summarise the most important information said by the teachers they met at school after listening carefully to every word told to Al-Douri and Hughes that morning.

Selway occupied himself in looking through the CCTV streets footage in the 48 hours that took place 24 hours around Radi's death, 12 hours before and after the incident.

There were four passages that lead to the footpath where Radi's death occurred. Selway went through them one by one. He couldn't of course spend 48 hours on each record, so he was trying to forward the footage and then stop it back to play normally whenever he sees a person or persons passing on the road. It was no easy task by any mean, because all the people of the surrounding towns walk their dogs there every day. Also, some people exercised there, the young running, the old walking.

That's why the detective decided to narrow his focus on just the strange hours, like late nights, early mornings and the exact time Radi went to do his exercise during that stormy morning.

There were actually two roads, with two passages on each towards the footpath, and each passage had a CCTV camera. He went first to the road that passes through the village located under Morobury's Castle Hill from which the woman who found the body came from.

He started looking at the time interval between 10 pm and 10 am, so if any suspect came across the passage couldn't have stayed at the footpath more than seven hours before the time of Radi's exercise.

He saw parts of the few cars that passed on the low road late that night, but there were definitely no people on foot as the camera was also showing the wind was hitting harder and harder the trees on the passage. He moved the cursor forward slowly to not miss any moving thing that could have passed through. Nothing appeared in the screen until the light of the day came about, he then saw a woman walking out her dog, when he checked the time, and he remembered the woman who found the body he recognised her immediately. Then after that he saw her running back through the passage. He concluded that what she told the police was perfectly correct.

After that he saw the police cordoning the area and blocking the passage. So, he moved to the second passage, again went through similar time interval but there was nothing there, absolutely nothing until the police blocked it after the incident.

Then he went to the two high passages which come from Bimport road, he went first to the smaller one. Also, nothing appeared there during the night. Then during the early hours of that Friday after the day light came through, he saw a man walking his dog, then two women exercising and later a group of people walking and running in a hurry, among them he recognised the Catholic priest he saw when he was going through the footpath himself and heard him thanking his god.

He then moved to the most important passage at which he and Radi usually met when they are entering the footpath or exiting from it. The passage was the widest and the camera covers almost three quarters of it, so there was always a possibility that a person could walk though without getting caught on camera if he walked extremely to the right side of the passage.

He couldn't notice any unusual activity during the night, and then at dawn as light was shyly invading the sky, he saw Radi running through. He was alone but it was clear that he was having difficulty running fast because of the strong wind at that time. Then couple of hours later he saw few people then group of people hurrying inside including himself and Max after people noticed the police activity and the news was spread about the incident.

When he almost finished his first review of this footage, Dobinson came in and handed him a paper on which she summarised the most important information given by the interviewees that morning at the school. The paper read:

- All interviewees said that Mustapha Radi was a good man, yet one of his students Tom Wright had accused him of blackmailing.

- The school head is almost certain that Tom Wright's issue was not drugs related.

- The teachers confirmed that Radi had a special relationship with the students as they had several exercises together outside the school every week.

- The school head and teachers noticed change in behaviour of some students in the second half of the past school year.

- The school head claimed that Radi had an argument in his house with a man in the night before his death.

- The school head said that she received a strange demand from the Ministry of Education, they wanted to move Radi from here to Newcastle, but she managed to turn down that demand after a call to Number 10.

- Rita and Jamie Cleman, a married couple of teachers, both confirmed that Radi asked them to cooperate with him to uncover what was going wrong with some of the students. At first, they agreed, but then when noticed that Radi was about to watch the students' activities outside the school and follow them, they decided to stay out of it.

- Laura Clark a teacher, felt worried about some students in the last month of the previous year, and those students didn't show up yet this year, and that could be for various reasons: they could have changed school, migrated to another country, they are ill or something worse had happened to them.

As Selway read that summary, Dobinson prepared two cups of tea. They then sat down on two chairs in front of the large window and shared their thoughts about what they have heard and seen so far.

"From what I read now and heard today, it seems that something unusual was taking place with the school pupils either during their time at school or outside".

"Yes definitely. I guess Al-Douri and Hughes will get their investigation jumping forward if they manage to talk to all the students who might be involved in a way or another in some illegal activities".

"What I am thinking also, is that if Radi was murdered, then there is a high probability that his death was related to this investigation regarding the young lads and those activities".

"Indeed, there is a link, if it's a murder. Have you found anything suspicious in the CCTV footage?"

"No not really. I haven't got enough time actually to watch them with complete time and focus; I wish that you take them as your task from now on. Please sit and watch them from tomorrow morning and try to watch the most important hours in their real times. Who knows? You might spot something I didn't see as I went through them rather rapidly".

"So, you don't want me to attend the future interviews".

"No, we have recorders. You better just stick with the footage right now".

Dobinson seemed unimpressed, but at last she said, "As you wish".

"By the way, can you please ring the Catholic Church as soon as you can?"

"What for?".

"I saw one of their priests in the morning of the incident and I saw some kind of happiness and relief on his face while giving a sign of thanks to the heavens. And he is one of the people who were near the body before the police arrival. I remembered him now when I saw the footage. I think I should ask him few questions".

Dobinson looked at her watch and said "It is quarter after 10. I don't think there will be any one in the church that late".

"It's a big church; there are fathers and nuns who live there. I don't know if they answer the main telephone at such time, but try it, you won't lose anything".

"It's definitely in the telephone book, let me have a look".

She stood up and opened a drawer near the main door of the office, she pulled out the telephone book, and after looking in couple of pages, she dialled the number of the Catholic Church, to her surprise she got quickly a reply

"Good evening. The Catholic Church, who is calling?"

"Good evening. This is the office of Detective Selway, can we speak to the head of the church please?"

"It's me; Father Sheridan speaking".

"Alright can you hold a moment please, Mr Selway will talk to you". She then waved to Selway who rushed towards the telephone.

"Good evening, Father"

Dobinson said in a low voice "Sheridan".

"Good evening, Father Sheridan. Sorry to disturb you at that time of the night".

"No problem. This is my favourite time of study and prayer. You are a detective, what is the matter? And how can the church be of help?"

"Do not worry. We only need to have a friendly conversation with one of your priests".

"One of our priests! Which one?"

"I don't know his name I am afraid, but I can describe him to you".

"I am not sure if I could be of any help on the phone. If you are close, it would be better to come here and drink a cup of soup with me".

"Yes. I am here in Morobury. I will join you after ten minutes or so".

Selway then collected his long coat and his cane. Waved the cane toward Dobinson and said "Go to bed now, you have a long day tomorrow watching the footage. Thanks for everything. Good night".

"Good night and good luck".

The church was hardly a ten minutes' walk from the office. And exactly after ten minutes from the phone conversation, Selway was in front of the gate ringing the bell. Few seconds later, Father Sheridan opened the door and invited the detective in.

They walked into a cosy study room, the light was so bright there, and that forced Selway to shut his eyes and reopen them slowly until they got familiar with the strength of light.

As they sat down, the Father immediately handed his guest a warm cup of Tomato soup.

"Oh. That's handy in such cold weather. Thank you very much".

"Your face looks familiar. I am sure I have seen you before".

"Yes, I used to come here sometime for a funeral or another public occasion".

"So, you are from the town then".

"Yes I am. My name is Roger Selway. Former army colonel, right now a detective"

"Nice to meet you; I wonder what a detective would want from a priest in our congregation".

"Well as you might have heard, a young man died at dawn last Sunday during that strong storm. And I came across your priest that morning he was one of the few people who came into the scene early, so I just need to check if he has any important information about the accident".

"I see. But I heard that the man's death was an accident. So why are you investigating?"

"There is some information that leaves the door open for another possibility".

"You mean a murder!"

"Probably, we don't know yet".

"And you told me on the phone that you don't know the name of the priest. We have four priests here. Can you describe him to me please; is he old? Young?"

"He is in his sixties I guess".

"Oh. That's father O'Shea".

"Okay. Can I talk to him?"

"Unfortunately, it would not be possible this week".

"Why?"

"Because he is abroad, he left yesterday to the Vatican, he won't return before next week".

"Oh. What a luck!"

"Is there anything else I could help you with?".

"Maybe, can you tell me a little bit about Father O'Shea? I mean what are his characteristics, his duties here? A little information about his background might prove helpful".

"He is a very active preacher. He travels on a regular basis. Among his duties some lecturing and in an interval time of some days he talks to people who want to confess".

"Is that all?"

"He is also popular among the young generation; many young lads gather for his lectures".

"And why is he that popular? Is he the most knowledgeable in your church?".

"Not really, he is popular because his lectures are not purely religious, he mixes them with politics and international affairs, I have warned him several times against that, but the others in the church are seeing no harm in what he is doing as long as it attracts the young girls and guys. And since 2013 we have seen numbers doubled while other churches are hardly having few old guests".

"And may I ask what he was possibly doing very early that Friday morning at the Castle Hill footpath?"

"There are few boxes in the area where people can leave money or jewels for the church. We collect them on a weekly basis. And it was O'Shea's turn last Sunday morning to collect them. There is a box at the footpath there, and regarding the time, it was the usual time for the collection before the path gets crowded".

"Interesting; Is there anything else you wish to add?"

"No. Not really" the father shook his head.

Selway stood up and thanked his host warmly for his time and he wished him a good night and left back to his house.

Chapter 21

Tom Wright was surprised to see all those strange faces at the office of the school head, he knew immediately that some troubles were coming his way. He looked to the three men and then to Ms Kane as he hoped to find any smiles, but there were none, not even fake ones. So, he braced himself to get hammered.

"Good morning".

"Good morning".

"Thomas, please sit here".

Al-Douri felt that it will be golden opportunity for him if he pushed the right buttons that would make the pupil gives out all the information he had. His strategy which he shared with Selway and Hughes was on showing big seriousness to the young lad, because the friendly approach that Ms Kane used with him before didn't give any productive result.

Al-Douri winked to Ms Kane, who accordingly said to Wright "Tom. I am sorry but we had to share your story with the authorities. And here they are Mr Al-Douri and Mr Hughes from the Police and Intelligence services, and Detective Selway. And they are here to talk to you, so please be cooperative or else they may pay you visit at home which something I know very well that you want to avoid, and I actually did my best to keep the story here in the school".

The pupil swallowed his saliva, and it was clear that his heart was beating fast. He then with a hardly audible voice said "Alright!" as he looked again at the serious faces of the three men.

"We heard your story that night when you were seen by your late teacher. And that when Ms Kane made you confront him you accused him of blackmailing you. Couple of days later he died in an accident, and he could be murdered." Before Al-Douri could finish his sentence, Tom stood up halfway and shouted "I have nothing to do with this. I swear."

"Sit down and do not disturb me when I am talking, you are here to answer when asked".

"Ok. Sorry"

"You were saying you have nothing to do with what exactly?"

"With the death of Mr Radi"

"Are you sure?"

"Yes. I am sure".

"Alright; let me get back to your story. You left 500 pounds cash under a public bench. To whom you left them and why?"

The teenager hesitated a little bit.

"We are waiting and remember to say things as they are; do not lie and do not hide anything" Al-Douri said firmly.

"Alright; alright"

The student looked again to those faces around him, then he forced the words out of his mouth "Answer to the first question: I do not know whom I was dealing with. Answer to the second question: Because someone blackmailed me and ordered me to give him money or else".

"Or else! What he or she knew about you that would enslave you to that extent and push you to give them all this money?"

Tom looked to the Ms Kane. Al-Douri immediately understood that the pupil didn't wish to reveal his secret in front of her, so he asked her "Could you please leave us few minutes with him on our own?"

"Sure!" Ms Kane replied while leaving the room quickly.

"Here you are. What is it?"

"A girl added me on Facebook last spring, and we had some intimate conversation, then we turned our cameras on, and you may know what happens in Cybersex".

"Yes, even if you shouldn't do that at your age. But keep going".

"After we finished our camera chat one night, the next morning she sent me a video of me recorded naked, and she threatened me to publish it on all the pages of my colleagues and my

174

teachers at school, and she asked for money to keep it between us".

"But you said earlier you don't know who you are dealing with. And now you are saying: it was a lady".

"Yes and no. I mean she gave me a name which is definitely not hers, also there is a man involved".

"Take your time and give me as much as details as you can. You had a cybersex session, tell me exactly what happened after that. Every single detail could be crucial".

"After you know, I was off, she waved goodbye, and we ended the chat. I turned off my laptop and went to bed. As I gave her my mobile number, she sent me a text message during the night; I only saw it in the morning. She said that she left me an important message on Facebook. So, I signed into Facebook to find a shocking video of me from the previous night, and with a warning message that this video could be sent to all people in my friends list. All what I have to do is to calm down and that I will receive a call from them in the coming hours on our landline. Of Course, I didn't want my mother to listen to our conversation or to pick up the phone herself, so I stayed all day next to the phone, pretending that I am reading a novel. And when they rang, I immediately answered, and there was a man talking. He said "*Hello Tom, be a good guy and listen to me. If you cooperate with us, you will be safe, we know that you are not a rich family. However, you still can afford to give us 250 pounds per month*". I told him "I can't", however he said "*I am not asking you if you can or can't, you have to find a way to gather such amount every month or else you know. We will text you by the end of the month and you should be ready with the first payment, and we will tell you where to leave it. We are watching you and if you tell anyone in school or police, we will expose you like a whore*".

"You are saying that they asked for 250 pounds per month, but you left them 500 in the last time; why?"

"Because I didn't pay the previous month"

"And for how long this has been going on?"

"April was the first month".

"So, it's six or seven months now".

"Six"

"That means you paid them 1500 pounds, or to be correct 1000 pounds because they didn't receive the last 500".

"Yes".

"And why did you accuse your teacher when he confronted you with the money?"

"Firstly, because I wondered how he knew that I am going to leave the money at that bench. Secondly because I recalled that his English accent and voice was a bit similar to the blackmailer".

"Interesting" replied Al-Douri.

There Selway interfered for the first time in the conversation "But if he was the blackmailer, why would he confront you with the money, he would have taken the money as usual" he said.

Tom didn't reply. But Hughes had a suggestion "What if Radi was involved in this blackmailing and then he decided to stop it for reasons we don't know, maybe he got enough money, or maybe the group he was part of had left the area, so he decided that the smartest way to clean his name is to pretend that he was caring for his students".

The pupil waved his thumb up to Hughes confirming that this was what he was thinking too.

Al-Douri and Selway stared at each other, and then Al-Douri said "Everything is possible, we will take this possibility into consideration". He added "Now let me get back to what you told us today. How did the girl get in touch with you first?"

"She added me on Facebook?"

"Is her profile still there?"

"No, she deleted it?"

"Have you saved any photo of her?"

"Yes, I have a couple of them at home".

Al-Douri handed him a little card with just his email printed on it and said, "Could you please send them to me by email today after school as soon as you get home".

"Ok" said Tom as he inserted the card into his pocket.

"One more question. Have you spoken to that lady? What she sounds like. Her accent sounded native English or else?"

"Frankly before the video session, our chat was only by messaging, and she never called me. Only texting me"

"But surely she spoke to you during the video session?"

"We hardly spoken to each other, you know" Tom blushed and turned his eyes shyly away.

"Ok Young man, Thanks for the information. Take care and let me know if they got back in touch with you. Don't leave home unless for school or for something very important. And don't forget to send me the photos you have".

"Alright; can I leave now?"

"Yes". Al-Douri opened the door for him. Then returned to his colleagues who were deeply thinking of what they had just heard.

Couple of minutes later, the school head returned to her office.

"Have you learned any important information?" She asked

"Yes, I think we have something to start with" Al-Douri answered.

"Anything else the school could help you with, for the time being?"

"Definitely"

At hearing the answer, Ms Kane had a more serious look as if she were telling Al-Douri to fire it away.

"I want to you to look carefully into the names of the other students that their performance and behaviour changed completely in the last six months or so. We need to talk to them, here in private. I trust we would find a way to get some information out of them".

"Ok consider it done. I will do so as soon as this afternoon. And I will try to speak to some of them at the end of the day before they return home, and I would get in touch if I managed to make a breakthrough with them".

"Thank you very much. Your cooperation is very much appreciated".

The three investigators left the school and Hughes drove the car to a pub where they sat down and ordered a coffee.

"Finally, things are moving" Al-Douri said.

"For you maybe yes, but for me I am still in the blue regarding Radi's death. Any news yet from London regarding the DNA test"

"No. Not yet".

"Can you call them and check again when they expect to release the result".

"Ok" Al-Douri then pulled out his mobile phone, dialled a number, then he waited.

"Hello, can I speak to Pinky?"

Selway couldn't hide his laughter; he knew it was some nickname. Al-Douri smiled back as he waited his "Pinky" to come through. It took nearly a minute before the man reached the phone. "Is there any news about the Morobury accident DNA sample?"

"We are making progress. We expect to send you the result within the coming 48 hours".

"Great. We look forward to it. Have a good day".

Al-Douri looked at Selway and said, "We will have it soon, he told me within the next 48 hours".

"Thank you. That's a relief".

"Tell me, have you found anything interesting on the CCTV footage?"

"I went through them quickly. Nothing caught my eye. However, Ms Dobinson will spend more time exploring them in the coming few days".

Selway then looked at his watch and said "I do apology, I must return home now. I have guests for lunch, so I better get home in order to cook and get things ready in time".

"We will drive you"

"Thank you very much, finish your coffee, there is really no need for that. My house is hardly ten minutes' walk from here and I do need to buy some fresh vegetables from a shop nearby".

The pub was hardly fifty yards away from the town's high street. Soon Selway walked on the pavement of the street, it was busier than usual at that time of the day because the weather was exceptionally nice. He then walked up to the right as he was taking a way back home which passed by a fresh vegetables shop. When he was thinking of what the things are he needed to buy, suddenly a young lad fell down in front of him. He rushed towards him and so did other people. The guy looked very pale. He checked his heartbeat; he is still alive. Selway told the people who gathered "He lost consciousness, please call an ambulance".

The town ambulance service was just half a mile away, so in around five minutes, the trained service men and women arrived at the scene, picked the lad into the ambulance and drove him fast to the emergency service at the Westminster Memorial hospital which was located behind Selway's house.

It was an unpleasant surprise, yet the detective had to stick with the lunch procedure, he murmured to himself "I will check on him at the hospital after the Watt sisters leave".

As soon as he walked inside the shop, immediately one of the ladies working there asked him "The usual list?"

"Yes please" he replied with a smile. "And please add some garlic and two Aubergines" he added.

Chapter 22

Around 1 pm, Selway hosted the Watt sisters for lunch. Ruth seemed excited as she looked forward to leaving Morobury to London to meet her lover there.

"Anne I am sorry that I had to leave you alone at this tough time, but you know this could be my last chance with Andrew" Ruth said.

"No worries, I will be fine. I only hope he really means what he says to you, and I wish you all the best" Anne replied.

Selway was listening to the conversation with interest, especially after he heard from Anne that Ruth's promised lover was a Don Juan who spent time with middle aged women for the sake of their fortune, so he can feed his gambling addiction.

"I hope you will still be reachable on your mobile phone when you are with your companion" The detective said addressing Ruth.

"Definitely yes; we are not heading to Venus yet" Ruth answered with a big laughter that showed the good mood she was in.

Selway wanted to keep all the contacts related to the investigation he led within touch, because at that time nothing was clear. He was deep in his thoughts as he smiled and looked to his two guests as if he was rather watching them on a TV screen and not on the same table.

He was reviewing the events in his mind. Radi died while he was under investigation about cybercrimes and drug trafficking, his student accused him of being his blackmailer. His death is still unclear if it was accidental or a murder. He had a clash with Mrs Clayton couple of weeks before his death, her son Barry is abroad, and no one knows for sure if he left before Radi's death or after. A very emotional goodbye was said by Mr Clayton to the teacher at the funeral. Why Father O'Shea looked relieved when Radi died? And Andrew, the gambler lover of Ruth Watt, joined the circle of suspicion for he could be planning to strike a big fortune if Ruth inherited her older sister.

In addition to all of that, Selway's mind was also worried about the fate of that lad who collapsed in the street few hours earlier. He didn't realise how far he went in his thought, until Anne watt shook his left arm. "Mr Selway, are you alright?"

"Sorry. I am so sorry; I was thinking about something".

"No worries. We have to leave now I am afraid, because her train leaves Millingham after half an hour".

"Oh. Don't worry about that, we can still drink a cup of coffee. I already booked her a Taxi, he will be here in 10 minutes, and the station is hardly ten minutes' drive".

He then left the table quickly, turned on his coffee machine, and three minutes later he served his guests two little cups.

"I hope the taxi doesn't arrive late, because I still have to pick my bag from the hotel" Ruth said.

"Don't worry, unless you haven't packed it" Selway said.

"No, it's packed and waiting at the entrance" Ruth confirmed.

"Very good, you will arrive in time" Selway reassured her.

As soon as the Watt sisters left with the Taxi, Selway had another look at the mirror, tighten up his top, and left to the hospital around the corner.

He walked into the reception, and asked for the young lad who came in through emergency services couple of hours earlier.

"He is in the intensive care section, room B" The detective was told by the receptionist.

There was another information desk at the emergency wing. And Selway asked the woman sitting there "Hello. Can I visit the lad in room B please?"

"No. Not now I am afraid, The Doctor told me visits are not allowed. However, you are the first person to ask about him. Are you his father or grandfather?"

Selway didn't appreciate that second suggestion as it made him feel very old. He then replied, "No. I only saw him today when he collapsed in the street".

"Oh, I see. Anyway, visits are not allowed right now".

"Ok no problem. Can I speak to the doctor please?"

"Dr Bateman is having his lunch at the moment, I guess. He should be here in the next half hour or so, if you can wait".

"Ok. I will wait. Can you please inform him that I want to talk to him?"

"Alright"

Selway then walked to the waiting room and took a seat. Sitting there, were only two women, a young and an old one, they seemed in distress, as they both had tears in their eyes, possibly because they had a family member in the intensive care.

Hardly ten minutes later, a man in white robe walked in and passed by the desk. The receptionist there stopped him. Selway saw her pointing towards him, and he knew immediately that the man was Doctor Bateman.

He was a young doctor, maybe in his thirties. He walked straight towards Selway. The detective stood up, they shook hands, and introduced themselves.

"How is he?" Selway asked.

"He is asleep now because I injected him with sleeping medics" Dr Bateman replied.

"And why is that? What is his problem?"

"He is a drug addict, and not any type, a dangerous drug".

"At that age! How on earth he gets such substances?"

"I don't know. By the way you are the first person to visit him, and he has been here for over three hours now. So that may tell that his parents are not in real touch with him".

"How sad"

The doctor shook his shoulders.

"Have you found anything on him that could show his identity?"

"Sorry but I don't know why I should answer all your questions. Jane (the receptionist) told me that you are not a relative. So why I should give you any information about his state".

At that Selway had to pull out his detective card. He waved it in the doctor face then said, "I am part of a team investigating many crimes in the area including drugs trafficking".

"Ah sorry again, please come with me to my desk and we can talk there".

They walked through couple of corridors, and then took few steps up to the first floor where the doctor office was located.

"Ok Doctor, can you please tell me what are we dealing with here? What is the actual state of the young patient?"

"He almost died, he was lucky that he collapsed in the street and was rushed to hospital, imagine if he collapsed alone somewhere behind closed doors, he would have certainly died in less than half an hour".

"You mean he had an overdose or something, we always hear about celebrities found dead at their homes from overdoses".

"Exactly! And the dose he took was a powerful mixture of cocaine and heroin and if he wasn't well built, it would have killed him in seconds".

"Good lord. Have you found anything on him that could give out his identity?".

"He had in his pocket only his mobile phone. I haven't tried the numbers in it yet". The Doctor opened the drawer of his desk and pulled out a smart phone, he turned it on and said "I looked quickly into his list of contacts, several names in it, but there is no indication for a home for example. Only people names; so, we can't really tell what the name of the lad is before we try and ring someone from his contact list.

"Ok. Go ahead then or give it to me and I will do it".

The Doctor handed Selway the phone.

Selway looked at the list, he picked the number of a female contact, and dialled it, it rang several times, but she didn't reply. He tried a male number, same thing happened, it rang for almost a minute but no reply. Dialled a third and fourth, same story, and the fifth line was shut.

"No one is answering. it's either he wasn't desirable for his friends so they are trying to avoid him, or maybe they are trying to stay away from trouble if they knew he is in hospital for reasons they may have knowledge of".

"So, what are you going to do now?"

"I will keep his mobile with me, my colleagues will be very interested in this story, and they may come here tonight or tomorrow to speak to you or to him if he was awake. Meanwhile I will try and call those numbers from my own telephone, if they replied I will try to get his name from them".

"But of course, those contacts would have several friends so how they would know which one you are calling for?"

"I will give them his number and I will take couple of photos of him now if you don't mind".

"Yes, no problem".

They walked back into the emergency wing, entered the room B. The lad was still there asleep. The detective took couple of photos by his mobile phone and left the hospital.

Meanwhile the school head had already talked with several students and managed to convince two of them to speak to the police the following day. She immediately called Al-Douri and told him that the next morning he will be able to talk to a female and a male student.

The Intelligence officer had just ended the call he received from the school, when he received a new call, this time from Selway.

"Have you managed to talk to more students?"

"Ms Kane had just called me to confirm two interviews tomorrow morning with two students".

"Great. I may have some very important news for you too".

"Really! What is that?"

"Today, after I left you to entertain my guests for lunch, a young lad collapsed in the street, and he was taken to hospital. I managed to talk to the doctor who dealt with him. He is a drug addict, and he could have died from an overdose. He won't be available for questioning before a day or two. However, I got his mobile phone and hopefully we can identify him soon".

"Very interesting, can we join you this evening, so we can go through this story together".

"Sure. You are welcome. Any time after 7 pm will do".

Selway turned off his phone as she stepped inside the old building in which his office was located. He wanted to check how things are going with his secretary.

On seeing him coming in, Ms Dobinson protested immediately "Oh my. What a boring task you have handed me".

"Found anything of interest yet?"

"Nothing significant on the first footage which I have just finished exploring. I am starting now the second one".

"It needs patience and concentration at the same time".

"But it's really painful. I sometimes fight falling asleep, and without turning songs on YouTube, the task would have been insurmountable".

"Sorry about that. But it's our job not to miss any detail no matter how small it is".

"You tell me now, how was your day at the school?"

"Fine, however the pupil managed to convince Al-Douri and Hughes that Radi could have been his blackmailer".

"I doubt that. A man who shed tears does not commit crimes of any kind. That what I learned from my experience".

"I told them too. But they are eager to not remove any possibility from the table. And in that, if we want to speak professionally, they are right".

"And have Ruth Watt left the town?"

"Yes, they had lunch in my place, and she left for London in the early afternoon".

Selway then told her the story of the young drug addict, and what the doctor at the hospital told him.

"Things are getting exciting"

"Yes, they are".

"Now that will give me a boost to keep looking into those footages, because I want to be of help in the investigations".

Selway waved his thumb up encouraging her to do as she just said. She then remembered something and asked "I almost forgot. You didn't tell me what happened last night at the church?"

"Not a big deal. The priest was not there. He is in Rome until next week".

"Ok. Anything else I could help you with today?"

"Yes. Maybe" The detective flipped his bottom lip with his finger then added "I don't like all these people going abroad when we must talk to them: Barry Clayton and the priest. And I certainly need to talk to the Claytons again, before they also vanish. But as you can see, we are busy with interviews, and we are always doing something related to the investigation. However, I should still be able to find time for a long chat with Mr Clayton tomorrow. Can you please call him and ask him if he can come to my house for dinner".

"I think you better talk to him personally and invite him".

"I know I can do that, but I want him to feel things are formal and not casual. So, call him first, if he answered tell him that I want to speak to him".

Dobinson dialled the Physicist number, after couple of rings, he answered. Dobinson said "Hello Mr Clayton. Detective Selway wants to tell you. I will pass the phone to him now".

"Hello Mr Clayton. Selway here, I hope you are doing well".

"I am fine. Any news in the investigation?"

"No, not really. However, I need to talk to you at the earliest of your conveniences. How about having dinner tomorrow in my house?"

"Tomorrow I was planning to watch a documentary on the TV in the evening"

"Can't you record it and watch it later".

"Yes, you are right, I better do that. Yes, I can of course".

"Ok. Let us say we dine here tomorrow at 8 pm?"

"Yes fine. See you tomorrow then and thank you for the invitation".

Chapter 23

In the evening Al-Douri and Hughes joined Selway in his house. Immediately they shared the contacts list from the mobile phone of the drug addict, and they started ringing the numbers they got. The first attempts for Selway and Hughes didn't work, but it did for Al-Douri. Hardly a minute later, they heard him talking to someone.

Hello Lucy----I hope I am not disturbing, please don't feel alarmed, the police are talking to you. ---- We are calling regarding one of your friends; he is in hospital after collapsing in the street earlier today. -----I hope you will help us identifying him. We only found his mobile phone in his pocket, and you are one of his contacts. ---- I will send you his photo in the next few seconds.

Al-Douri then attached a photo of the lad and sent it through to that friend called "Lucy". Hardly a minute later, "It's Peter Hoare" Lucy replied.

Ok thank you very much for your great help. Can you tell us a little bit about him, how do you know him?

"I was his teacher two years ago, all what I know is that he comes from a very wealthy family. He was an ordinary student of mine".

"And at which school?".

"In Morobury, but I changed school last year as I moved north to Stoke on Trent".

"Ok thank you".

Al-Douri then turned to his colleagues and said "We got his name. Peter Hoare and he is a student in the secondary school. So, we are indeed dealing with a gang targeting young lads with both sexual blackmailing and drug addiction, and they have been in the area for nearly a year".

"It's also the same period of time that Radi spent in the area before his death" Hughes remarked.

"I don't think Radi was a gangster, and I believe it was a coincidence that he lived here in the same period of time. And maybe he paid his life because of that coincidence especially when he got his nose into it" Selway defended his neighbour.

"Probably you are right, but as I said previously, we can't remove any suspect from our list, just because you feel that he couldn't be part of it. What if he was forced to be part of it? What if he was also being blackmailed?" Al-Douri suggested.

A minute of silence invaded the living room in Selway's house after this suggestion, which sounded very plausible.

"Ok, but you are getting luckier than me. Your investigation is moving swiftly as many victims of the gang you are after started to appear on the scene. But my own investigation is still very foggy, we still do not know if it was an accident or a murder, and we can't prove it either way" Selway said.

"You are right. I fully understand your frustration. However, I feel strongly that the two cases are related, so when we advance in our case, you will automatically benefit from it" Al-Douri said optimistically.

"I hope so. But my frustration comes from my expectations that solving my case would help you solve yours and not the other way round" Selway said while massaging his moustache.

Hughes tried to cheer the detective up, "Fingers crossed things will go smoother for you once the London team releases the results of the DNA of the blood sample found on Radi's sleeve".

"Ok. I am looking forward to that". Then he turned to Al-Douri and asked, "Have you received any interesting information on the list of people who rented the Claytons annexe before Radi?".

"I should have them by tomorrow morning. So, once I finished my interviews at the school, I will forward them to you by email".

"You are talking as if I am not going to be present at the school interviews!"

"Ah do you want to attend that as well?"

"Of Course, I do. Radi was a teacher there. So even if I believe the crimes related to his students have nothing to do with him, but it still somehow all connected".

"Alright, no problem; you are always welcome to join us at the school interviews tomorrow morning, but I thought you wanted to interview other people again like the Claytons".

"Mr Clayton will be my guest for dinner tomorrow evening. So don't worry the two schedules will not collide, I know how to set my priorities properly".

Before returning to their isolated hotel, Al-Douri and Hughes agreed to sit and check with him the previous tenants of the Claytons annexe once they receive details about them from the main office.

Selway fed his dog and sat alone in the living room thinking of all what he heard and seen so far. *The big picture is nowhere near clear, even though there are pupils who experienced sexual blackmailing or drug addiction, which is something the police have been suspecting for some time, what's new so far, practically nothing apart from the fact that Radi personally investigated the issue, or at least he was involved in it somehow.* As he went up to bed, he felt sorry for his secretary that he handed her that so boring task of checking the important interval times of the CCTV footage minute by minute. But then he said "This is her job. I better sleep as soon as possible because the next day promised to be a fully loaded one".

The next morning Brenda, a pupil of 16-year-old, stood like in a trial looking at the faces of the stranger men around her. She then whispered few words in Ms Kane ear. The latter then told the investigators "She is very shy; she is not able to talk in front of you".

"What do you suggest then?" asked Al-Douri.

Selway interfered and suggested "How about a woman as interviewer?"

Ms Kane then looked at Brenda, who she shyly nodded her head positively.

Selway said to Al-Douri "I will call Ms Dobinson and she will interview her". While Selway rang his secretary, Al-Douri suggested that they interview Martin the second pupil, and then at the arrival of Mr Dobinson she takes care of Brenda.

Ms Kane sent Brenda back to her class and told her that she will call her back once Ms Dobinson arrived.

Martin was 18 years old and in the last secondary school class before joining University. He possessed a strong personality, and he didn't mind speaking in front of the school manager.

He had almost a similar story to Tom. A sexy girl lured him into a Cybersex video chat, and then they blackmailed him. And the amount he paid per month was five hundred pounds, as his family was in a better financial state than Tom's. So, it was clear for the investigators that the blackmailers picked their targets carefully and they knew beforehand their financial state and how much they can afford to pay.

The only difference between Martin and Tom was that he was asked to leave the money in a different public place and that was behind a temporary parking sign located near a hair salon. Also, the blackmailers didn't bother to ring him on the phone, so he thought all the time he was dealing with the lady, for they kept sending him messages to his mobile through various internet platforms.

However, he said he didn't receive an order to pay the current month which was September. So August was the last month he paid. And in total he paid them 2500 pounds over the period from April to end of August.

During the Q and A session with Martin, Ms Dobinson arrived, and she started already questioning Brenda after Hughes gave her few instructions on what information she must focus most.

And the conversation between Selway's secretary and the young girl went as follows:
"Hello Brenda. My name is Ms Dobinson, and I am here to help free you of the burdens you have been carrying on your own for months. Please be very frank with me and don't worry about any intimate information you may give me. Be courageous and just feel free to say everything you have on your chest".

Brenda nodded her head positively.

"Can we start?"

"Yes"

"You have admitted to Ms Kane yesterday that you have been the victim of a sexual blackmailer, what can you tell me about that? How it all started and how did you fall for it?"

"It started when a handsome chap added me on Facebook, and you know as a young lady I would like to show my real friends that I do know some handsome guys, so I accepted the friendship request"

"When was that?"

"During the first week of March"

"Ok thanks. And how things developed later?"

"He started sending me photos and poems and kept saying good things about every photo I posted".

"Were his photos nude ones?"

"No at the beginning, for nearly a month it was only romantic kind of contact".

"And then?"

"Once he felt that I am responding well to him, he wanted to arrange a Rendezvous face to face, and he claimed that would be possible after 11 pm, because he claimed he worked from 1 pm till 11 pm every day, so during the day I am in school so we can't meet other than between 11 and midnight. I apologised because I couldn't go out after such time at night. And I suggested that we wait for an event like a birthday party of one of my friends or so to meet. Few days later, he asked why we don't do video chat; this is a better way to see what we really look like. As I was very attracted to him physically, I said to myself why not. Once the video chat started, he immediately started removing his clothes one by one, and I was like pulled by a magnet, I couldn't resist, and I fell for it. The next day, the entire dream turned out to be a nightmare"

"Did he call you?"

"Yes, he did it on the landline number even I didn't give it to him myself, so I was frightened to the core".

"And what did he say?"

"He said he wanted to see me the next day at 11:30 pm near the memorial cross next to the hospital, or else he would publish my video on the school Facebook page. I begged him not to and told him that I can't do what he was asking. He insisted that I can and if I don't come out, he would ask me to pay him 1000 pounds every month. At that I told him no, it's something I don't have any access to, so I would rather agree to meet him".

"And you went?"

"Yes, I went to the Cross location late at night, and I stood alone there under a light rain shower, but no one was there, then when I wanted to return home some ten minutes later, he sent me a message on my phone and said that there is a plastic bag on the corner of the cross little wall and I have to pick it up, hide it from eyes, and take it home with me, and later he will tell me what I do with its content".

"Interesting and quiet exciting! And what was in that bag?"

"I picked it without looking at the content in darkness there, then I rushed back home, it was almost midnight; I was frightened as hell as the rain went also heavier. I smuggled myself inside the house, and then when I became alone inside my room, I turned the light on and discovered that the bag is filled with smaller packs each contains some white powder".

"And of course, you had an idea what that might be?"

"Well, I only saw it in movies and on TV. So yes".

"And what happened next?"

"He sent me a new message saying that I should wait an order from him in a couple of days' time, and that I should be ready any time during the evenings to execute what he might order me to do".

Dobinson nodded her head showing that she is following every word that came out of Brenda lips. Then the latter went on "It was clear for me that I have to distribute the stuff for him. I told him what if the police caught me. But he promised that I will be protected all time, and my identity will be always concealed. He also sent me by delivery a hooded top to help me do my job as discreet as possible. And every now and then I received an order to go to a certain site and leave the bags for people who were buying them"

"And what are those sites? Can you name them to me please?"

"I left some at the bottom of public benches along the Castle hill footpath and the memorial garden. Some in the walls near the Supermarket. However, the majority of distribution took place at the Catholic Church. We used to attend lectures of a priest there, and the clients were usually some of the attendees, we leave the bags in their hands from behind, and they never look at who is handing them the bags. Of course, I wasn't alone, but no one was allowed to look at the other face, or he or she will get punished, even the addicts who are buying the stuff didn't look because if they did, they wouldn't be able to get the stuff anymore".

"Very interesting; but you didn't feel that you are doing a very bad thing!"

"Of Course, I did, but I had no choice I am afraid. Also, he used to tell me to not worry saying that the stuff is legal in many European countries such as the Netherlands etc.."

"And you are not afraid now that he might now know that you told the police and that he might publish your video?"

"Of course, I am afraid, but I haven't heard from him for over a month now, even his Facebook profile is no longer there, so maybe he is no longer after me or no longer active!".

Chapter 24

When Ms Dobinson re-joined the team as they left the school building, Selway read immediately in her face that she got very important information out of her young interviewee. And as soon as they sat on their very isolated corner table inside the nearby pub, Dobinson fired up the information she heard from Brenda.

Dobinson didn't speak; she only turned the recorder on. And her face went full red from excitement, as she looked at the eyes of her three colleagues and read all sorts of feelings on them. Seriousness was the most dominant expression.

Al-Douri said "This is a very important witness". He then dialled quickly the school number and asked the manager to send him the address of Brenda. As soon as he received it in text, he then called Chief Constable Owen and told him that the location should be watched and protected 24/7, and that Brenda should be fully protected in every step she takes.

Al-Douri then returned to the table chat "We have to protect her. Those criminals would do anything to hide their traces. She is the first proof we have that we are dealing with a gang. It's now confirmed to us that both, drug trafficking and Cyber blackmailing, were done by the same person or group" he said.

Selway showed his approval and added "It's clear that they are very professional criminals, because they study their victims very carefully. They know that young girls could not handle the pressure the same way young boys do, and they know that they are less likely to steal money out of their parents in order to pay for blackmail, so the best way is to get a different use of them, something they could handle and ease the pressure off their chest for a while every here and now. We are indeed dealing with a very smart criminal or criminals".

Hughes spoke for the first time and said "But you didn't notice that all those activities seemed to have ceased since Radi's death. The two pupils who we interviewed said that they no longer received any instructions or order for a month or two lately. Brenda also confirmed same thing. For me there is definitely connection to Radi's death; and as things are so far, he seems to me the suspect number one, because since his death regardless of if it happened by accident or by murder, these activities seem to have stopped all of a sudden".

A minute of silence invaded the table. Hughes words were very logical, even Selway and Dobinson who usually defended Radi on every occasion couldn't find a window for argument this time.

Suddenly Al-Douri received a call. It was from the MI5 Headquarter in London. They informed him that the files of the previous tenants of the Clayton's annexe are now ready, and they were sent to his email address. After he ended the call, Al-Douri winked at Selway and told him "The details of the previous tenants of the Claytons annexe have landed in my email inbox, and I will forward them to yours immediately".

"Thank you. And what are your plans this afternoon? Shouldn't we check with hospital to see if we can speak to Peter Hoare?"

"Indeed. Will you call the doctor please? He met you, we haven't met him yet".

Selway dialled the Doctor number, but it was off, so he left him a voice message asking if the guy was awake, and whether possible to question him that afternoon.

"I left him a message, because his mobile is switched off, maybe he is busy in an operation room or something".

"Ok. How about you come with us, and we can look together into the tenants' files. And then while at our hotel we try to contact the doctor again".

"Not a bad idea at all". He then looked at Dobinson and said, "You have a spare key of my house; can you please feed Max and then return to office to continue your CCTV inspections ". Dobinson nodded her head in accord and said, "Ok don't worry, I will do that".

"Thank you very much" Selway said and drew the first smile on his face that day.

Half an hour later they took their seats inside Al-Douri's hotel room. He immediately opened his laptop and forwarded the files to Selway. Once sent, he opened them as Hughes and Selway surrounded him behind the screen. The files were for five tenants. First file was about the oldest tenant, she was a painter, and she died the previous year. So, the trio agreed that the woman is no longer of interest. That conclusion reduced the number of the tenants to four. The second file was about a Polish man in his thirties, he works in construction. He rented the annexe for two years 2010 and 2011. He was married and has two daughters. According to the MI5 information, he relocated to different towns and cities in the following years, and he is now living in London. His record is clean of any wrongdoing. The third file included information on a nurse who used to work at the hospital nearby, she stayed in the annexe for three years 2012, 2013 and 2014. She then moved through the NHS system to other hospitals, and she currently lives in Exeter, and she works at a hospital there. As the annexe was very close to the hospital and it's most convenient for a nurse, the trio decided that this tenant also should be removed from the list of potential suspects.

The fourth file contained information about a man in his early forties. He is a musician called Alfred Smith, and he is gay. He lived in the annexe in 2015 and now he lives in Koln in Germany. Selway spoke for the first time and said "This one seems interesting; do we have full contact details?

"Yes. We do have a big deal of contact details, his address in Germany, his email address, and even his Skype ID"

"Good. Let us talk to him as soon as we finish checking the last tenant out".

The fifth and final file was about an old lady in her late seventies, she lived at the annexe in 2016. She is a widow. Her children live in the United States. She now lives in a care home. The trio agreed to remove this lady out of the loop.

"Have you got Skype on this laptop?" Selway asked

"Yes" Al-Douri answered.

"Ok, sign in then, and try to contact Alfred Smith".

Hardly a minute passed before Smith was added to Al-Douri's Skype list of contact. He didn't appear online though. He left him a message after an attempt of video call had failed.

"Send him a message by email as well. Maybe he is not using Skype often".

Al-Douri agreed and dropped him a line by email. Hughes asked "Can you now reattempt the Doctor number? We should talk to that lad in the hospital".

Selway dialled the doctor number, this time it rang but it still no answer. So, he left him a second voice message. Couple of minutes later, they heard a ring, this time it was on Skype. Alfred Smith was ringing them back. Al-Douri immediately answered the call and left his seat in front of the camera to Selway, as the interview was related to Radi's death.

"Hello Mr Smith. Thanks for calling back".

"Hi. How can I help you?"

"I want to ask you few questions related to the year you spent here at the Claytons annexe in Morobury".

"Ok. Fire them off".

"Have you had an affair with Mr Clayton?"

Alfred looked surprised of the straightforward question. He laughed a bit then said, "Yes and no".

"What does that mean?"

"I mean, we had some little fun from time to time, so I don't know if that would be called an affair or a relationship or any name".

"So, no love involved?"

"To be honest, it was one sided love".

"He was fond of you?"

"I don't think so. I fell for him, but I don't think it was mutual".

"I see. Are you a jealous person?"

"I could be sometime".

"Well. The last tenant who rented the place had died couple of weeks ago and we are suspecting a foul play".

"You are not implying that I had motivation to kill him because of a jealousy crisis. Are you?"

"Perhaps"

"No. Not me, I can't hurt a fly. Besides I haven't been to the United Kingdom for over a year now".

"Why should I believe you?"

"Because I am saying the truth; also, Mr Clayton is no longer an interest of mine". Alfred then waved to someone in his room, then another man appeared, he looked in his fifties. Alfred then explained "This is Guntram, my German husband. I am very faithful to him. Satisfied now?"

"This sounds convincing. However, we hope to talk to you again if necessary".

"No problem, you are such a handsome man, and you are welcome to call anytime". The two men laughed as Selway turned reddish as he said "Ok. Alright, thanks for the compliment. Have a nice evening. Thanks for your time. Bye for now".

After the call, the two officers were looking with a look full of surprise at the detective. He knew that they were surprised about his question regarding Mr Clayton. But no questions were asked as Selway's mobile rang in a persist manner and it was the Doctor from the hospital. He informed them that his patient is now awake, and he can talk.

Hardly half an hour later, they were rushing through the hospital door. However, the Doctor, who seemed to have been waiting them, showed up immediately as soon as they walked in. Selway said "We know where the room is".

"Only one person is allowed in, I am afraid" The Doctor replied as he blocked their way before they reached the room door. The three investigators looked at each other, and as the drug case was Al-Douri's, he was the one who finally entered the room to interview the lad.

"Hello Peter. I am here to ask you few questions regarding your situation".

The teenager nodded his head positively. And Al-Douri went on "The Doctor told us that you had a drug overdose that almost killed you. How do you get those drugs?"

The guy didn't speak. He only raised his right arm and rubbed his fingers on each other in a sign signifying "Money", meaning that he had been buying them.

"Who is the seller?"

"I don't know"

"You mean that you never met the seller".

"Never"

"And how you were making deals?"

"He asks me to leave money in some public places, and then he asks me to collect the drugs from specific places also".

"Was that the only method?"

"Sometimes he gave me drugs by hand from behind and I wasn't allowed to turn around".

"Can you explain that better please?"

"Sometimes, I used to go to the Catholic Church and attend a lecture given regularly by a preacher. There we were asked to keep one hand behind our back while sitting in the lecture, and warned to never look behind, and the seller passes by and hands us the bags".

"How often did that happen?".

"It used to happen on a regular basis, once a week or so at the beginning. But as I am wealthy, I was able to buy large quantities".

"And when did you buy the last package?"

"A month ago, or so, I bought something that could last for half a year. You know"

"The doctor said that no one of your parents showed up yet and you are here for more than 24 hours now. Can you explain that?"

A pale smile covered the boy's face as he said "I am a black-eyed kid. My mother and father are separated, they both live abroad running their businesses, and they left me here with my old frail grandfather".

"And he won't be worried about your where about?"

"He is handicapped. He is confined to a chair. He has servants at his large house. And this is not the first time I sleep outside without prior notice"

The lad started coughing heavily, and he looked in distress suddenly, so Al-Douri rushed outside and brought the Doctor in, who then gave him a signal meaning that was enough of questioning for the day.

Chapter 25

The trio left the hospital and walked straight to Selway's house located hardly 100 yards from the hospital gates. Hughes had also parked the car there, but as soon as Al-Douri shared with his two colleagues the information he had from the teenager, Selway's antenna captured immediately the link to the Catholic Church once more. Selway insisted to invite them in because he wanted some action to be taken immediately to get hold of that Catholic priest as soon as he returned from Rome. He opened immediately the suggestion "We heard earlier from Brenda that she was asked sometimes to attend the church during the lectures of this specific priest called Father O'Shea in order to deliver the drug packs to the clients. And now Peter confirmed that this time as a client who was buying the stuff. I also saw that same priest thanking heavens and looked a bit happy the morning Mustapha Radi's body was discovered".

"When did you see him looking happy?"

"At the time when Radi's body was discovered, I was running into the footpath like everybody else to see what was going on, and he was standing there and about to do a U turn when I saw him relived thanking heavens and almost smiling. So, if he is also involved in the drug trafficking, that means he could be directly or indirectly having a role in all of this".

"Interesting. He could be a homophobic zealot"

"And more interestingly, the head of the church told me that the lecture of this priest got popular because he added some politics and international affairs into it, and he seemed to be a big fan of the Russian President Vladimir Putin and his war on the Syrian people".

"Hmm. That's taking us to a completely new level".

"Therefore, I believe you should get to this priest as soon as he lands back on the British soil. We should speak to him even if he is not directly involved, he would certainly hold some important useful information if not about Radi's death, then at least about the people who attend his lectures".

"Ok, I will contact the related authorities as soon as I get back to the hotel. Anything else you want me to do for you in the coming 24 hours and remember tomorrow we should get the DNA result from London. So, we have to be well organised in order to deal with all these information flooding at us almost every hour".

Selway massaged his balanced moustache as he was trying to remember *what he might still need from higher authorities regarding the case*. He then said "Yes. I do need from you two very important requests".

"Ok. Go on"

"First I need to get access to the Facebook and Skype profiles of Mustapha Radi, and I believe this is a very important matter not only for my case related to his death, but also to your case if you really still believe he might be involved in a way or another with the cyber blackmailing and drugs activities".

"Very important point indeed; and I have to tell you that we have already requested that from the high office who will get things arranged with the two internet firms. So, what's the second request?"

"I need you to get some information related to an attempt made by the Ministry of Education to relocate Mr Radi from this school to a Newcastle one, for that strange request happened couple of weeks before his death".

"We will do what we can. Now we have to leave you to arrange your dinner as you are receiving Mr Clayton. And I will be in touch tomorrow as soon as we get the DNA result".

"Thank you in advance for everything".

They said goodbyes with smiles as the three were feeling excited, for the two investigations seemed to have picked some speed in the previous forty-eight hours.

Meanwhile at the office, Dobinson was having a celebration of her own. She was replaying few seconds of one of the CCTV footages again and again. She said to herself "It's definitely the shadow of a person walking".

She managed to spot the shadow of a human walking from Bimport main passage into the footpath. Although nothing of the person appeared on the camera but the streetlamp reflected a walking shadow on the ground, and it was impossible to tell if that shadow belongs to a man or to a woman.

Dobinson took a note of the exact timing of this appearance on the video file, and there she found also important information, that this person went into the footpath nearly half an hour before Mustapha Radi run in.

That finding pushed her into looking with more focus into the videos she had, as she felt she could find something as interesting or even more. And maybe since she started that task, it was the first time she felt enthusiastic about it.

At 7 pm, Selway welcomed in his house Mr John Clayton. They immediately walked to the dinner table as the detective said, "We better have our dinner first before the food goes cold".

"Ok and this way I would eat in peace while you keep your questions for after dinner".

"Yes, don't worry. I won't dare harming your appetite".

As they finished, Clayton admitted that his old neighbour was a very good cook because he appreciated the tasty meal. However, the host fired at him a suggestion that he never expected, "So how about replacing your wife by a handsome man?" Selway asked.

Clayton who was getting off the table almost trapped himself by the leg of his chair when he heard those explosive words.

"Calm down. I know everything, no deed to hide. Let us wash our hands and get back to sit and talk it over" Selway added trying to calm his guest down.

Couple of minutes later they faced each other in the living room. Selway asked his neighbour to be frank and to tell him everything related to his relationship with Mr Radi.

The Physicist took a deep breath and said "I have discovered in the last ten years or so that I am getting more and more attracted to men. Maybe because my wife became less active sexually, I don't know, but it is what it is. And after I have tried some fun with men, I found it very fulfilling and good for my wellbeing. It took off my stresses and in it I found some good and enjoyable escape from my work".

"I understand that. No need to explain to me why you are attracted to men, you are mature enough to decide what to do in your private life. However, if you feel you want to take things off your chest please do, but I am mostly interested in your relationship with your late tenant".

"I want to be totally frank with you. I have encountered Mustapha first time in a gay chat room couple of years ago. As we were both very attracted to each other, he came couple of times to a hotel nearby and as we enjoyed our time together, we wanted to meet more often. I suggested that he applies for the post of Sport teacher as the school here and relocate here if successful".

"So, it wasn't a coincidence then"

"No, I am afraid, we arranged it".

"Interesting! Go on"

"He applied and got the job. And of course, immediately I proposed him the annexe which had been free before his arrival, so my wife didn't notice anything unusual because I advertised the annexe with the estate agency".

"Very smart, yes"

"And I spent the best year of my life with him here next door. And everything was going perfectly good for us until hell broke loose when my wife walked in the annexe and saw us together naked in bed. So, you know there were not several explanations for what she saw. And she went mad since. She insisted that he must leave immediately and of course she warned me against meeting him again".

"But how did your wife walk in? Did you keep the door open? And how did she enter a place without knocking on the door?"

"I don't know, she didn't give me any chance to ask her those questions. All my attempts to talk to her since have failed. But I am sure the door was locked".

"Maybe she used the original copy of the key, the one you hold as landlords".

"No. that wasn't possible because I am very careful with that and since Mustapha rented the place, I kept that key with me all the time".

"That means the door wasn't locked. You know Mustapha could have forgotten to lock it".

A serious look appeared on the face of Mr Clayton "Let us say what you are saying that the door wasn't locked, but definitely it wasn't open, so how my wife would come in like that without knocking or ringing the bell".

"Sensible question; I think we have to find the answer from her, so I should visit you tomorrow morning".

"I hope she will be able to explain and ease my fears".

"Your fears of what?"

"I had some dark thoughts that Mustapha might have deliberately kept the door open for her to see us, maybe he wanted us to get divorced so he can get me exclusively for himself".

"Possible even if it doesn't sound logical to me. Have you talked to him about it?"

"Yes. At first when my wife came in, I was shocked and of course my first reaction was to jump out of bed, put my clothes on and went home to try to calm her down. But later when those thoughts came to my mind, I confronted Mustapha with what I am thinking. He denied it and he was very upset because I doubted him".

Clayton had tears in his eyes as he added "That was the night previous to his death. So, it's very hurtful for me that our story ended with such a clash, and if the truth turned out to be that he didn't plan anything related to my wife, I will feel sorry - about doubting him - until the day I am gone".

"That's why you were apologising to him at the morgue".

"Yes"

"And you were wearing beige trousers when you had the argument with him that night"

"Yes. How do you know that?"

"Because Mustapha was chatting to someone, and his camera was on when you had the argument".

"Who?"

"I will tell you when we finish the investigation. But look me in the eye right now and tell me frankly have you felt mad because of that thought and you decided to get revenge?"

"You mean I killed him".

"Yes"

"No. Whatever the state of rage I am in, I am a mature man and I love Mustapha. Even if he did that for real, I would always count it as an act of jealousy. But yes, I was angry when I confronted him, and I should have been kinder in discussing my doubts with him".

"I looked carefully into the profiles of your previous tenants. One of them was gay, so you had same type of relationship with him?"

"No one was like Mustapha. Yes, I had couple of fun encounters with the musician, and he was very fond of me, but I didn't find him really my type, so I wouldn't call it a relationship".

"What if Alfred Smith might have felt jealous and he could have somehow discovered your relationship with Mustapha. Do you think he could have killed him?"

"Alfred! No. He is a very sensitive light-hearted guy. I wouldn't believe my eyes if I saw him doing such thing. So, if you are asking me my opinion about his personality, my answer is a definite no".

"Alright I trust you. Tell me now what time is best to get your wife to talk to me in the morning. At what time she wakes up?"

"Best time is around 10 am, and I will inform her that you will be visiting".

Chapter 26

It was the first time Selway got a deep sound sleep since the investigation started, as he felt that things begun to move towards unravelling what really happened at dawn during that dark stormy day. He woke up unusually late, it was quarter after nine, and it was Max who woke him up after he waited in vain for his breakfast to be served in time. The detective fed the dog, took a long warm shower. He was thinking of the busy day ahead, especially the result of the DNA test of the blood found on the sleeve of Mr Radi. He was also thinking of what information he could get from Mrs Clayton in the coming hour or so.

At 10 am he knocked on the door of the Claytons. Few seconds later Maria the maid opened the door for him and said, "Mrs Clayton is expecting you and she will join you soon, please follow me". It was sunny but very cold morning. The detective followed the maid who guided him to a glassy room in the garden, where one could enjoy the sun rays and at the same time keep the chilly wind away. She asked him what he likes to drink, and he replied, "Any fresh fruit juice would do".

"How about Carrot Juice?".

"Prefect. Thank you".

After a minute he was welcomed by Mrs Clayton who drew an artificial smile on her face and shook his hand while taking her seat in front of him. "Beautiful garden; and a nice way to enjoy the sun" he said as he smiled back at her.

"It seems you have forgotten that I am an Architect. So yes, everything in my space should be as good as there is".

"All my respect"

"John told me that he told you what happened. You know, with that tenant I mean". Clayton pushed the words out of her mouth in disgust mixed with anger.

"Yes"

"So how do you feel about it if you were in my place?"

"We will talk about that later. Let me know first how you ended up inside the annexe that day? You are not going to tell me that you heard a noise, and the door was open. Are you?"

Blood resurfaced on the woman face, as if she was being reminded of something she doesn't want to remember. Again, she fired her words in an outrage stroke "I will be frank with you. Someone sent me a message on my mobile phone and told me that my husband is in bed with that guy at that very moment. Of Course, I was in total disbelief, but then I checked John whereabouts, he wasn't in his room or on his desk, so I walked out to the annexe, and as you might have noticed the annexe door has a handle, so I moved it, and the door was open. I walked in and I could hear their voices in the bedroom, I walked into the corridor and to my shock they were there in bed together".

"So, the door wasn't locked"

"No"

"Hmm" The detective squeezed his mind as his finger teased his bottom lip. Then he asked, "Have you kept that message you received?"

"Yes. Because I am considering divorce"

Maria interrupted them with two cups of carrot juices, then left.

"Is there a number on that message or was it sent online?"

"No, it wasn't through social media, it was from a mobile number to mine"

"Have you got the number?"

"Yes. It is on the message, but I have tried many times to ring them back, but it's always shut".

"Can I see that message on your mobile if you don't mind".

"Ok. I will be right back".

As his mobile was silent for the interview, he felt it vibrating in his pocket, he pulled it out and found a message from his secretary informing him that she found at least one important detail in the CCTV footage that is worthy of exploring.

He replied that he will join her at the office sometime before sunset and told her that he had still a couple of questioning sessions and reminded her that The DNA blood result could show up at any time.

As he clicked send, he saw the shadow of his hostess regaining her seat. He smiled at her as she handed him her mobile open on the message, she received about her husband affair.

"Thank you" he said.

The message read "Could you ever imagine the great scientist in bed with a young lad from the middle east? If you can't imagine that you should walk into that annexe and see for yourself. Eyes do not deceive, if heart does!"

"Sorry that you have received such a provocative message. Do you allow me to forward it to my mobile with the number of the sender?"

Mrs Clayton sucked deeply her e-cigarette then opened her both hands without answering by words, Selway understood what she meant, *do as you please*.

He forwarded the message to himself, and as he finished, he received a message from Al-Douri. He checked it quickly and it read "We will receive the DNA results after two hours. However, I have received some info related to the request made by the ministry of education regarding moving Radi from Dorset to Newcastle, and my informer confirmed to me it was a private request made by women who know well each other, you know what I mean".

"Ok got it" Selway replied.

Then he looked back to his hostess. And he asked her "I have a question related to the aftermath of your discovery"

She waved her hand for him to ask.

"Have you tried to make some high-profile contact in order to remove Mr Radi from his job here at the school?"

Clayton threw a scary look at him and said "No".

"How many people know about this affair other than you two and of course your late tenant?"

"I don't know"

"What do you mean by you don't know?"

"I mean, I don't know with whom they could have talked about it"

"You mean you haven't told anyone about it yourself?"

"No"

"Not even your son?"

The woman suddenly stood up and said "You have no feelings, you know. I have accepted your interview request, and you have been asking me all the time about this affair. Have you got no heart?"

She didn't allow him to reply; she checked her watch and said, "I am afraid I have to end this conversation here, as I have got other engagements that I should keep up with in time".

The detective thanked her for her time and left.

Soon after he returned home, Dobinson joined him for lunch, and of course she was eager to tell him what she had discovered on the CCTV footage. But when she was in the middle of explaining to him the shadow she saw on the ground at the main passage to the footpath, the doorbell rang. Max barked once. His owner complained about this sudden visit, and wondered who that might be, he rushed towards the door and opened it. Al-Douri and Hughes walked in. Al-Douri handed him immediately a printed paper and said "The DNA Result, I have already forwarded a copy to your email, but I brought you this paper with me because I know you will be too excited to see the results and I wanted to spare you the hassle of signing in in order to see it. Selway hungry eyes went through the lines like a whistle. And then he looked back at his two guests and said "So it's not Radi's blood"

"No" replied Hughes.

"Does that mean we are now officially dealing with a murder?"

"It's now a big possibility, but we still can't confirm that".

"Confirm what?"

"That someone had deliberately killed Mr Radi".

"By accident or deliberately, he didn't fall alone, or else from where this blood had come to his sleeve?"

"Maybe from the person who for some reason picked up the knife?"

"I don't know, but you might become sure that someone caused the death, if you hear from Ms Dobinson what she saw on the CCTV footage".

"What did she find?"

Dobinson who was listening to them talking, joined the conversation for the first time and said "There is definitely someone who walked from Bimport into the footpath at approximately twenty or thirty minutes before Radi went through. And no one can tell me that someone before dawn - at a hell of a weather - was going there by coincidence at that specific time".

Al-Douri said "Well. You have caught something important in investigating your case then. I am happy that we are making swift progress in our case too".

Hughes then pointed out to a small paragraph printed at the bottom of the DNA blood result "Have you read this?"

Selway looked back and said, "No. let me see". "Oh, they are saying that the DNA doesn't match any DNA they have in the database for criminals in the country" he added.

Al-Douri suggested "But of course you will soon reduce the list of your high suspects, because we will take samples of their DNA and see if one of them matches that".

"Well, the two main suspects for me are both abroad at the moment and that annoys me so much".

"Who are these two?"

"Father O'Shea and Barry Clayton; the first seems to be linked to both cases: the crime and the drug trafficking. And the second was seen shouting in anger about something unknown to us for sure but I guess his anger was related to the affair of his father, because when I interviewed his mother today, she was afraid to say that she has told him about it".

"Can't we get their DNA samples from their clothes or something?" asked Dobinson.

"We better wait their return because if we are to tell the Claytons and the Church that Barry and Father O'Shea are main suspects, they might warn them, and they may not return" Al-Douri replied.

"Any way, we know that the priest will return this weekend. Regarding Barry if we can issue an arrest warrant via the Interpol and the Europol to get him wherever he might be at the moment" said Selway.

Hughes explained "An arrest warrant can't be issued at the moment, because we don't have anything against Barry other than that he was angry about his father's affair with Radi. We need more proofs to be able to release an arrest warrant".

Al-Douri and Hughes stood up and were about to leave the house. Al-Douri said "Anyway let me know how things develop with you. We have to leave you now because I have some interviews scheduled related to my case. The drug trafficking activities proved to be so vast".

The two men left. After walking with them to the door, Selway sat down, said nothing and went on massaging his moustache thinking deeply about his next move. He even forgot totally that his secretary was still there until she spoke and said "I should leave you too. Do you want anything particular from me?"

"Yes. You found a person moving to the footpath via the main passage before Radi. Now you should focus on the footage time after the death. We may get something about when the probable killer did leave the footpath".

Dobinson opened the door but before she left, Selway said "Please take Max for a walk or I tell you what. I will do that myself. Have a nice rest of the day"

Half an hour later, Selway was about to go out with Max when Al-Douri called him and told him to check his email because he sent him the list of friends Radi had had on Skype and on Facebook, so he could check them out.

Chapter 27

As soon as he received Al-Douri's message, Selway jumped upstairs, turned on his laptop and signed into his email address. He was eager to have a look at the circle of social media friends that Mr Radi had. It was a very cold afternoon, and even though the heating was on all day long, Max found refuge under his master chair. And as the detective was over excited to open the content of his email account, he accidentally pressed his right foot on Max's who barked, out of his pain, a low bark which sounded like a question mark.
Selway said "I am so sorry, but I haven't noticed your presence somehow". The detective went through the names of Radi's Facebook friends and their respective online profiles. There were people of all ages, some foreign some local. From the activity report he didn't seem to have a very active profile on that social media website. He then went through the Skype list, and there were a larger number of profiles, and as he had expected, the majority were of men over fifty years old. Selway for a start focused on the names that might be resident in Dorset, he said to himself "How about a jealous lover who has

discovered the relationship between Radi and Clayton, but it takes a mature man to be disturbed mentally in order to commit murder for the sake of a relationship". He then said, "I don't know". He printed the list of names with small photos shown next to them, and decided to show them to Ms Watt as she might recognise some of them if they were close in real life to her adopted son, and they were not merely internet connections. He checked his watch, it was around 6 pm and it was almost the sunset. He rang Ms Dobinson "Are you still at the office?"

"Yes, about to return to the hotel, it would be warmer for me in bed there to check the remaining parts of the cameras footage".

"Can you wait for another fifteen minutes? I want you to show me that shadow you saw on the footage".

"Ok, see you then".

Selway joined her couple of minutes later, and there he sat as she played the video at the precise moment the shadow appeared reflected from the streetlight. After repeating it several times, Selway said "You have done great job by spotting this. The timing says it all really. A crazy weather, someone going through the passage minutes before Radi, he or she definitely wasn't there for exercise too. Actually, Radi was crazy to walk out that dawn, but we know that he did that on regular basis. He did exercise at that time whenever he got the opportunity".

"And of course, the killer, if there is one, knew that too"

"Definitely; it must be someone very close to him, someone who knows that he usually exercises at dawn or someone Radi personally had informed the day before that he will go out regardless of how strong the storm will be".

"Who were the closest people to him?"

"Well, the sisters Watts and Clayton the father. These three were the closest to him".

"I don't think his adoptive mother, or her sister have any motivation to get rid of him. That leaves us with Mr Clayton, but you seem to know him very well. Is he really a trustworthy good man?"

"I don't think John Clayton could do such thing, but who knows?"

"What if it was him but not deliberately?"

"What do you mean?"

"I mean maybe he tried to surprise him, and by mistake the young fell down by accident. And we both heard Mr Clayton at the morgue apologising to Radi and saying he didn't mean it".

Selway eyes went wide open "Very plausible scenario as strange as it may seem. However, when I questioned him the second time, he said that what he meant by his words was an apology regarding an argument they had during the night previous to Radi's death. But again, who knows if he told me the truth or not?"

The two looked at each other for few seconds, then Selway added "But if this is really what had happened, and as an accident, that means this would be a very painful tragedy, and it would be so painful for Clayton to recover emotionally from it, and as far as I can read face expressions, I don't feel there are signs of guilt on his face, unless he knows very well how to control his emotions".

Suddenly Selway's mobile rang, it was Al-Douri who said that he got more and more witnesses saying that they received drugs at the Catholic Church during the lectures of Father O'Shea, and that he received permission from top officials to raid the church and search the priest belongings even in his absence. Selway asked his secretary to keep exploring the CCTV footages, he then joined Al-Douri and the police team for the raid.

It was 8 pm when the police unit stormed into the church. Selway and Al-Douri apologised to the head of the church because of the raid, but they showed him the official order to carry it out without prior notice. The priest belongings and space were scanned inch by inch by dogs, drug and metal detecting machines. No drugs were found but suddenly a police officer went out with a Swiss small knife.

Selway, Al-Douri and Hughes were stunned once they saw the knife in the palm of the officer hand. It was exactly how Anne Watt and Ms Kavanagh (the woman who discovered Radi's body) described it to them. And with the initials M.R inscribed on it. It was beyond any doubt the knife of Mustapha Radi. So, there was only one explanation: the priest was the person who picked it up from the scene, so was he also the killer? Of course, that was the question which occurred instantly in their minds. And Al-Douri remembered that Chief Inspector Owen told him that at their arrival Father O'Shea was saying a prayer near the body, so he must have done that deliberately to kneel with his monk robe and pick the knife without being noticed by the people who gathered there that morning. Once the search was over, Selway asked the head of the church about the exact date of the priest return.

"This coming Sunday, he arrives to Heathrow around noon, and he should arrive here couple of hours before sunset or so" Father Sheridan replied.

Al-Douri made it clear to Father Sheridan to never mention anything related to the raid to Father O'Shea if he got in touch. And then the group of policemen left while Selway and his two colleagues stood outside in the street. Selway insisted that they should come to his house to rearrange their conclusions and plan their next move.

Meanwhile Ms Dobinson was on the verge of another exciting discovery in a different CCTV footage. As she focused on the time interval exactly after the supposed time of the death, one of the cameras in the lower part of the footpath, had caught a very tiny corner of what it looked like a dark coloured car.

She called her boss, and the latter told her to join them in his house immediately. Couple of minutes later, the four of them gathered in front of Dobinson's laptop screen as she played the footage on the right spot, then she started explaining what she was seeing "At first I noticed that the light became stronger than just the road lamp light, and when I focused too much, I clearly saw a few inches of the front corner of a car with its light on. The car stayed there for nearly twenty minutes, and then suddenly it vanished, because the light of the road returned to normal, and the corner of the car disappeared".

"Unfortunately, the car didn't pass in front of the camera; that would have given us a big clue" Hughes commented

"Yes, but that leaves us with two possibilities: First the car went in reverse and left the place without getting caught by the camera, the Second the corner of the car was not one of the fronts but rather the back" Selway concluded.

"Whatever the position that car was in, it was clear that it was related to the accident or the crime. Because the time it was there was as if the killer came in by it, committed his(her) crime and then left, or also it could have been someone was waiting him or her to drive him (her) away from the scene as fast as possible" Al-Douri said

Selway raised his thumb up for him approving what he heard. He then said "And after Radi's knife was found in the priest belongings, there is no more doubt that Radi's death and the cyber blackmailing, and drug trafficking are all connected. The priest is certainly involved in all of this".

Hughes protested "You are not telling me that the priest has been blackmailing those pupils. Are you?"

"Well not necessarily him, maybe he is just a member of a group" Selway answered.

"But something is still strange in this knife story. Why if the priest is the killer would he return to pick up that knife which actually belongs to the dead man?"Al-Douri wondered.

"Of course, there are still many questions and things to observe regarding the priest involvement into all this, but we can't deny that he is directly involved. You've just told me that all your interviewees today claimed that they picked drugs from the church during the lectures of this specific priest. And Radi's knife was in his possession too, so he definitely knew too much about what's going on even if he is not fully involved in it".

"So, what do you think? Should we give it a go and get his DNA to see if it matches the one from the blood found on Radi's sleeve?"

"Absolutely" replied Selway

But then Hughes surprised the three of them by pulling from inside his jacket an old-fashioned underwear. Al-Douri was first to comment "Don't tell me you picked it from Father O'Shea's room. Did you?"

"Yes, I thought ahead and smuggled it out when I got the chance to".

Selway took it from Hughes, and then he approached it in a disgusted way to his nose and said, "I am not sure if it's going to be any help, because it smells washing powder, so it's not recently used".

"Then forget about it then. But how sure you are that the head of the church won't warn his colleague about our raid?" Dobinson asked.

"Don't worry about that. We are not police, we are intelligence operators, and now every electronic or communication device in the Church is under surveillance. Also, our team in London is listening to every word spoken at the church from now on" Hughes boasted.

"Not enough. They can still ring him from any outside telephone and that includes and telephone cabin in the street" Selway protested.

"Don't worry; the few telephone cabins in Morobury, Millingham and the surrounding villages are all under surveillance 24 hours a day".

"Ok. No complaint about that. We only have 48 hours before his scheduled return. Will you get him at the airport? Or will you leave him to return here?"

"That's why we are here now; we need to discuss our next move very carefully. Will it be wise to get him as soon as his plane lands and then confront him with the knife and question him regarding the two cases; or would it be wiser to leave him unsuspected and watch him after his return and see with whom he might communicate".

"I wonder how he would be able to find an explanation about the knife. I think this will be enough to force him to say all what he knows".

"In my opinion the second option is better as long as he would be always under our control, if he gets us to others who are also involved in crimes then that would be great, if he led us to nothing then we can still arrest him at any time, confront him with the knife and question him until he gives all the answers we need"

"I will take more time to think about a final decision. We still have two days and God only knows what could happen during the coming 48 hours".

"You are right we still have time, but can't you see with me that if the priest is really involved directly in all of this, he is definitely having one assistant or more. I don't know if he drives a dark car, but if he doesn't and we want to take what we saw on the CCTV footage in account, that mean he has one accomplice or more".

"You are aright; maybe it's wiser to let him loose as he may lead us to the network he works with. Because he might get protective towards his accomplices and refuses to answer our questions properly".

"Also don't forget to review what the law enforcement rules are regarding arresting a religious figure"

"Ok. I believe I have plenty of things to arrange, so we better leave you now, and I will inform you once we make a decision about the priest"

"Alright; I look forward to that"

Al-Douri and Hughes stood up, then the first remembered something, he said "I almost forgot to ask you, have you found anything useful in the internet friends list of Mr Radi?"

"I have checked them quickly earlier today, plenty of names, so it's hard to say really who were the closest to him or if he ever met them in real life. But I think Anne Watt will be of help in this tomorrow. I will invite her for breakfast, and I will let her go through the names to see if she recognises anyone".

Chapter 28

The following morning the detective hosted Ms Watt for breakfast. As they went through their coffees, Selway asked her if she heard any news about her sister.

"She only contacted me one since. She seems enjoying her time" Anne replied. She asked him about the latest news of the investigation. He didn't give her many details; however, he told her there was some significant advance and he mentioned of course that the DNA test of the blood found on her son's sleeve doesn't match his DNA, which means the case is leaning more and more towards a homicide. After they finished their breakfast, Selway opened his electronic tablet which was handier than the laptop. He moved his chair next to Watt's. He opened the file that contained the list of profiles that had connection with Mustapha. And they started checking them one by one. Watt went on and repeated "No, No, no" for some dozens of profiles, so the detective almost gave up on finding something special out of those internet profiles, and he started opening them in a faster rhythm. Then suddenly Watt held his hand and asked, "Can you please get the last couple of profiles back". He then went slowly backwards. Then she said "It's him. What is he doing in Mustapha's friends list?!"

"Who is he?"

"Andrew Johnson, my sister's boyfriend"

"The one with her in London now?".

"Yes"

"And what's strange in the story? Maybe they met each other because of your sister"

"No, I don't think so, because she never mentions her affairs in front of Mustapha"

"You mean they never knew or met each other"

"Not of my knowledge. No!"

"Maybe Ruth spoke about Mustapha to her lover, and knowing his full name he added him to his Skype"

"Possible but for what reason?".

"I don't know. However, it's important that you confirmed his presence. Now at least I know what Ruth's boyfriend looks like".

"I will try to talk to her later today and I will ask her if they ever talked about Mustapha".

"If you want to listen to my advice, you better not telling her anything"

"Why?"

"Because they definitely have talked about him during their conversations, the man would have definitely asked her about her family, and she of course had mentioned you and Mustapha to him"

"You are right. But I felt surprised because Mustapha never mentioned the man in front of me, and he had the habit of telling me about every new in his life ".

"Do you know what this man drives as a car?"

"Yes. Why are you asking such a question?"

"Nothing really, I am just checking how much do you know about him".

The detective didn't want to alarm her, so he changed the subject and managed to keep going with the profiles, but none of them were of Radi's direct circle apart from Mr Clayton, the school head and teachers, and some university friends. These the ones Ms Watt was sure that her son had met them in real life.

Selway had plenty of questions to ask about Mr Johnson but as he didn't want to turn Ms Watt suspicions, he decided to ask the direct questions he had in mind about the man in the next occasion. The woman checked her watch and said, "It's almost ten thirty, and I have a delivery expected at the hotel between eleven and noon, so I must leave you know, for the delivery requires my personal signature".

"Ok my lady. Thanks for your time and your help so far. I wish you a very good rest of the day".

After Ms Watt left to the hotel, Selway sat down looking at Max who stared back at him barking in a low friendly voice. The detective eyes were set at the dog, but his mind was thinking and rethinking all what he had heard and seen since this investigation started. Suddenly a call on his mobile disturbed his thoughts. He looked at the number, it was Al_Douri. He clicked the green button quickly and immediately the voice of the intelligent young man came through

"Hi. Heard any good news from Ms Watt?"

"Well yes and no. I mean there is someone who is raising my suspicions to some extent; however, I need another chat with Ms Watt before allowing myself to ask for your help in getting every single possible detail about him and his history".

"Ok. As you wish"

"Tell me what you have found on the Church Hall camera. You definitely have some thrilling information. Don't you?"

"Unfortunately, nothing! It seems they are still moving ahead of us, or at least they are committing their crimes with a very high level of professionalism".

"Why? What gave you such impression?"

"The electronic system in the Church has been definitely hacked. When we got the recorded files out of the hall camera, the majority of them were broken and unplayable, so we couldn't get any of the lectures on record. We are definitely dealing with well-trained criminals, and I have more doubts now that it's not one or even two individuals, they could be a gang".

"What a shame. And have you made up your mind about the arrival of Father O'Shea?"

"I hoped to get something out of the church camera, but since we are still in a total blur. I think it would be wiser if we allow the man to return in a normal fashion to his duties, and then we watch his movements and hopefully he could lead us to his collaborators or to the perpetrators if he is being used without knowing for what purpose".

"Since yesterday that was also my opinion. However, you have to be very clear and sharp with the other church members that they should never mention the police raid to the priest".

"Don't worry, I have already sent Hughes there. He will gather them all and make it clear to them that if any of them informed the priest or warned him, they will face the law in obstructing the way of justice. Also, he will give them a frightening indirect impression that we have planted hidden cameras and microphone in all the rooms of the church, so they have to take that in account".

"Ok good then. Let us wait and hope the fish moves into the net".

"Tell me what are you going to do with the DNA samples? I mean how we will get DNA samples of the priest and the Claytons senior and junior. These are the three we agreed last time that they could be directly involved in Radi's case. If the blood found on the victim doesn't belong to them, we can then take them off the list, and if it belongs to one of them that means we are done with your case".

"You are right. Regarding the priest, I don't think we can get it before we see where he will lead us in the investigation because we can't ask for his saliva or blood sample without raising his suspicions. Regarding the Claytons, I believe I can easily get a sample from the father, first because he is a friend of mine, and because he can't refuse, for any refusal will make him first suspect. Regarding his son Barry, we can use the DNA of the father, and if it matches a fatherhood test with the blood on Radi's sleeve, that will give us immediately the conclusion that his son was the killer or at least the suspect number one".

"Very smart thinking, you got me on this. Ok go ahead with demanding a DNA sample from Mr Clayton and let us see where it will take us".

"Ok deal".

As soon as he ended the call with Al-Douri, the detective dialled the number of Mr Clayton. But he got no answer, so he left him a message asking to call him back urgently. He then stared again at Max thinking of what he has just heard from the intelligence officer. To get the camera of the church hacked, that means a very well organised crime is at work. How much is it in connection with Radi's supposed murder? He wondered to himself. But if the perpetrators are that sophisticated in technology; that means they could have planted their own secret cameras, microphones or other devices in any area of interest for them.

And while he is thinking of that he slapped his front head forcefully by the palm of his left hand. And shouted "Oh my. How stupid I have been to forget such an important thing".

He then redialled Al-Douri number; the latter answered almost immediately.

"Oh! I need your help urgently"

"What about?"

"I have a mobile number we should know whom it belongs to".

"Have you tried to call it?"

"Nope, not really, because I am sure it was used for specific reason and then turned off".

"Well, what is it?"

"I will send it to you in a message now".

He ended the call then sent the number given to him by Mrs Clayton. After that he wondered why not giving a try. He dialled the number, but the line was shut as expected. However, he felt excited about getting to know where that number was sold. He felt hungry, but it was no surprise as the afternoon had already started. So he went to the kitchen, fed the dog. He then checked if his secretary needs him to order anything for her. She told him that she had already cooked some Ravioli at the office kitchen, and she expected to finish the footages checking before the end of the day. He decided on making some stir-fry as he had some Turkey meat. While cooking them, Mr Clayton returned his call. So, he invited him in immediately. He prepared the table with two dishes, few minutes later the doorbell rang announcing the arrival of the old neighbour.

Mr Clayton apologised "I am afraid I can't join you today, because I only woke up hardly two hours ago, and I had already my breakfast, so I can't consume any food before 4 o'clock or so".

"What a Shame. These stir-fry smells great and taste great too" Selway said as he chewed the content of one fork.

"I will not disturb you. So, I won't ask why you called me until you finish. I will turn the TV on if you don't mind"

Selway's mouth was full of food, so he waved his hand and nodded to his guest to do whatever he wanted.

Ten minutes later he joined him in the sitting room, and in his hands, he carried a tiny plastic tube. He approached his surprised guest who wondered "What is this?"

"I need a sample of your saliva if you don't mind".

"What for? A DNA tests!"

"Yes"

"Why?"

"I am sorry, but it's required for the investigation"

"I believe you should have an official order to get me giving you what you want"

"I know, but I want you to cooperate with me and so we can win time. Official papers will take time to issue, and I believe it's best for both of us to do it as friends, and at our own pace".

"Just explain to me why you want it, and I will make up my mind to cooperate or not".

"Because there was blood found on the sleeve of Mr Radi, and after testing it in the lab in London we are sure now that the blood doesn't belong to Radi".

"So, you are thinking now of it, as a murder. And you are trying to see if that blood matches mine".

"Exactly"

The scientist took the tube from the detective, spat inside it, closed it and returned it to him.

Chapter 29

The MI5 men and women were spread all over Heathrow airport, and the message was clear to watch the Catholic Priest like his shadow. Even couple of them have followed him all the way from Rome and they were sitting right behind him on the British Airways plane. So, the man wasn't able to breathe without being noticed. The plane landed peacefully, and the priest, as he was member of a religious congregation, was able to pass the airport checkpoint through the VIP gate. Couple of minutes later he received his luggage and walked outside the airport to the Coach stop. He seemed to have planned his trip all the way back to Morobury.

After waiting nearly half an hour, the coach from Heathrow to Morobury departed the airport and two intelligence officers managed to get on board. The Priest opened his mobile phone for the first time since his return to the British soil. He then dialled a number, and after few seconds they heard him informing someone of his arrival and that's he will be at the church after four hours. The plane arrived around noon, so the man had an early morning journey from his guestroom in the Vatican to the airport. And hardly after twenty minutes on board of the coach he fell asleep, as there were another four hours before arriving to his final destination.

One of the agents called Al-Douri who had his team waiting at several corners around the Catholic church. And he told him that the fish was on its way and that he made a call informing someone of his arrival time. "Yes, don't worry, we heard the call. He was talking to the head of the church. So don't worry. Keep an eye on him until he arrives here" Al-Douri replied.

"He is in a deep sleep".

"Ok but don't do the same".

At that time, the knife has been returned to its place in O'Shea's room, also the underwear was returned after it was refused by the lab as unhelpful. So, everything was in the same state the priest had left it in before his Rome trip. Even the police had sent one of their officers under cover as a new member of the clergy supposedly sent for training purpose for a month. His mission was to keep an eye at the movement inside the church and assure that no member of the church would ever warn the priest about the investigation.

Everything was perfectly set in place when the coach unloaded the priest and his luggage at the parking in front of the town hall. The church was not far, so the old man picked up his bag and walked to the church.

It was a normal return as he received greetings from the other members of the church. Father O'Shea withdrew later to take a shower and get some rest before dinner.

At dinner table he was introduced to the supposed clergy trainee - the undercover police officer- Brother Kevin O'Hara. He didn't suspect anything. However, he was busy answering other brothers and sisters whenever they asked him about his trip. And that's why the tea after dinner took a longer time than usual, as everybody was interested to hear the priest talking about Rome, and he also happily showed them some photos and videos on his laptop.

Everything looked very normal, and it was nearly 11 pm when all members withdrew to their rooms, however the agent had deliberately stayed late and as his room was the usually guest room next to the priest's, he tried to re-open a discussion with him. As the two of them walked towards their rooms, the young man said "I love the photos you took inside the pope wing at St Peter. I only wish to see them again".

"I will reopen the laptop for you now if you wish, I have slept enough earlier, so I am highly unlikely going to sleep before 1 or 2 o'clock, so we have plenty of time to have a chat. I want also to know your story and why you decided to join the church".

The priest opened the door of his room, asked his guest to sit on the chair, turned on his laptop, and asked him to wait for him as he went to the loo. The undercover police officer was sitting on the chair with his back towards the door and he was looking at the laptop screen as it was starting. And that was the last thing he saw before someone gave him a big blow on the back of his head.

At dawn of the next day, there was a storm gaining momentum. One of the church sisters who used to say an early morning prayer on the grave of her parents buried in the church graveyard was on her knees next to the two graves. She finished quickly saying her prayers as she felt drops of water announcing that heavy rain is soon to be unleashed from the sky. She stood up and as she turned her face towards the church, a thunder and lightning struck illuminating the entire yard. The woman was struck dumb as her eyes fell on a body hanging from the large tree at the corner of the yard. Her heart was beating fast as she approached the tree, then the lightning struck again, and she saw a priest hang by a rope on a brunch of the tree.

She screamed out loud and hurried inside the church. Everybody was still asleep, but she entered quickly the room of the oldest sister and woke her up.

"What's going on?"

"The Father"

"What Father?"

"Father O'Shea"

"What happened to him?"

"He is out there hanging from the tree"

"What? Maybe you had a nightmare"

"No. He is dead for real"

"Let me put on my robe. Go summon Father Sheridan"

Couple of minutes later, the two sisters and the church head stood in front of the body of the Father O'Shea. It was a real grotesque scene especially at that time of the day, and with wind and rain flooding down. Father Sheridan advised them to not touch anything. They went inside, and he called the police and Al-Douri.

The police arrived at the scene after some ten minutes from the call. Al-Douri and Hughes arrived some ten minutes after the police. Load of photos were taken. Also, Al-Douri hurried to check where was the man they planted inside to keep an eye on the priest. They didn't find him in his room, then they had to force their way inside the priest room as the door was locked. And there they found their man on the floor with blood on the back of his head. Hughes held his wrist quickly and said, "His heartbeat is so weak; he should be treated quickly". They carried him to an ambulance and straight to the emergency services at the hospital close by.

Al-Douri was standing in front of the hanged body in a state of a complete shock. Inspector Owen who didn't like the intelligence handling all those crimes stood next to him and said "Things seem to be spinning out of control. Eh?"

Al-Douri didn't reply. He then dialled the number of Mr Selway. And after several attempts he managed to wake him up "Hurry up to the church. We are facing a new disaster".

The detective couldn't believe his ears. But he jumped out of bed, put on his thick house robe and as soon as he opened the door, he noticed the raining weather. So, he returned upstairs put on his long winter coat and boots. Max who was asleep on the sofa next to the door didn't bother to even wake up.

After some ten minutes' walk, the detective arrived at the scene. The body of the priest was hanged from the tree, and under it was a long wooden chair from the church kitchen chairs. The scene had all the components of a suicide.

Al-Douri briefed him of what happened, and how they found the police officer almost dead too, inside the priest room, and what he heard from the witnesses.

Selway wondered "So what do you think? Is it a suicide?"

"I can't say anything. We have to speak to our officer to see what happened to him" Al-Douri replied.

Owen interfered into the conversation "Radi's accident, and now this priest. Two horrible deaths occurred at two stormy dawns. Are they accidents or Murders?"

"We are not certain of anything yet about both death cases. Even though there was blood other than Radi's on his sleeve we are still not sure one hundred per cent that it was a murder, or at least a deliberate one. And this one seems to be suicide. However, it could be also very much a murder" Selway replied.

"Are you telling me that after weeks of investigation you still have no clue of what is going on?" Owen went on.

Al-Douri looked very annoyed by Owen remarks. However, he tried his best to control his temper before firing out the following "I am not on this case by my choice. It was the order of the interior ministry. And we are making big progress in the case related to blackmailing and drug trafficking".

"Where is the progress and people are losing their lives?"

"I don't think it's time to bully each other Inspector Owen. We had lots of hope to get information from this dead now priest, but for some reason he or somebody else didn't want us to get this information. And this death if it proves anything, it proves that we are walking in the right direction".

"Ok anyway, it looks a suicide to me. The priest is not a weak man, and I can't see who could force him into hanging. It seems he decided to put an end for his life for some reason" Owen pointed out

"No. Not a Catholic priest" Al-Douri disagreed. "I don't think a Catholic priest with his level of devotion to his faith would commit suicide and lose the chance to enter paradise" he added.

"But it looks totally impossible that he was forced into doing it. If someone was threatening him by a gun, he would rather have got himself shot than got hanged"

"Hold on you both; let us see first the autopsy result, and what the morgue doctor would say about the cause of the death. If it was the hang, it could be very much a suicide" Selway said.

"What do you mean?" Owen asked.

"I mean what if he was killed before the hanging was staged" Selway clarified his idea.

"Yes clever. My disappointment had got the better of me. He could have been killed and then put on the rope to appear as suicide" Al-Douri agreed with his friend.

After the forensic team finished their work, the rain had ceased, and the morning light erased totally the darkness. The body was then collected and sent by ambulance to the morgue. During this time Al-Douri was making several calls. Soon after, the New Scotland Yard Police rang Owen and told him to leave the case to Al-Douri team. Again, the man stared unpleasantly at the young intelligence agent before withdrawing with the three officers of his.

"Good God. He is so annoying"

"He is. But I think we also share some responsibility, because maybe it was better to arrest the priest at the airport".

Al-Douri shook his head in frustration. A minute later they were joined by Hughes who had also a gloomy face that morning.

"What is the news at the hospital?"

"I left our man in the intensive care. They did all what they can. They replaced the blood he had lost at the accident, but they won't know before hours if he is out of danger or not"

"And if everything went alright. When can we talk to him?"

"Not before 24 hours, unless he recovered very quickly; and that is possible because he is very well-built young man".

"Ah. It is another nervous wait then. Don't you see with me how much of waits we had in this investigation? Plenty of waits either for DNA results or for the return to people from abroad etc" Selway complained.

"Calm down. I can feel how upset you are. And you are not alone. I and Hughes are upset too. We all want this nightmare to end as soon as possible, but things take time, and we can't force our rhythm on events. Bad surprises are always a possibility" Al-Douri concluded.

Chapter 30

At lunch Selway hosted Al-Douri, Hughes and Ms Dobinson at his house. It was necessary to unite their efforts as they felt the only decisive line that could have led them to the criminals has been cut. They built many hopes and wishes on Father O'Shea whom they lost forever at the dawn of that day.

243

They ate their meal which was ordered from a restaurant, in total silence, as each one of them sunk in his own thoughts and analysis regarding the tough weeks they had. Selway was waiting many results and first of them the DNA test of Mr Clayton, also another portion of his mind was assessing that strange gambler Andrew Johnson, the boyfriend of Ruth Watt. Ms Dobinson was rearranging in her mind what she was going to say about the CCTV footages after she went through all of them for days. Al-Douri was hugely upset because he felt everything would have been now in a better place if he arrested Father O'Shea at the airport instead of allowing him to skip to his own fate, while Hughes was feeling useless because he felt the entire case they came to Dorset for could get buried with the body of the dead priest.

They were moving like robots after they finished filling their stomachs. They were walking in an automatic way to wash their hands, and then took their seats at the living room without a spoken word.

As she was not involved in the bad decisions they made lately, Ms Dobinson had the courage to break the long silence. She announced that she finished looking carefully into the CCTV footages and her conclusion was "We know for certain that someone or at least one person walked into the footpath dozens of minutes before Mustapha Radi. Also, we know that a dark big 4X4 car which highly likely to have been driven by the potential criminals did also move at the downhill road. However, we cannot identify the sex of the person nor the manufacturer and the colour of the car. And that leads us to one definite conclusion that Mustapha Radi was not alone that dawn at the footpath".

Selway spoke on his turn and said "And as we know now for sure that the blood found on the sleeve of Mr Radi was not his own. That confirms that another person was in very close contact with him when the accident or the crime took place. It's crucial to wait for the results of the DNA tests of the samples taken from Mr John Clayton here yesterday and from the body of Father O'Shea at the morgue this morning. We know also that Mr Radi's knife was found in the room of the priest, and it was totally clean from any trace of blood. That gives us the conclusion that the priest picked the knife from the incident site but why? Was he the killer? And if so, why he didn't leave the knife which actually belongs to the dead man at the scene? If the knife remained at the scene, then that could have erased any suspicion about foul play at all. There is some big secret in this story, and I still cannot put my finger on it. However, I hope the DNA results would clarify some of the mist surrounding Radi's death". Hughes interrupted the detective and said, "But you are confirming something we cannot be sure of!"

"What is that?"

"You are saying that the priest picked the knife from the scene, but how about a different scenario? What if the true picker of the knife had hidden it at the priest room?"

"It's a possibility. Yes, but how strong is it?"

"It could be very strong if the two crimes were committed by the same person or persons, and that person is a member of the clergy".

"A member of the clergy! Can you please explain?"

"I mean we are talking too much about Father O'Shea because the drugs deals were done during his lectures, and also because you saw him the morning Radi's body was found, and because when we raided his room, we found the missing knife. But are we not forgetting that the church contains other people? I mean if we focus on the church members, any one or more of them could have arranged the drug deals during

245

Father O'Shea's lectures. Also, they could have easily messed with the Church cameras whenever needed. They could have planted the knife deliberately inside the priest room and that could have been done since you first made the contact with the church, and you informed them that you need to question the priest. Also, that member or members could have also forced Father O'Shea to commit suicide".

"Chapeau bas to you Mr Hughes, it's a very possible scenario; I have to admit, I didn't go that far in my analysis" Selway praised Hughes.

Al-Douri felt proud of his colleague and joined the conversation saying "So I believe we have to re-question every resident in the Catholic Church. Let us do so after we manage to talk to our man in the hospital. He could have some very valuable information of what happened last night".

"May I ask? Are you following contacts with those young guys and girls who had been blackmailed? I mean are you checking if they have been contacted lately by the blackmailer or blackmailers?"

"Yes, I do ring them every day. And none of them heard again from the criminals since the death of Mr Radi".

"That means they ceased their activities since they knew the police is after them".

"Or it also means that Mr Radi was the blackmailer or one of the blackmailers either by choice or forced to do so. You remember the young female pupil whom they used to deliver the drugs to their clients. So, for me we have many questions and hardly any answer. Yes, we feel we are making progress because things are happening before us on the ground, but in reality, apart from the dead priest we have no clear suspect to deal directly with".

Silence invaded the room once again, because the words were harsh but at the same time very true. The two deaths cannot be confirmed as murders, they could be accidental and suicidal. The knife left in the scene, its disappearance from the scene then its reappearance in Father O'Shea's room. A criminal or a gang are using people to sell their drugs and bring them the money while staying away from the scene. It's a real puzzle of puzzles. They felt as they were dealing with some supernatural evil power. It was there, they can see its deeds, but they can't see it for what it was.

The detective stood up, waved his cane, touched his moustache and said in a strong voice "It's true that this is the first case for me as a detective. But I am fully certain that we will get to the bottom of it. You told me that you will let me lead the team. And I am speaking now as leader of the team. From this moment onward we are no longer separating the two cases, we will go together for the two cases as one case. And to be in full concentration we have to exist at one place. Therefore, I hope you will accept my invitation to be my guests in this house, there are enough rooms. So, you leave your hotels immediately and you come here from tonight, and we plan our next moves together.

The other three looked at each other. Then they said "Alright. Let us do this". Al-Douri then added "But you will accept that we all pay when it comes to food and bills, because we don't know how long it will take us to get the job done".

"Ok. No problem" Selway replied.

The next hours were busy with the relocation process, and of course the most disappointed with the sudden process were the hotels owners who out of nowhere lost some regular income especially at that time of the year when few tourists came to North Dorset. In the other hand the most benefited from the situation was Max who found himself suddenly flooded by gifts as the three other humans joined his master.

At sunset, Al-Douri received a call from the hospital located next door. The doctor told him that the police officer was now awake, and they can talk to him after half an hour as he was having his dinner.

In time, the three men left to the hospital while Ms Dobinson stayed behind to prepare the dinner. The doctor showed them into the room and left them with their colleague. The first to speak was the patient himself Officer O'Hara said "I am so sorry. I knew from the doctor briefly what happened and that father O'Shea had committed suicide or something of the sort". Al-Douri comforted him by saying "Don't worry. This is part of our job. Surprises are not always nice. Please set your mind back to what happened yesterday since you joined the church family. I want to know everything since we left you there. Any small detail could prove crucial for the investigation".

The officer took a deep breath then said "When you left me there, Father Sheridan guided me to my room which was usually open for any guest. And when I put on the Monk dress and re-joined the other members sitting in the main room, some smiled, and some looked in not so impressed way. So, I felt I should calm their nerves a little bit by saying I hope the priest will be clean and no harm to the church reputation will take place, and I assured them that all the investigation has been done secretly so far. However, Father Sheridan said they accepted me to go undercover because he knows that we don't trust that the church members are not going to warn Father O'Shea that he was at the centre of the investigation. And who could deny that? Later they tried to warm things up between us as much as they could, and they sounded friendlier. However, I felt uneasy. Then when Father O'Shea arrived, he went straight to take a shower; he changed his clothes to a church one, and then joined us all on the dinner table. I didn't notice any one of them trying to warn him about anything, they were just talking in a normal fashion. They asked him about his trip and what he enjoyed most there. And after dinner he opened his laptop and showed them some videos and photos he took while in the Vatican".

The officer paused a little bit, he drunk some water, then went on "It was getting late, and at almost 11 o'clock, all withdrew to their beds, and I was left alone with him. I hesitated to open a new chat with him, but then I said to myself my room is next to his and I may not get another golden chance to get to know the man, so after he collected his laptop and walked towards his room, I walked after him quickly and before he entered his room I said "Please brother I was impressed by some of the videos inside the Vatican and it would be nice to see them properly, maybe tomorrow if you don't mind". He told me that he took enough rest in the coach trip and after his arrival, and that he won't sleep before another couple of hours, so he invited me to his room as he was also curious to know what made a young man like me join the priesthood. I was of course delighted to get the chance for such a conversation. So, I accepted the invitation, he showed me in, and asked me to sit in the only chair in the room next to his bed. He turned on the laptop and told me he will be right back as he wanted to go to the toilet. The back of the chair was towards the door, and I felt him leaving the room, and I was looking at the laptop screen when I got a very strong hit on the back of my head. And I woke up here couple of hours ago

"No one talked to him privately?"

"No. I don't think so, unless someone met him outside the main room when he was off to take a shower. But it's highly likely that no conversation took place"

"And did he look worried, sad or depressed?"

"No, not at all and that's why I was shocked when I heard that he committed suicide during the night".

Al-Douri felt very upset because he hoped for some information that could shed some light on what happened that night, but the officer's account made the story even more complex. Selway read all the expressions on his colleague's face, and he felt big sympathy for him. The nurse knocked on the door and disturbed them as it was the time for an injection. The three stood up and Al-Douri said "Ok dear. Rest well, we will see you again tomorrow, and if you remember anything call me immediately. Have a good evening".

Chapter 31

The state of silence invaded Selway's house once more after they returned from the hospital. Ms Dobinson read the disappointment on their faces, so she avoided asking them about what they heard from the injured police officer.

She continued setting the dinner table, and after some ten minutes she called them to it. They were taking their seats when Al-Douri received a call from London, he withdrew to the living room while waved his hand for them to go on and not wait for him. The other three started their meal and it didn't take Al-Douri too long to re-join them. The three of them were looking at him with several questions marks painted on their curious faces. They managed to notice quickly some relief on the young man face. He noticed that, so he tried to tease them a bit. He said "Nice food. Thanks Ms Dobinson". "You are welcome" she replied. Hughes didn't wait, he fired his words immediately "Come on, what was that call?"

"Well, it's related to Selway's part of the case. They managed to give me the identity of the buyer of the telephone card who called Mrs Clayton to inform her about the affair of her husband". The detective ears tuned on immediately and the spoon stopped at once in his plate. And he asked "Who is that? Do we know him or her?"

"Yes, you do know him very well!"

"Me?"

"Yes You!"

"Who is this? Don't tell me Ruth's boyfriend".

"No. It's Mustapha Radi"

Selway and Dobinson looked stunned, while Hughes said quickly "You see. I always told you that this guy was not necessarily a victim in all of this".

"Are they sure about that?"

"Yes. That's what they have on their record".

"And did they give the address of the shop where the telephone sim card was bought?"

"Yes"

"And where is that?"

"Here in Morobury".

"Ok we will go there first thing in the morning".

Dobinson who met Radi accidentally after his affair was uncovered by Mrs Clayton and still remember how heartbroken he was, defended him fiercely "I am sorry, but it doesn't make sense to me, that someone in a deep love relationship would dare take such risk of losing it in order to achieve what exactly?"

"Maybe he wasn't in a true love story" Hughes said.

"You didn't see how upset he was, he was burning inside out when I met him accidentally at the restaurant that evening. I still can't see what he would benefit from telling Mrs Clayton what was going on between him and her husband"

"Maybe he was upset because the plan didn't go the way he wished" said Al-Douri.

"What do you mean?"

"I mean, he maybe has thought that the affair exposure would lead to a divorce between the Claytons, but instead the first decision taken by Mrs Clayton was to end his tenancy and throw him out of their lives".

"This entire story is screwing my head" admitted the detective. "If Mustapha Radi was indeed behind that message that means I am a big failure on recognising how good a soul is. Yes, the guy gave me the impression that he is hiding something related to his private life or something, but he didn't look as someone capable of evil deeds".

"Well love is blind and can turn someone into some crazy deeds. And he was still young, so it's possible".

Dobinson then said "We can't but keep an open mind about that possibility, because as you know he lied to me that night when

I asked him what was going on and he claimed he had an affair with a woman"

Selway protested at that remark "No one would expect a gay man to speak with a lady he met for the first time and tell her straight forward he is gay and in an affair with a married man".

Silence returned for a minute, then Max disturbed it by barking next to his master who looked at his watch and said, "Oh it's time for your cookie, you never forgive messing with your routine". He opened the drawer brought two cookies for the dog who announced his thanks immediately.

Selway then asked Al-Douri "Any news yet about Ruth's boyfriend Andrew Johnson?"
"No. Not yet, because I told them to prepare a full file about him. And this takes a bit of time".

"And have you asked about the car he drives or owns nowadays?"

"Of course, I did. That was at the top of my demands. Don't worry I know very well what you are thinking". They smiled to each other for the first time since the early morning of that day.

As it was a long hard day, at 10 pm they started withdrawing to their rooms. There were two bathrooms available with douche cabins, so there were no queues. By 11 each one of them was in his bed trying to get a good sleep before they kick off the following day of their investigation.

At 9 am the time at which the electronics shop located at the Tesco Supermarket usually open. Selway and Al-Douri stood there and waited the two employees who were opening the door of the shop. As soon as they both settled down inside, the two detectives went in, showed them their professional cards. Then

Selway asked "We have information regarding a mobile line, I mean sim card which was bought from here and registered under the name of Mustapha Radi. Can you please check your data to see if this information is correct?"

One of the two guys turned on the main computer at the shop, and after nearly a minute, he asked how the name was spelled. Al-Douri replied "M U S T A P H A, then the last name R A D I". The guy typed the name into the system and hit the search button. Few seconds later he got the profile, he then turned the flexible screen towards the detectives, and said "Yes we have got him here on the record. I will print the profile for you including a copy of the passport he provided when he bought the telephone card".

Selway and Al-Douri starred at each other few seconds, and Selway said "I can see that the date of the operation was in August. Do you remember the man when he came here and bought it from you?"

The guy behind the computer replied "No. Not really, I am afraid, as you know we see dozens of faces every day, so I don't think I remember anything about this". But then the other guy came forward and said, "I think I can remember that name, he looked again at the screen and said, "Yes I remember selling this card".

Selway eyes widen in delight mixed with excitement, and asked "Did he really look like the photo in the passport?"

"To be frank with you, I am not sure". The guy closed his eyes few seconds as he was trying to remember that specific moment, then said "I can't really say. My memory is failing me". Al-Douri looked unimpressed then asked, "What is the process of selling someone a sim card?" The salesman replied "we ask for an id card, a passport or driving licence. And in the case of Mr Radi, he handed me his passport, I photocopied it and returned it to him after entering his details with address etc..".

"So, you can't be sure if it was the man, you saw looked like the one on the passport photo?"

"If it's the man I am remembering, it was a cool night, and he was wearing a scarf hiding big part of his face. A scarf the Arabs wear, the white and black one linked to the Palestinian cause, I guess. He was coughing heavily, seemed to have a flu, because he was wearing a top like in winter. But with the passport and an Arab name on it, nothing indicated it could be another person".

Al-Douri and Selway shared a glance; then the salesman added "Wait a minute, I think he wasn't alone. If it's the right man I am remembering, there was a lady with him, she came after him hurrying him up, and they left immediately".

"Do you remember her face, age, height?"

"She was also wearing similar scarf and hat, yet her face was clear, I would say she in her 30's maybe 40's. Pale white skin, not tall, not short"

"If you see a photo of her, would you recognise her?"

"Maybe"

"Ok thank you for now. Can we please have your own mobile number?"

"Yes sure".

The guy wrote it down on the papers he printed for them. Al-Douri collected the papers, and they returned home.

As soon as they regained the car, Selway dialled the number of the housemaid of the Claytons.

"Good morning, Maria"

"Good morning, Sir"

"Detective Selway here, I hope I am not disturbing"

"No, I have just handed Mrs Clayton her breakfast, and I am now at the kitchen alone and in peace for the next half an hour hopefully".

"I won't take more than a minute or two. I just want you to remember very well, have you ever walked with Mr Radi towards the phone shop inside the Tesco supermarket. I mean he was buying something, and you waited for him to finish before you returned together".

"Hm. Well actually we went several times to Tesco together, so it's hard for me to tell really if such episode had happened. I think I need more time to focus my mind and try to remember".

"Ok no problem, take your time and let me know your decisive answer, yes or no, as soon as you remember".

"Alright. I will do so surely".

"Thanks. Have a nice day"

"Same to you Sir"

The car had already arrived back to Selway's house. So, they entered the house, and Al-Douri briefed Dobinson and Hughes of what they heard. Dobinson who was refusing to believe that Radi could have done so, took immediately the paper and saw Radi's profile with his passport and house address on it.

Dobinson asked, "Have you tried to call the women Radi may have gone there with?"

"I called Maria, the Claytons housemaid, she said she needs some time to remember if she ever saw him buying from the electronics shop. That's one person that came to my mind immediately because we know that they used to go there together, but of course the woman could be someone else".

"Well, the other woman I saw in his company was the school head. Have you called her?"

"But the guy told us it's a lady in her 40s or 30s. And the Ms Kane is in her late fifties I guess"

"But she was wearing scarf, so you don't know"

"You are right"

Selway dialled Geraldine Kane's number, and after dozens of seconds she opened up the line.

"Hello Ms Kane. It's detective Selway"

"Hi. How are you? And how is your investigation going?"

"I am fine thanks. And the investigation still requires some efforts. And I hope you might be able to give us a hand"

"Surely, how can I help?"

"I need you to remember if you ever walked with Mr Radi into the Tesco supermarket?"

After few seconds, Kane said "No. Never, we have been to my place, I visited him once at his place, and most of time we meet in pub or a restaurant and of course here at school, but we never went shopping together"

Mourad Mourad

"Maybe you met him there accidentally"

"No. I can assure you that we had never been together inside the supermarket".

"Ok thanks for this confirmation. May I ask you a favour please?"

"Sure! Go ahead"

"Can you please check with the school female teachers if any one of them been at Tesco with Mr Radi, or met him there by coincidence?"

"Ok. I will call them now and I will ring you back when I finish".

"Your help is very much appreciated. Thank you".

As he ended the call, a noise came from the main door, it was the postman pushing some letters and brochures through the letterbox. Ms Dobinson was closest to the door, so she got them. She checked them one after the other.

"What are they? Anything significant?" Selway asked

"One from your bank; an advertisement from window cleaners; and two monthly printed magazines from the art centre about their coming schedule".

"Two! Why two?"

"One under your name, and the other was going to Mr Radi's address".

"Ah yes. I almost forgot that his mails were diverted to here".

Suddenly Al-Douri mobile phone went on, the call was from the morgue and the doctor there said that his report about the priest's body was ready, so they could go collect it.

Immediately Al-Douri, Hughes and Selway hurried up to the car. In few minutes they were inside the morgue talking to the pathologist.

"The time of death is between midnight and dawn; we can't tell the exact hour I am afraid".

"And was it really a death by hanging?"

"The death happened definitely by pressing on his neck, but if it's a suicide by the rope we can't confirm"

"What does that mean?"

"Aren't there any traces of the rope on his neck?

"There are rope traces on his neck and we all know that the rope was round his neck. But there is also a possibility of him being murdered by neck pressing before being put on the rope to make it appear like a suicide"

"So again, we can't confirm if it's a suicide or a homicide"

"I am afraid not, because if there is a murder and it happened few minutes before hanging the body with the rope that makes it almost impossible for us to really say the difference. And mind you I am saying this as possibility, and it may not be true, the man might have committed suicide. But I am telling you this because I can't confirm in my official report either way as cause of death".

"Ok thank you for your effort".

Al-Douri exploded from anger as they regained the car "This is impossible. Either we are dealing with a professional criminal ghost or ghosts, or we are really facing some strange series of coincidences. I mean what if that priest accidentally was present during Radi's fall. Then for some personal reason he committed suicide. I can't wait for that DNA test of his to see if it matches the blood on Radi's clothes or not".

Chapter 32

Dobinson noticed the frustration on their faces as they entered the house. And her employer informed her of the result, so she no longer wondered why. Things around them were happening but for them nothing was certain yet. They felt like walking blindly on a road and they hear people being killed without having the ability to see what was exactly happening and identify who were the killers, if there were any.

Few minutes later, Selway received the awaited call from the school head who informed him that none of the female teachers have ever been in the company of Mr Radi outside the school premises. And while they were debating if Radi was really the man who bought that sim card, Selway received a call from Maria whom in her turn confirmed that, as well as she can remember, when they shopped together Mr Radi never walked into the phones shop.

Selway then told them "You see, we have now all the confirmations from the women who were seen in public with him that he never been there. So again, I think there is something fishy in this story".

"But you are always assuming that he must be innocent even though plenty of findings so far pointed to his involvement into the criminal activities we have been investigating". Hughes complained.

"Not only that but you are also assuming that all those women are saying the truth, but what one of them lied?" Al-Douri suggested.

"You are both right. My short friendship with Mr Radi had pushed me several times to think in a partial way" Selway admitted.

Al-Douri received a call from London. They told him that they sent him by email all the information available on Ruth's boyfriend Andrew Johnson. He immediately told Selway "We have got something you asked for?"

"What? Clayton's DNA Result?"

"No. The gambler's profile"

"Oh yes".

They surrounded Al-Douri behind his computer as he opened the email and the attachments linked to it.

It included several photos of the man, and the attached note said "He has been on up and down financially for almost three decades. He is an addict gambler; he dated many rich people from both sexes for the sake of their financial support to his addiction. He is lately dating Ruth Watt, they own a luxurious yacht, and he drives a dark blue 4X4.

After hearing what the note said. They shared a glance at each other faces. Then Selway said "He had bisexual affairs, and that explains better his appearance on Radi's friends list".

"And his car is a dark coloured 4 by 4. And that fits the size of the car which its corner appeared on the CCTV footage" Dobinson noticed.

"I must have to admit that his profile with his history of relying on easy money also could push him into criminal activities such as drugs selling and Cyber blackmailing" Al-Douri said.

Hughes protested "But you are forgetting that he is not resident here, and maybe never been here. And that drives all those suggestions away".

"He still can be part of a group which is active here recently. His profile fits if he and his girlfriend wanted to get rid of Mustafa Radi in order to become the sole inheritors of her sister's huge wealth" Selway said.

"Interesting point which I think came across of our minds all since we heard of him. But that would put Ms Anne Watt in danger. Don't you think?" Al-Douri wondered.

"He or they won't act that quick, or they will turn attention to them, however we must keep an eye on the older sister" Selway replied. Then he dialled the number of Ms Watt, and after nearly a minute she replied

"Sorry for disturbing your nap. I won't take much time"

"Any news?"

"No not much. But I have a question that I forgot to ask you earlier"

"Go ahead"

"You were asked to come here by Mustapha, right?"

"Yes, because he wanted me to oversee his relocation to a new house"

"Did he invite you both? I mean you and your sister? Did you come from London by train or by a Taxi?"

"He naturally invited me, you know, but when I informed my sister about his request, she was keen to see the area, and also her boyfriend proposed driving us here, so it happened this way".

"So, Ruth's boyfriend, Andrew Johnson, the man you don't like, drove you both here?"

"Yes. I actually accepted the offer for Ruth's sake".

"So why were you surprised to see him in Mustapha's friends list?"

"Because I don't think they have ever met each other!"

"Not even here! I mean your son was waiting you when you arrived surely"

"Well if we came by train, he would have waited us. But he didn't see me here until after I checked in at the hotel".

"You mean Ruth's boyfriend drove you here and left immediately?"

"They drove me here to this hotel, while they checked in together at a hotel in Stokeminster. You know they needed their privacy"

"But when I and Inspector Owen first came to the hotel to inform you about Mustapha's death, you and your sister were at your hotel"

"Yes, she joined me in the hotel in the early morning, because her boyfriend left for London for a business of his own"

"Ah. Alright"

"Why are you asking all those questions?"

Selway didn't want to alarm the lady, so he said "I was just rechecking some facts about Mustapha state of affairs the days before his death, and then your answers made me ask more questions out of curiosity. Take care. Talk to you soon".

As soon as the detective turned off his phone, he said "Damn I knew it. He was here in the few days that preceded Radi's death"

"Who was?"

"The gambler"

"Interesting"

"Yes indeed. He was staying in a hotel in Stokeminster and he drove his 4X4 around. And as you know the road caught by the lower CCTV of the footpath, is the road that goes to Stokeminster. So, I am afraid some kind of evidence is starting to build up"

"Yes, but what he has to do with the death of Father O'Shea, and the knife found at the priest's room?"

"There must be an explanation for all of this"

"Any way, I think the DNA Tests are the main key in this case".

As Hughes finished his words, Al-Douri received a new call from London and this time it was the DNA main laboratory. They informed him that they sent him the results of both DNA tests, the one of Father O'Shea and the one of Mr John Clayton.

Again, they surrounded him as he checked his email inbox, the message explained the following: *"Compared to the blood*

found on Mustapha Radi's sleeve, Father O'Shea's DNA is 100 per cent negative. It's definitely not his blood.
Compared to that same blood sample, Mr John Clayton's DNA doesn't match it fully. However, the blood belongs to one of his close cousins, a father, a mother, a son, a daughter, a sister or a brother. That means the blood is not Mr Clayton's but belongs to one of his closest family members".

They all said at once "Barry Clayton, his son".

"He was the main suspect since the beginning. His anxious mother, his state of anger described to us by the housemaid, his connection to that racist political movement. All fit the bill. But where on earth is he right now?" Selway said in despair.

"Don't worry, we will get him, the Europol and the Interpol have been asked to try and locate him, and after this information, they could move and arrest him wherever he is. I will contact London immediately so they can issue an arrest warrant" Al-Douri played Selway's worries down.

The MI5 agent then stood up walked toward the corner and spoke to his colleagues about the matter. As soon as he finished, Selway suggested "I am sure that his mother is in contact with him somehow".

"We took that into account, all the Claytons lines are under surveillance and so are their internet activities"

"But she can still make a call from the street or from an internet cafe"

"We have done what we can, but now as we have a confirmation of his son involvement, we will be watching her every move".

"I do have a better idea" Selway claimed.

"What?"

"How about shaking her and forcing her to react" the detective said.

"What do you mean?"

"I mean we should let her know that the blood found is definitely her son's. And that he is now the number one suspect. She will definitely make a move to warn him, and that's how we can locate him" Selway explained.

"Brilliant idea, but we can't go straight and tell her that in her face" Al-Douri said.

"We must think of a way to convey the message to her indirectly. So, she won't suspect that we know she knew" Selway agreed.

"The only way I think is through the housemaid, because I doubt Mr John Clayton would cooperate with us against his son" Dobinson suggested.

"You are right. Ring Maria on her mobile and pretend that you are not hearing what she is saying, then ring the landline of the Claytons and ask to talk to her because her mobile seems to not work properly" Selway told his secretary.

"And then" she said.

"And then you ask her to come here for a questioning session. Of course, she would ask permission from the Claytons and at that Mrs Clayton will be waiting her impatiently to know what the questions were about" he said.

Dobinson dialled the maid's number. As soon as she replied, Dobinson pretended not to hear her, "Alo Maria. It's me Ms Dobinson. Hello. I can't hear anything".

In the meantime, Selway dialled the landline number from his landline phone, as soon as he got an answer. Dobinson ended the first call and took the second.

"The Claytons, the Lady of the house speaking"

"Hello Mrs Clayton. Ms Dobinson the secretary of Detective Selway speaking. Can I speak to Maria please? I have tried to reach her on her mobile, but I couldn't hear what she was saying."

"What do you want her for?"

"Mr Selway needs to ask her urgently couple of questions, so I hope you won't mind her coming here now".

"Ok. Speak to her". "This is Ms Dobinson; they want to ask you questions" Clayton was heard telling her servant

"Hi Ms Dobinson, how can I help?"

"Can you please come here immediately?"

"Can I go there right now?" She was heard asking Mrs Clayton. Then she said "Ok. I will join you in few minutes".

As soon as the call ended, they clashed their hands palms in high five celebrating that they managed to turn the attention and the curiosity of Mrs Clayton.

Al-Douri asked Hughes to go there by car and wait to see if Mrs Clayton would leave the house later.

Ten minutes later Maria joined them with some seriousness on her face. Selway went directly with his words "Tell me, how far are you ready to go in order to catch the murderer of your friend?"

"Oh. Was he murdered then?"

"Many findings point that way. Yes".

"I would definitely go as far as my ability allows me to".

"Even if that means risking losing your current job!".

The lady looked to the three faces around her then said "Yes"

"Ok. You don't need to worry about your job; if you lost it, we would get you another one".

"So, what can I do to help?"

"Look we received today a DNA test result confirming that the blood found on Mustafa's sleeve was Barry's".

Maria's hand went immediately up to her mouth expressing her shock.

"And this should not come as surprise for you because you described to us previously how furious he was when you last saw him leaving the house and he was shouting of wanting to kill someone".

"True".

"As you know Barry Clayton has not been in the United Kingdom for couple of weeks now. And we need you to help us finding him".

"How ?!"

"I will tell you what to do if you promise to keep this between us and remember you could be sent to jail if we know that you warned the Claytons about our plan".

The woman said courageously "I promise to do as I am told. If Barry is really the killer, then he deserves to be punished for his crime".

Selway smiled for the first time and said "Ok my dear. Here what you have got to do. Mrs Clayton will definitely be curious right now to know what we have been asking you about. So, we expect her as soon as you walk into her house to ask you what we wanted. And you should tell her, that we were asking about Barry: When was the last time you saw him? Did he really travel before Radi's death? Did you ever hear him clashing with the late tenant? Then she will ask you what did you answer? And you would claim that you said you didn't see him for a while before Radi's accident, and that you asked us why all this interest in Barry? And that Dobinson confined to you that his DNA confirms that the blood found on Radi's sleeve was his, and that the Europol and Interpol will get him soon wherever he is".

"Ok. It won't be easy though".

"We know it's not an easy task, but that is what you have to tell her. And please try to act emotionally a little bit while conveying this information to her. Alright?"

Maria nodded approval.

"Then off you go" Selway gave her the green light.

Chapter 33

As expected, hardly half an hour after Maria returned to the Claytons house, Mrs Clayton rushed outside and walked down the street to the first public telephone cabin. Hughes was well equipped in his car by the best detection machine ever made, so he was able to hear her breath and detect the number she was dialling. He parked the car on the opposite side of the road and waited there. The woman was clearly nervous as her coins fell down as she was in hurry to insert them into the machine, then she decided it's best to use her credit card. "Oh God. Come on". She then dialled a number and waited but she doesn't seem to get an answer. She tried it again but to her frustration she seemed to have fallen on a dead end. Then she looked on her mobile phone as if she was getting out another number. Then she dialled that one. This time there was ringing however no one answered. She tried it again and after giving up she left a vocal message "Please tell Barry your mother called and she is warning you of coming back home, they are after you. Do not return, and I will transfer money to your bank account. Please send me a message or an email confirming that you received this message. Take care. Bye for now".

The woman walked back home nervously, her face full of anxiety and fear. Hughes recorded that and drove back to Selway's home. Couple of minutes later, Al-Douri sent the two numbers they got to the Europol and the Interpol. Also, he received confirmation from London that they had issued an arrest warrant for Barry Clayton wherever he is in the world. As soon as all of this was done, silence invaded the living room. Then Hughes broke the silence "I think things are becoming clearer now. Can I give you my understanding of the situation so far?"

"Go ahead"

"From the first interviews we conducted Mrs Clayton seemed to have known something that we didn't, and when Maria described how furious Barry Clayton was after he knew about the affair between his father and Mustafa Radi. It became obvious that he had a strong motive to kill the tenant. The DNA Blood test has proven his involvement, we know that a person, apparently him, walked into the footpath some twenty minutes

270

before Radi. So, he is indeed the killer, but maybe he didn't mean to kill the teacher, it could have been a fight between the two that led to Radi's death. However, I don't think that accident is related to the drugs trafficking and the cyber blackmailing. For these two I believe Radi was involved in them, he was the blackmailer and the drug dealer, otherwise how do you explain that all those activities ceased immediately with his death? So, for me the case is solved as follows: Barry killed Radi accidentally. And Radi might have got his punishment for the ordeal he caused to many people during his first year in this area".

"And how do you explain the knife in the room of Father O'Shea and his death?"

"Regarding the knife, it could be that the priest witnessed the fight between the two young men, and after Barry left by the car that waited for him, the priest went down and checked Radi's body, and saw the knife so he decided to hide it in order to make the entire event looks like a fall accident. And about his death it could be a real suicide, for some reason he was depressed, and he decided to end the suffering once and for all".

"I would have agreed with you that the priest saw a clash between Mustapha and Barry if that was happening during the day. Because Radi's death occurred at dawn, at time hardly anyone can see clearly from a distance anything. Also, you seemed to forget that the knife was still near the dead body in the morning, and it was seen there by the woman who informed the police, but when she returned later it was gone". Al-Douri expressed his doubts on Hughes' analysis.

"Well, it could be also that the priest saw Barry going into the footpath and then he discovered Radi's body and saw the knife next to it, he gathered the puzzle together and thought it belonged to Barry, so to hide it he picked it up before the people and the police arrived"

"This scenario is very possible".

"However, if we are to agree that the priest accidentally picked the knife, his death is still look suspicious to me because don't forget most of the drug operations happened during his lectures"

"I would rather say no not suspicious. Maybe he was involved somehow in the drug ring, and he felt depressed because of that, then maybe he repented and decided to punish himself "

"Also, possible"

"But don't forget that our man confirmed to us that he saw no sign of depression or sadness on the priest that night"

"Well if a believer believed that he had repented and that he is making peace with God, he wouldn't look anxious, would he?"

Silence gained the upper hand. Maybe because Barry's involvement in Radi's death was certain, and the possibility of the priest suicidal repentance - even if suicide is a big sin in the church - sounded a very credible theory to all of them.

Then Dobinson broke the silence "So what now? We wait until Barry get caught, or we should try to get his mother to speak what she knows, because she clearly knows that her son has done something wrong?"

"She will never tell us anything. Maybe she saw him returning home that morning and he told her what he had done, so she asked him to leave the country until things settle down. That's the best information we could get of her if she confessed, but she won't. So, we really know since the beginning what she has been hiding. So, talking to her won't change anything in the situation" Selway said. He then added "However I think I have a better idea. I will have my dinner out with Mr Clayton tonight. He is unaware of what is going on unless his wife informed him. In both situations he would definitely like to talk. And I need to hear some clarification not only regarding his son but most importantly regarding his late lover. They had some two years love affair, so he definitely knows Mustapha Radi very well. I want to know his opinion in our suspicions regarding Radi's involvement in blackmailing and drugs. Did he notice anything during the time they spent together? Any information no matter how little could be crucial to solve the puzzle" Selway added.

The detective dialled the number of his neighbour who answered almost immediately as if he has been waiting the call.

"Good evening"

"I wish it was that good"

"Did your wife tell you?"

"Yes, she did. She is in hysterical mood, and she went mad on me because of the DNA test. You tricked me into this"

"Please do not despair. The Death of Mustapha Radi could still have happened accidentally, so investigation is still on going. Maybe we can talk it over in the restaurant if you accept my invitation".

"What do you mean by: accidentally?"

"I mean they could had had a fight and wrestled, and then Radi died accidentally".

"Ok I agree to meet you. But I am not really up for dinner. How about the Sports Club pub, it's wide and we can easily find a table to talk there"

"Alright, see you after half an hour at the Pub".

Meanwhile Al-Douri received a call from London about the two numbers that Mrs Clayton called. He was informed that one of them is totally dead. The second is located in Venice in Italy, and they will try to catch the holder as soon as possible. As soon as Al-Douri shared the information with them, the detective raised his thumb up and said "Well, things seem to be moving at last. Let us hope all the mist surrounding these cases will soon be completely gone".

"Would you want me to drive you to the pub?" Hughes asked. "No. Thanks. Plenty of time to walk down there" The detective replied as he balanced his hat on his head, threw his cane up and then caught it with his right hand while renewing the wax on his moustache in front of the mirror by his left hand.

"Should we wait you on dinner?" Dobinson asked

"No. Because I don't know how long my conversation with Mr Clayton will take. So please have your dinner without me, but don't forget Max" Selway replied while the dog barked gently when he heard his name. The detective sneaked himself outside as his dog tried to follow suit, but his master stated "No my darling. You are not going anywhere, you stay here". He then winked and addressed his guests "please go out with him for a walk after dinner". The door was then slammed in the face of Max who expressed a sad noise.

The moon was shining brightly that night. Selway was about to take the opposite side of the road when he heard Mr Clayton shouting at him from behind. "I got you". "Let us walk together all the way then". Mr Clayton was usually a smiley person, but he looked grimed under the streetlight. And that was understandable due to his son being the first suspect in a possible murder. "I want to hear more from you about that possible accident theory" he said.

"Are you preparing a lawyer?"

"Of Course, I am!"

"It's just a suggestion. Your DNA sample is 100 per cent related to the DNA of the blood found on the sleeve of Mr Radi, so your son is somehow involved in the death of your late lover".

"Is there any percentage that the DNA test result could be wrong? You know I have been in close contact with Radi for the last two years. Even the track suit he was wearing that morning was a gift from me for his birthday. Could the blood have got to it somehow?"

"Come on. You are a scientist. You know how accurate DNA tests are. And the blood on the sleeve was fresh, some hours old. So, there is no denial it's your son's blood. I understand your wishful thinking but no. We can discuss the possibility of them wrestling each other from the top of the hill all the way down and accidentally Radi's head hit the rock.

"Alright. Alright"

The two men arrived at the pub which was a bit crowded that night as there were some of the football and rugby teams' players with their coaches. Most of them saluted Mr Clayton "Good Evening Professor". "Good evening, everybody" Even couple of them including the rugby coach slammed his hand as he passed by.

They took a seat in the darkest corner of the pub and continued their conversation.

"So, tell me now are they really after my son?"

"But of course, my friend; there is an international arrest warrant. Sooner or later, they will arrest him. I have little doubt about that".

"So, you mean the only exit for him is that to confess that death happened accidentally as they wrestled each other".

"Dear John look me in the eye, if your son killed that man deliberately. Would you still want to defend him?" The Professor closed his eyes, took a soufflé then said "No".

"Alright then calm down. What happened had happened. All what we can do is to wait and see what your son will say about Radi's death".

Tears went down on the cheeks through the grey beard hair of Mr Clayton. Selway tapped him on the shoulder, and said "I understand your frustration, disappointment, anger, sadness, all this mixture of feelings. Your son who is certainly very precious to your heart might have killed deliberately your lover. I can feel the fire burning inside of you right now".

The man exploded in tears and said "It's my fault. Why do we have to pay the price for the love of our lives? Why? And God damn it's a very heavy price indeed".

The waiter brought them two beer glasses. Selway asked his friend to calm down and drink his glass.

"John, Tell me about Mustapha. Please take all your love feelings towards him aside and give me an insight to the soul of that guy".

"What do you want to know exactly?"

"I mean you spent enough time together for nearly two years, so you definitely had known him close enough. And I tend to trust your judgement".

"I still don't understand. The guy is dead, and what brings his characteristics into our conversation now!"

"My colleagues are suspecting him to be in a drug trafficking ring, and/or he was a cyber-blackmailer. I mean someone who could blackmail people to give him money or else he would publish their intimate videos or photos etc.."

"Mustapha!?"

"Yes"

"No. He was a very sensitive guy. He thinks hundreds of times before making a move because he wanted to study all its sides and once, he feels certain that no harm in it to others he commits himself to it. No, he was not that sort of guy. You saw how fit he was, he was not into drug or cyber-sex"

"I share with you the same opinion even if I have known him for two weeks only. However, there is still a possibility that he was forced to join a criminal ring"

"What that supposed to mean?"

"I mean someone might have caught him in an intimate position in videos or photos and then blackmailed him to do some dirty deeds or else he will get his scandal published".

"Maybe"

"Maybe you can help me by remembering your time together, have you ever felt him worried, anxious about something, any unusual behaviour that might caught your attention"

Mr Clayton took a deep look around the place as if he was trying to gather his memories. And after couple of minutes of just drinking, he said "I can't remember any. Also, I feel my head almost exploding. I think I need some rest. If I remember anything of the sort, I will let you know".

Chapter 34

At night the wall of the backyard of the Claytons home witnessed some unusual activity. A key was turned into the garden backdoor hidden between trees. And steps rushed inside the garden keeping as close as possible to the walls, as automatic lights turned on whenever something moved inside the garden. The steps stopped at the door of the annexe that Radi used to live at. A key was turned into the door.

Mr John Clayton who wasn't able to sleep that night, looked outside the window of his room towards the garden as he saw the light came on, however he didn't suspect anything as the light often comes on for any moving creature, animal, bird etc. He was thinking of what he heard earlier from the detective. He was thinking of the best lawyer to hire for the certain case that was waiting his son, also he was trying to remember some of the moments he spent with Radi in the UK and abroad, and he couldn't remember any suspicious behaviour from his late lover. And after long period of thinking, sleep finally got the best of him.

He woke up couple of hours later at the voice of his wife screaming and shouting hysterically outside the house. He puts on his bed robe and run downstairs and walked outside. There she was standing in front of the annexe screaming and pulling her hair like mad. She had never seen her before in such state, and he knew instantly that something very serious had happened. He rushed towards her, she shouted at him "Don't touch me, don't say a word, it's all because of you" while she pointed her hand towards the annexe.

The door was half open. Mr Clayton walked in and there he saw the body of his son on the floor. Few seconds later he was pushed forward by the emergency service crew who rushed in from across the road as soon as they heard the screams of Mrs Clayton. The medical staff confirmed that Barry Clayton was dead, and soon the police came forward. Selway and his companions were the last to arrive. Immediately Inspector Owen showed his fury at them "Of Course you are the last to arrive because you have been handling the case very well indeed. This is the third death in less than three weeks".

They didn't reply. Selway and Al-Douri went immediately to the head of the forensic team and asked him about the body. "We need to do some work at the morgue, because there is no outer violence on the body, also he is too young to die naturally from a heart attack, so we have to check and see" he said.

Photos and videos of the scene were taken. A police officer was asked to search the body before they move it to the morgue. There in the pocket he took out train tickets and two passports, and a smart phone. Owen took them immediately from the officer and he opened them while Al-Douri and Selway looked from behind his shoulders. They were a British passport and an Italian one, both with Barry's photos on them, but the second was under an Italian name Alberto Chiesa. The train tickets were for these trips: Rome - Paris - London - Millingham.

"He knew that police were after him, so he returned using a forged Italian passport" Al-Douri said.

Selway took the last ticket of the journey from London to Millingham and the date was three days ago. "So, he was here when Father O'Shea died" The detective pointed out.

The forensic team asked permission to remove the body and they got it. Hughes checked the phone, it was open. He dialled his number and the number showed up, it was a British number, yet not the one previously known for Barry Clayton. He then went into the calls' history, and there he found the number of Mrs Clayton called less than hour ago. And in the messages inbox there was nothing neither sent nor received, however there was a drafted message which seem to have been wanted to be sent to Mrs Clayton. Selway waved to Dobinson. The latter asked everybody to leave the annexe for the police crew, and then accompanied the Claytons to their house while trying her best to ease the pain of the mother.

Hughes took a seat as he read out loud the message "Am sorry mum. Sorry to have been such a bad person. I have to confess to you that I was involved with Mustapha in drug trafficking and cyber blackmailing, and that what made me very mad when you told me about his affair with my father. So, I attacked him that morning, even though my intention was not to kill him, but we wrestled our way down the hill then his head hit the rock and died instantly. I met Father O'Shea at his arrival at Rome airport, he informed me that the police found blood on Radi's body, and they are suspecting a murder. However, the stupid priest told me how he picked mistakenly the knife as he thought it was the weapon, I used to kill Radi, so he took it and hide it. I couldn't bear his stupidity, and also because he was involved with me and Radi in the criminal activities I mentioned, so I decided that he should go too. I don't know why I did that, but I did it. Please forgive me and find me a way out of this, please.

Selway, Al-Douri and Owen were stunned by these confessions, because it clarified everything that had been going. Hughes then waved the phone and boasted "You see, it's exactly the way I saw things since the beginning. I knew Radi was not that clean chap he appeared to be, and there you have it my dears".

"So, it was a trio of criminals who took each other off" Owen said. Selway didn't say a word. However, Al-Douri said "It's important that we wait to see the cause of Barry's death. Also, we need to talk immediately to his mother". He then asked Owen if they have trained dogs on drugs. The latter immediately called the office, and he said, "They are on their way".

Al-Douri said "If what Barry said is true that means they should have some place to hide the drugs, we have to search the entire Claytons' site including the gardens".

Hughes went out to check if they can talk to Mrs Clayton. Dobinson replied, "Not now" she is completely under the shock, maybe in the evening it could be possible".

He told them that the woman can't talk at the moment. Selway took a seat in the corner as he sank deep in his thoughts "Was it really that simple? Was Radi really a bad guy after all?" He looked at the police men talking to each other, yet he heard nothing of what they were saying. Because yes, he was on the case, but he lost his way in the investigation completely. "Maybe it's not for me as a profession, I do trust people easily. I am no detective. I better admit it and end it now before similar embarrassments in the future" he murmured to himself.

He was taken back to reality by the trained dogs coming inside the place, they started to sniff, then they rushed toward the cupboards at the corner of the kitchen, and they started barking loudly and crazily. One of the officers opened the space, and then the dogs started moving their paws in several directions at the floor inside the cupboard. Another officer handed his colleague a metal tool in which he pulled up the extreme side of the wooden floor, and after several attempts he uncovered several kilos of different types of drugs. Hughes who was the most enthusiastic for the discovery turned around and looked at Al-Douri and then Selway at the opposite corner, and he waved his two thumbs up shouting "Game over".

Al-Douri's mobile rang persistently so he had to answer it. He walked outside. It was the London office confirming that the owner of the telephone number called by Mrs Clayton, the day before, has been caught by the Italian police and they are waiting a signal from the United Kingdom on what to do with him. Al-Douri who was upset of how things unfolded so far was about to tell them let him go, but then he thought it was better that he consulted his team members first before giving their final say. Hughes and Selway joined him outside as Owen and his men and dogs shut the doors behind them for, they got everything recorded and ready to be reported. The detective expressed his wishes to talk to Mr Clayton while the two intelligence officers said they will return to his house where they will write their official report about the cases they have been investigating.

Selway knocked on the Claytons door, Maria opened it. She had tears in her eyes as the atmosphere inside the house was gloomy and very sad. He asked her about Mr Clayton. She said, "In his room".

"Can you please ask him if I can join him?"

"Ok. Please wait a minute".

"She walked up stairs, then few seconds later she came down and waved her hand welcoming the detective in a sign that he can walk inside the man's room. As the detective walked in the corridor, he heard Mrs Clayton crying and his secretary Ms Dobinson trying to calm her down. He closed his eyes and thought "How sad!". He knocked on Clayton's door, he didn't hear an answer, so he opened it and walked in. The man was sitting on his bed. His eyes were fully red flooded with tears.

"I am so sorry for your loss".

The man nodded in a sign of thank you, but he didn't speak.

"I know it's not the right time to say what I am going to say, but sooner or later you have to know it".

"To know what?"

"Your son was sending his mother a message in which he confessed killing Mustapha Radi accidentally, they wrestled each other, and Radi's head hit the rock. Exactly the same scenario we both imagined last night".

"So, what I am supposed to feel right now, delighted that my dead son was not deliberately a criminal".

"Sorry but this is not the full story"

The man slammed his right hand next to him on the bed, expressing his carelessness of whatever the rest of the story might be.

"According to the message found on Barry's phone, He and Radi and Father O'Shea were involved in drugs trafficking and Cyber blackmailing for money. And he had killed the priest two days ago".

A sudden surprise mixed with denial and anger appeared on the face of the Professor. "What? What on earth have you just said?"

"I am telling you what was found on a message in your son's mobile phone. He confessed killing Radi accidentally, then the priest who seemed to have expected that Radi would be targeted by Barry, saw a knife next to Radi's body so he picked it up in order to protect Barry. He didn't know that it was Radi's knife. By doing so he opened the eyes of the police that the death was not an accidental fall. Your son didn't forgive him for that, and because he was also his partner in other criminal activities, he decided that it would be better to get rid of him in a way that would look like a suicide. Maybe because he heard that the knife was found in his room, and he was afraid that he might talk to the police under pressure about the cyber blackmailing and drug trafficking. Whatever his motives were, your son - according to the message - was confessing to his mother that he killed the priest".

"I remember that morning when Mustafa's body discovered I woke up and the late Father was here talking to my wife, and they were talking about something he did, and my wife seemed relieved to have done it"

"Maybe they were talking about the knife he picked from the scene of the crime!"

"But why would Barry do evil for money, he got everything a man his age would dream of?"

"I also asked myself the question, but I saw myself his mobile phone, the message, also he had a forged Italian passport he travelled with to get unnoticed by the police on the borders, also the police had just seized dozens of kilos of heroin, cocaine and other drugs from inside the annexe you rented to Mr Radi. So, I can't really see how anyone can have any doubt about this story any longer".

"And you said Mustafa was also part in all of these criminal activities?"

"Unfortunately, yes!"

The house owner suddenly jumped out of his bed and said "This story is puzzling my mind. Well Barry was not a wise guy or even a good one and I know that. But Mustapha I don't believe he was involved it at all".

"Any way you should prepare for the funeral. It should not take the morgue more than 48 hours to give the cause of the death of your son. Even though with all what we have seen so far, it's highly likely a drug overdose".

"I want to know how his mother knew he was in the annexe. Don't tell me she has known that he was here all these days"

"I doubt so, because when Your DNA result came out and she knew that definitely Barry is going to face a trial, she tried to call him, so there must be another explanation"

"I want to know that from her" Clayton said while walking towards the door.

"But she is in a hysterical state at the moment, she won't talk".

"I want to know this right now".

The detective had no choice but joined his host as he walked downstairs and then to the living room where his wife and Mrs Dobinson were sitting on the sofa. As soon as her eyes fell on her husband, she shouted out loud "Get out of my house you selfish bastard. I don't want to see you. Go away". Dobinson tried to calm her down, while her husband for the first time since the investigation started, approached her and shook her with his both hands "I will go away, but first give me an answer I want to hear. How did you discover Barry's body? Were you hiding him there?"

"He called me from a strange number. And said mum please help me? And I asked him where are you? He replied: At the annexe". She then fiercely added "Now leave me alone. All of you, get out of my house, get out now". The woman went mad, and understandably so, she forced them all outside the house including her maid.

Chapter 35

Two days later the coroner issued his report about the cause of Barry's death. As expected, it was a complication of a dangerously overdosed mixed cocktail of drugs that nobody can sustain.

The following morning people gathered at the church cemetery for the funeral. The scene was very dramatic, and the most affected was clearly the mother, and to lesser degree her daughter and son who returned from abroad to say one last goodbye to their brother. Also at the funeral was his closest friend Stephen Sumpter who had returned the previous day from Italy after spending hard time under arrest there because Mrs Clayton left him a message for her son on his mobile phone.

After the burial, the family left back to their house. Al-Douri was speaking to the school head informing her that the Claytons and the Watts will refund the money taken from the school students. Also, authorities will help accommodate addicted people in rehab centres in the area until they recover fully from the deadly addiction to proscribed drugs.

He then joined Hughes and the others. "It's time we return to where we came from. Our job here is done, even though we didn't do big deal in our investigation really. Thank you, my friend, for your hospitality. See you in another case maybe"

"I don't think I will remain in this job as detective I am afraid. I was very incompetent" Selway said in a very low tone.

"Don't say that. It was just your first case, and this profession is not always a win. Believe me" Al-Douri advised.

Owen interfered "What have you done with the media regarding publishing the information about the case? It's our duty to inform the public in an official manner".

Al-Douri was prepared for that question "I have asked London to give the story a final script and they will announce it at the beginning of next week. Because we don't want families to get loads of hurt at one go. Let them breathe a little bit. Because if we tell parents of the pupils involved, some of them might cause some chaos for the grieving families. Better wait the situation to calm a bit down" The MI5 agent said.

"Alright"

The police and intelligence men waved goodbye at Selway and Dobinson who in their turn walked back towards their office close by.

"So, it's all over then" Dobinson said.

"Yes, I am throwing the sponge immediately" Her boss replied.

"I don't mean your career. I meant the case"

"Of course, it did. Do you still have doubts?"

"Yes"

Selway then stood still and asked his assistant "What about?"

"The dark large car down the road; who was in it?"

"It couldn't be linked to the crime at all. It also could be Barry's car"

"Hmm, but why he would have the car down there and then he comes from the upper side?"

"It could be the way he planned things as he knew he will be down the hill at the end of the task. Also, we don't know how much the priest was involved with Barry in this, so it could be also that the priest was the one who walked from the upper side while Barry came by car and then left by it".

"Possible"

"Come on, apart from the confessions of Barry, his blood did match the blood found on the Radi's sleeve, so it's over. We didn't handle it well. We have been useless. Please change the subject; I don't want to talk about it".

"That means I am losing my job".

"Yes, I will pay you an additional three months, and you go search for a new job"

"So can I return to London tonight?"

"You need to clean the office computers from everything related to the private detective business because I think I will put it for sale or rent from next month onward. So, it's better you leave for London at the beginning of next week"

That night Selway slept for the first time deeply and soundly since Radi's death. He woke up late, looked at the clock it was 10:10 am. He walked downstairs, called Ms Dobinson, she wasn't there, he then saw a bit of food in Max's plate, so he understood that she woke up, fed the dog and left to the office.

While standing there thinking of what he will have for breakfast, the postman pushed some letters through the door letterbox. Selway went into the kitchen put some eggs on the boiler, then walked towards the main door and pulled the letters. One from the council, another from BT, and the third had a stranger's name on it. "A mistake by the postman, I will hand it to him back tomorrow", Selway said that and he was about to throw the letter on the table when he noticed the address, it was the annexe of the Claytons, so it was destined to where Radi used to live, however the name on it wasn't Mustapha Radi. He tried to recall the names of the previous tenants, but no success. He went upstairs brought his laptop, turned it on at the kitchen table, prepared eggs with some melting cheese and made a sandwich with a glass of milk. He then opened the file of the tenants. He checked the names one by one. None of them matched the name on the letter. The letter was from Sainsbury's Supermarket, it seemed to be including an offer or something.

"It could be some mistake by the database of the company" he convinced himself. However, after finishing his breakfast, he decided to call Mr Clayton.

Mr Clayton mobile was shut, so he tried the landline number, and his call was received by Mrs Clayton

"Sorry to disturb you, but I have received a letter addressed to your annexe. And the name on it doesn't match any of your family members or the previous tenants".

"What is the name?"

"I will text it to you now to your mobile"

Mrs Clayton brought her mobile from her room, read the text, and replied to the detective

"Oh yes. I know him"

"Who is he?"

"He stayed less than a month at the annexe before Radi moved in".

"But you didn't mention him among previous tenants"

"Because we felt it was irrelevant because he wasn't really a tenant, he didn't pay for his stay. John decided to host him here temporarily while he was looking for a house to buy".

"Why is he a friend of his?"

"Not really. But as you know John is involved socially as member of the managerial board of the Sports club, and I guess the man was about to sign a contract with them there or something. So, it was just a temporarily stay until the man finalised the papers of buying a house"

"Is this his full name?"

"Yes, I think"

"Ok. Thank you. Have a nice day".

Selway immediately called his old friend Chief Inspector Smith who saw immediately the number of the caller, and he started the conversation directly "Hey there. What am I hearing?"

"What?"

"Al-Douri told me that you want to end your career"

"Yes. This entire investigation proved how useless I am. I couldn't judge the good from the bad really".

"It's a hard profession, or you believe yourself is going to win every case you get involved in"

"Anyway, I am not calling to argue about my future"

"Why are you calling then?"

"I have a name of a man. And I need you to gather for me information about him"

"Ok"

"I will text it to you after the call. But please let them bring any information even if it's primary, not necessarily the full history".

As he ended the call, Max barked several times. His owner understood that he wanted his morning walk. So, the detective wore his tracksuit and left his house. As he walked towards the footpath entrance, a large black car left the Claytons house and passed by, he recognised in it, Barry's friend, Stephen. The car was leaving slowly as it just regained the Bimport road, so Selway didn't know why but he waved his hand and stopped the man".

"Good morning"

"Good morning" The guy replied while appearing shaky as if he had just hidden something.

Selway showed him his card and said "I need to talk to you; can you just drive slowly to my house? It's just here around the corner"

"Alright"

The car stopped at a temporary parking at the outside corner of Selway's garden. The guy waited in the car until the detective opened the door of his house and then returned and asked him to come in. Once Stephen left his car, Selway sent his hand at where he saw his sudden guest hiding something, he then pulled his hand with some white powder in it. "That what I expected!".

Stephen didn't appreciate the movement, but he had to obey his host orders, so there inside the house he found himself sitting and being questioned.

"Your name is Stephen Sumpter?"

"Yes"

"And you are the closest friend of Barry Clayton?"

Yes"

"Is this your car?"

"Yes"

"I think Barry drives a similar one"

"Yes, same model but his is dark blue, mine is black. We bought them at the same offer"

"You travelled with Barry from here few weeks ago"

"Yes. Nothing was planned, he came to me in the morning and told me that we are flying to Italy, and everything was booked, so I just packed some clothes and we left"

"I learned from his father that you usually spent several hours together every day. So, you certainly were together the night before your sudden trip"

"Yes, we were together till late that night"

"What do you mean by late? What hour exactly and what were you doing?"

We were at a night club in Millingham, we left around 1 pm, I drove him up here and I was about to return home, when he suggested that it was still early. So, we decided to try a new set of drugs we were just given"

"By whom? You know that I know now that you are on drugs, and you know now the entire story of who was involved in the drugs ring"

Stephen moved his tongue from right to left and said "Look I want to be honest with you. I have heard from Barry's parents what he had confessed, and I am surprised about him confessing to being part of the drug trafficking"

"Why?"

"Because when it all started, we used to receive together our weekly portions from an unknown source. So how now that source became Barry himself?"

"Well maybe he joined the ring at a later stage"

"Possible"

"This is not the most important thing for me. I want to know what you did that night and at what time you left Barry".

"All what I remember is that Barry woke me up inside the car, and told me to go home"

"Wait a minute. You arrived to Bimport at around 1 am and then you stopped the car because Barry said it's still early to go to bed and you started sniffing something new you had just bought"

"Yes"

"And what happened next?"

"We were talking and after two sniffs I lost consciousness, or I fell asleep I don't know. All what I remember is that Barry shook me and even bit me to wake me up. So, I woke up and I felt scared

"Why?"

"Because Barry had blood on his clothes"

"Where did it come from?"

"I don't know, I mean I asked him, and he said he didn't know. He wanted to go home so he asked me to leave and told me to look at the time"

"What time was that?

"20 minutes - quarter to 6 am"

"And where were your car parked?"

"Exactly at the same spot where my car is outside right now but in the opposite direction"

"Here at the corner of my wall"

"Yes"

"And what happened next?

"I returned home, and I took a shower, I was about to sleep when Barry rang me and said that he is coming, and we are travelling immediately"

"Just like that?"

"I know it sounds surreal for you, but I had never refused to go with Barry anywhere, we were close friends since our first day at school all the way up to the University"

Stephen then had some tears in his eyes,

The detective brought him a glass of water. After he calmed down, Selway asked him "And what happened next?"

"He arrived by his car, and we left for London Heathrow and took the first plane to Italy, and it was leaving just immediately, it seemed to me that he picked the destination according to the timing. He was like fleeing from a ghost"

"And you didn't ask him why all of a sudden this was happening?"

"I asked him, and he just didn't want to talk about it. He handed me the staff and just said enjoy and stop asking questions".

"So, you didn't know that Radi was found dead that morning"

"No. Not until a week later, when we were about to leave Rome to Athens, Barry received a call from Father O'Shea. And then Barry confessed to me that police are suspecting him of Radi's death. So, he left me the choice to keep travelling with him or we separate there until things get clearer"

"And then"

"Maybe I shouldn't have done so but I decided to stay away from the trouble. I remembered the blood on Barry's clothes, so I thought foul even though Barry swore to me that he didn't do anything or at least he can't remember doing anything. But I was a coward and I left him alone".

"Where did you leave him exactly?"

"At a hotel in Rome, I left down to Venice where I stayed until I received a voice message from Mrs Clayton and few hours later the police arrested me and transferred me to London, then

I was released when Barry died after he confessed of his crimes".

"And did the drugs suppliers contact you while in Italy?"

"Yes, they sent an email to Barry?"

"What email?"

"bcbimport@live.co.uk it's an email account we were asked to create so they contact us wherever we are without being noticed"

"Please write to me your full address and telephone number here"

The detective handed him a paper and a pen. The guy wrote his address down. The detective said "I will not take more time from you. Thanks for answering my questions".

The detective saw him off, and he immediately dialled the number of the rehab administration and gave them the details in order to check if they still can save the young man from the poison he was feeding to his body.

He then went upstairs, took his clothes off, and took a long hot shower. There he was thinking, there is something strange in this story, yet he can't tell what it is. *Can people on drugs do something that they forget couple of hours later? Possible but not necessarily true.* Then an idea jumped up to his mind. *The car was parked just on the corner of my house, and it might have been recorded by one of my CCTV cameras.*

He finished his shower, put on his home gown, and he made himself a cup of tea as he turned on the cameras system in his small wooden room filled with screens.

His system was run on deleting automatically every 21 days. So, he smiled as he found the footage of that day still available, and if he waited another 48 hours, he would have lost it for good. After several clicks he retrieved the scenes of that stormy morning, He turned on all the cameras monitors on an interval of time from 10pm to 1 am and watched the events unfolding.

The first few minutes there were nothing other than the trees around the house going left and right, up and down in front of the cameras because of the windy storm. However, his interest was focused on the camera he had at the corner of his garden wall and the one on the top front of the house, these were the ones that could record the parking spot. Around 5 minutes after 1 am, a 4X4 black car arrived and parked at the spot. So, he knew that Stephen was telling the truth. However only a corner of the car appeared on the camera located on the top of the house, and only the car top was caught by the camera located on the garden wall. He kept watching minute by minute because if someone emerged from the car, he should be able to see them. Then at about 2 o'clock another 4X4 dark car stopped at the opposite side of the road, he could see its back, yet he couldn't see if someone emerged from it. He felt angry, and he started walking inside the room as he was staring constantly on the monitors, he wanted to see something that could shed the light on what really took place that night. Maybe his prayers were to be answered, as the storm took its toll on the pomegranate tree in the garden, and one of its branches pushed the camera which in its turn turned its lens to a more vertical position, and there was the shock as he was able to see two persons dressed in black doing something inside the parked car which was Stephen's. He couldn't see exactly what they were doing, but one of them suddenly turned his face towards the camera, and it looked familiar. Then he was able to see some kind of a bottle in his hand, and then the second person stood still as if relaxing from long time on knees. It was clear the second person was a woman, because he could see the form of her breast and long hair under the head band.

Minutes later they left the place, and he looked up to the street camera, the other car took off few seconds later, so they came by that car, done their business whatever that was and then left. He checked the time of the footage; it was 35 minutes after 3 am.

He knew what he had just seen change the complexity of the entire story, and suddenly he felt the passion about his career returning to his veins. He then dialled the number of Chief Inspector Smith and told him to join him with some well-trained officers. Smith was surprised by the demand, but he couldn't refuse.

Headsham was hardly quarter an hour drive from Exeter, Smith took three officers from the main police station there and drove off to Morobury.

Meanwhile Selway got dressed nattily, and he walked down to the hotel where he asked to meet Anne Watt. She came down and they sat at a lounge table. She said "Good you came, because I wanted to call you to tell you that I am leaving tomorrow, I called Ruth, and she will come with her friend to collect me"

"Glad that you did"

"What?"

"Glad that you called them, because you are all invited to my house tomorrow for lunch"

The woman looked surprised. She then opened her handbag pulled out a cheque and handed it to him "Thank you for all your effort. And I am really sad that my son was involved in those crimes".

"No, my lady; Please keep the cheque, I said since the beginning I am not doing it for money especially this case, and also I haven't finished my job yet"

"What do you mean? But the police closed the case. Didn't they?"

"Tomorrow please be with your sister and Mr Johnson at my house at 1 pm and you will know everything you would wish to know".

He then returned to his home, he called the Claytons and told them to come over with their housemaid. Mr Clayton told him his wife won't come. But Selway asked him to tell her that "Roger Selway will show you that your son was innocent, and he was a victim". After telling that to his wife, Clayton replied "Ok, she said she will come".

The detective then called Barry's friend Stephen, the headmaster of the church and one of his nuns. And of course, he didn't forget to call Inspector Owen, Al-Douri and Hughes. The last two tried to apologise because they were busy getting information for their coming case, but Selway threatened to never talk to them again and insisted they should be present because there will be a big surprise confirming to them the case was not over.

He called the school head Ms Geraldine Kane, and asked her to be in company with two teachers a male and a female.

He finally called his office and told Ms Dobinson to come over and help Mrs Brown to cook for the guests coming tomorrow.

Later Selway received a message from Smith that he will be with him in the next hour. The message included also the details he got about the man he asked him to investigate, the one who stayed briefly at the annexe before Radi rented it.
Max barked heavily as if he was protesting that his morning walk didn't happen really, as it was cut short by the presence of Stephen Sumpter.

"Alright, alright, we have got some half an hour, let's go"

He took the dog out and programmed his mobile on the address finder application. The address as he had imagined was there, he was standing under a two floors house situated across the street from the Catholic Church. Also there stood a dark 4x4 car in its garage.

Suddenly Max clashed with another dog passing by, Selway calmed his dog down and kept walking, did a u turn and returned home.

Few minutes after Selway's arrival to his house, Chief inspector Smith and his men arrived there too. Selway explained to them the plot from A to Z, and together they prepared the stage for the lunch of the following day.

Chapter 36

The next day at 1 pm all guests arrived at Selway's house. The detective insisted they had their lunch before he reveals the newfound facts to them. Mr Clayton protested "Do you think we can eat while our minds are thinking of what you have in store?"

Selway's excuse was" If I tell you right now the true story, you won't eat later. You will be too excited to think of staying for lunch. So, you better force yourselves and eat just now"

They gave up, and they took their seats to the tables set for the occasion. An hour later they gathered in the vast living room. And Selway started his show.

"Several people in this room had the motivation to kill Mustapha Radi and to keep things hidden from the eyes of the investigators. I start with you two Mr and Mrs Clayton. Mrs Clayton you had all the hate in the world for Mr Radi since you discovered his affair with your husband. You literally tried at first to send him away from the town by using your connections in high places to remove him and send him to a school in Newcastle, and when you failed, you tried to force your husband to never contact him again, and to be certain of that you informed your son Barry about the affair, and of course by informing him you made the latter go mad. You had also hidden from the investigators the fact that you told the priest Father O'Shea about the affair of your husband, you also warned your son abroad by a message you sent with the priest himself. So, who knows it might be you who plotted the entire affair, maybe it didn't go perfectly according to plan as both your son and the priest lost their lives. Yet maybe if Radi wasn't killed that day, you would have killed him another day.

All the guests looked at the woman who blushed off completely, and then the detective turned to her husband "And You Mr Clayton. You had that secret affair, and you went mad after you felt that it might be Radi himself who informed your wife about it. And you actually had a big argument with the guy few hours before his death, and your argument was caught by the Skype camera of the school manager. Also, you were seen at the morgue asking Radi for forgiveness. So, it could have been a moment of blind anger, and maybe with no intention of killing the man but it happened accidentally during a fight between you two.

The detective then turned toward Stephen Sumpter and said "And here comes Barry's closest friend who had seen him more than his own parents on almost a daily basis for over two decades. Stephen wanted me to believe that he lost consciousness in his car that night, and that Barry covered with blood woke him up, and then he returned home without knowing what happened to Mustapha Radi. And the two fled this country to Athens then Rome. Mr Sumpter you are a drug addict, so why would I believe you weren't involved in that drug ring too. You are as bad at university as Barry, so whatever he was capable of, you would be capable of too, if not more".

Selway then picked Ruth Watt and her boyfriend Andrew Johnson "Ms Ruth Watt and Mr Andrew Johnson; welcome to the list of our main suspects. You too were in this area during the night of Mr Radi's death; you were capable of cooperating to get rid of him"

"Nonsense! What for?" Ruth shouted

"Money, money, money. Maybe You want to be the sole inheritor of your older sister when she dies. And of course, the history of your lover Mr Johnson tells loads of how much he loves easy money and how much he needs it every day in his gambling addictive life".

Mr Johnson wanted to complain but Selway said "Shush. For now, I am going to tell you the story and how it happened from A to Z, and I will reveal to you the names of the killers, because there is a killer and a lady that assisted him.

Roger Selway took a deep breath and said the following while all eyes and ears were tuned to him:

In this mysterious case the same killer killed Mustapha Radi, Father O'Shea and Barry Clayton in order to erase any evidence that could point towards his involvement in the Drugs Trafficking and Cybersex Blackmailing which rocked North Dorset in the last year or so. In fact, the killer wanted to bury those activities in this area with the bodies of the three victims. He could have been successful, and he could have got away with his crimes if weren't to a very tiny mistake he made before he started his criminal activities here.

Everything was going fine for him until he noticed that Mustapha Radi started following his clients, so he planned to get rid of him in a way or another. He knew of Radi's sexual affair with John Clayton, so he used the keys copy he made of the Annexe keys to borrow the Passport of Mustapha Radi in order to buy a telephone card from which he sent a message to Mrs Clayton in it he revealed to her the secret of her husband. Not only that he also timed his message to reach Mrs Clayton when her husband was at Radi's place, and to pave for her the way he unlocked the door so she could enter the annexe and see for herself what was going on. By that he managed to push the Claytons to end the tenancy agreement with Mustapha Radi, but the latter insisted to remain in Morobury when he decided to relocate to another address.

And then the murderer saw Mr Radi taking the money left under the public bench by the student Tom Wright. At that moment he realised that soon the police will be talking to his victims, and he decided that his business can no longer continue as usual in North Dorset. He knew that it was time to shut down the ring of his activities in the area, and that he had to do whatever it takes in order to manipulate the authorities and convince them that the activities have ceased because those who were their perpetrators have died accidentally or got rid of each other.

How did he murder Mustapha Radi, Father O'Shea and then Barry Clayton? The killer knew everything related to Mr Radi's daily routine. Because he had access to the Annexe, he knew that Radi had a Swiss knife, he even used his scarf and his passport to manipulate the Claytons and us. So literally he became a living ghost of Radi in the days prior to his murder. And he first met Barry Clayton and Stephen Sumpter at a night club in Millingham where he heard from Barry how upset and angry, he was from his daddy's affair with Mustapha Radi. He decided to act swiftly guided by the stormy weather, he handed Barry and Stephen through his assistant a new drug which was actually a strong sleeping pill with a severe effect of three hours. Then he drove carefully with his assistant behind their cars. They saw their victims parking here outside my house at around 1 am. He waited from distance until the two guys fell asleep; he then drove forward and parked his car across the road and rushed with his assistant to Stephen's car. There the murderer used a Swiss knife to open a wound in the rib of Barry Clayton, his assistant is certainly a nurse or a doctor or have good knowledge in medicine, because she managed to get enough blood to fill half of a small bottle, then she put on the scar a strong medicine that cut blood immediately, and then did some stitches to not keep it open. However, they wanted to give Barry Clayton the impression that he had done something bad he can't remember, so they deliberately left some blood on his clothes. Then the two divided their efforts, the man took the blood bottle and walked into the footpath some half an hour before dawn which is the usual time for Radi's exercise, while the lady drove the car to the downside road in order to wait her man there after he gets the job done.

Al-Douri interrupted Selway and said "But what if Mr Radi didn't exercise that dawn? That could have put the killer's plan in jeopardy"

"Not necessarily so. The blood bottle could have been used another day" Selway replied. Al-Douri nodded approval. And then Selway continued his narration of the events.

The killer wearing a heavy jacket put the blood bottle inside one of its pockets and waited behind one of the trees at the top of the cliff at the middle section of the footpath. As soon as Radi appeared running in front of him, he left his hide and pushed him off the cliff and then jumped down behind him and hit his head at the rock. After he was certain the man is dead, he opened the bottle of Barry's blood and threw its content on the sleeve of Mr Radi. The plot was first to appear as an accidental fall and if police went smart and discovered it was a homicide, at best they could discover the blood on the sleeve and that would lead them to Barry Clayton as the murderer.

The couple then left the scene by car and followed the investigation from distance. What happened next is that Emma Kavanagh discovered the body, she went back home and called the police. During that time Barry woke up and he was shocked to see his wound, he woke his friend up and told him to go home, as he was in pain and wanted to return home because the light of the day had already erased the darkness of the night. As Barry run toward his house with blood on his clothes, he was seen by Father O'Shea. The latter felt something was wrong, and because Mrs Clayton confessed to him the previous night that she informed her son about his dad's affair and how worried she was because Barry went mad about it. The priest remembered the footpath where Radi exercised and so he decided to go check things there. Once he saw the body, he immediately rushed down towards it, his eye caught the knife. As he was in a hurry, he thought automatically it was the tool of the crime, he picked it up and then started some kind of prayer near the body as people started to gather. Then Kavanagh returned to the scene with the police, and she noticed the disappearance of the knife, and then we discovered the blood on the sleeve.

At that time, Mrs Clayton woke up at her son coming home late and she saw blood on his clothes and the scar on his body, she didn't know exactly what happened, but she assumed that he might have done something bad to Mustapha Radi. She wanted him to leave the country immediately, so she woke him up and told him to travel abroad without any delay. And he did, because he himself felt that he might have done something wrong under the influence of the drugs. Then later the Priest came and boasted to Mrs Clayton that he picked the knife from the scene in order to protect her son. The two of them remained in contact, and as the investigation evolved and investigators showed interest in the knife and the blood, she paid a trip for the priest to Rome in order to warn her son to never return because the police are not taking it as an accident but rather a homicide.

The murderer received the news about the disappearance of the knife and as he used the Catholic Church as a main site for drugs trafficking, he had already planted very advanced electronic devices inside the church so he can hack the CCTV system of the site and at the same time watch the development of our investigative activities there. Father O'Shea was one of his main acquaintances there and he seemed to have known from him that he will be travelling to Rome. The assistant of the killer travelled also to Rome with the priest on the same plane, and as soon as she found Barry's hotel, she suggested to him help with a forged Italian passport. Barry then found himself obliged to part way with his friend Stephen after he informed him that he was in trouble with police because he was a suspect in Radi's death. Stephen then left Rome to Venice and left Barry alone, an easy target for the criminals.

From there the killers told Barry that the Europol was after him and he will get caught if he keeps moving in his original identity, so they convinced him to return home under cover and prepared for him an Italian passport and booked his trip all the way to Millingham by train via Paris and London. The assistant of the killer boarded the train with him from Rome to Paris.

The murderer then met him at Paris – Gare du Nord Station and he returned with him to Millingham via London. The killer then kept him in his house which is located on a high ground and across the rood from the Catholic Church. Everything was timed to perfection with the return of the priest who seemed to have known the killer big deal because they share the same political interest. The killer knew of the knife found in O'Shea's room and watched the police activity inside the church. He knew he must get rid of Father O'Shea because he was afraid that the latter might get in touch with him and that would have put him under the spotlight. That's why he entered the Church as a Sunday worshiper and hid himself inside the building which he knew every corner of it. He prepared everything for the priest return, and he stayed behind after the Sunday mess. So, when police came in and planted everything, he had been already inside the compound which he definitely had visited and watched on a very regular basis for over a year. Of course, his eyes focused first on the police officer planted inside the church, so he decided to get rid of him. He was hiding inside the priest's room when the latter came inside with the undercover policeman. As soon as the priest withdrew to the toilet, he hit our man by a statue and almost killed him. And then later he caught the priest at the toilet door and suffocated him with a rope which he used later to stage the hanging scene to give us the impression that the priest committed suicide.

Then when the body was discovered and the church was crowded, it was very easy for him to slip away and return to his place nearby. There he prepared for his last crime, to get rid of the entire story from A to Z. He gave Barry Clayton a deadly cocktail of drugs, and then brought him into the annexe which he had his keys and he had already filled it with drugs. He of course typed the supposed drafted confession of Barry Clayton and called his mother after he played the few words, he recorded from his victim previously at his own flat. And then he left the door open for her to discover the body of her son. And we all almost fell for this evil plot.

Ladies and gentlemen let me now introduce to you the killer: Mr Pascal Marchandise, the French coach of this town's Rugby Team. His real name is Laurent Malho, he is a French army veteran but with history of racist crimes, and lately involved in money laundering for the kremlin oligarch and he heads a group of networks for drugs trafficking and cyber blackmailing.

As Selway introduced the murderer, Smith's men then brought him forward. Mrs Clayton said furiously "You! You son of a bitch! We opened our house for you".

The most shocked was her husband who was struck dumb for nearly a minute before jumping of his seat and catching Malho by the neck before the police officers took him off the murderer.

Malho was a big man with muscles like a bull. And he looked so confident. He never shied away from staring back at all those who came to Selway's house that day. He then said to Selway "I heard all what you said; however, you haven't mentioned what was the mistake I made?"

"You were sent an offer brochure from Sainsbury's Supermarket under your name at the Annexe address. And that was your undo, because the Claytons never mentioned you when we asked them about the tenants who rented the place before Mustapha Radi".
Mrs Clayton interrupted the detective "Because he didn't rent the place. John brought him to stay as long as it took him to find a place to buy" she said.
Mr Clayton continued what his wife started "I was asked by the management of the Sports Club to do so. They had just invited

him from France as their new Rugby Coach, and he was successful with them this season. That's why I was surprised when I heard from the club owners that he refused to renew his contract and he decided to relocate to Scotland as he got an offer from a club there. But now I understand the reason behind his wish to move away from this county".

Selway looked at Malho and said "So you were about to relocate your dark activities to Scotland. Eh?"

"These bloody supermarkets they never leave you alone" Malho said angrily.

"But I don't think there is a Sainsbury's here in the area. So where did you subscribe with them?" Selway wondered.

"I was still in London. There was a Sainsbury's store near the hotel, and at that time I was already given the address I will be staying at my arrival here, so it was a stupid step from me to give it to them as my address" explained Malho.

Al-Douri spoke for the first time "We had the name of Pascal Marchandise in our list of people who relocated to North Dorset recently, but as a successful Rugby coach we classified him in the category C one category below Mustapha Radi, which is the category that is highly unlikely to be involved in outlaw activities" he said.

Hughes then joined his colleague as if he was trying to ease the guilt they felt for not looking better in their list of possible suspects "When we arrived here, the suspect was at the most successful period for the Rugby club and he was very popular, and that's why we decided to put his name among the least dangerous" he explained.

Al-Douri still had a question to ask, he looked towards Selway and Smith and said, "But how did you go deep and find out his real name and his criminal record?"

"If the Claytons told us about his stay in the Annexe early in the investigation or if his name popped up in the letterbox before when it did, we would have played it down I am sure" admitted Selway. "It was all about the timing" the detective added.

Selway sipped some water from a glass on a table in front of him and continued his conference "And when it comes to did, we did dig for information about Malho aka Marchandise, I have to explain to you how I uncovered the truth".

All eyes focused again on the handsome moustached detective as he went on explaining how did manage to catch the murderer "The stormy weather when Mustapha Radi was killed had already redeemed itself an hour or so before the crime occurred".

Selway looked at those faces around him, and he saw the biggest interest shown on the face of Laurent Malho. The detective rearranged in his head the events according to their time and importance then said "It was all discovered thanks to slight information I have gathered throughout the investigation. But the turning point was when I invited Stephen Sumpter (the friend of Barry Clayton) to a questioning session in my house, and he parked his car at the public parking just at the outside right corner of my garden. Then he informed me that his car was parked just at the same spot during the night of the first crime. As I have a security system of cameras around my house, I went through the recordings of that specific night and I discovered that at the time when Barry Clayton and Stephen Sumpter were asleep in the car under the influence of drugs supplied to them by the criminals, a couple of criminals parked their car at the other side of the road, then they came to Stephen's car. My cameras weren't able to catch what was going on but thanks to the storm the wind forced a brunch of the pomegranate tree to move the camera located to my garden wall into a lower angle. And there I saw a man and a woman in black doing something to the unconscious then Barry Clayton, and then I saw the face of the man and I recognised him immediately because I saw him twice once when he was at a training session with his team around the town and I was walking with the sisters Watt, and the second time I saw him at the Club Pub when I had a drink there with John Clayton. At once I knew who he was, immediately I looked up at the website of the Rugby club and I got his name and nationality. The name was the same at the Sainsbury letter. Once I noticed that he is French, my memory jumped back to information supplied to me randomly by my secretary Ms Dobinson who at the time of the party celebrated by the "White Cross" Movement told me that one at least of the four foreign ladies who stayed at the Grosvenor Arms Hotel and attended the party was speaking French with a man late at night at the hotel, so at that I assumed this lady was the assistant of the Rugby Coach in his crime especially that I saw the four ladies when they left the hotel in the morning of the crime and one of them looked completely exhausted".

Malho shook his head in disbelief at all these strange coincidences that led the detective to the truth which he tried in every possible way to bury forever. Selway sipped some water from his glass and continued "I then called my best friend Chief Inspector Ronald Smith of the New Scotland Yard and told him what I saw and I asked him to get the photos of the four ladies and copies of their passports from the Hotel administration, and to look which one of them is the assistant of the killer. I suggested to him that she is highly likely a medic, a doctor or a nurse. I leave now the speech to Chief Inspector Smith".

All eyes then turned to Mr Smith who in his turn stood up and said "After couple of calls to my colleagues in London and the Europol, it was easy to locate the suspect as she has been using her official papers. She is called Adelina Mutu, and she has double nationality -French Romanian. Mr Selway was right, because she is a nurse, and the Europol arrested her at her workplace in a hospital in Paris. She confessed everything to ease the penalty on herself; she informed us how she met Malho and fell for him. And how he asked her to help him get Barry Clayton wounded safely by a Swiss knife to make the accident as if Mustapha and Barry clashed together and Mustapha caused the wound to his attacker, and of course to get some of Barry's blood drawn in order to manipulate the police. Also, she confessed of using her annual holiday to travel at the same flight from London to Rome with Father O'Shea in order to locate Barry Clayton there and lure him into returning to England using a fake Italian passport that was left for her inside her hotel room there. So, this is the point that we will be following with Mr Malho later because he seems to be part in a very large global criminal network that is highly likely linked directly to the extreme right movements in European countries and we assume it could be also linked indirectly to the Russian government".

Malho looked defiant "You will get zero information from me. I would rather die than allowing you more success against us" he said.

"And who do you mean by us?" Smith asked but the murderer looked away in complete arrogance.

Selway then finished the conference "We learned Malho's history after the French Intelligence services agreed to lift the veil from his record once we showed them enough evidence of his criminal activities across the channel. From now on it's the role of the MI5 and the MI6 to follow suite with him and the network he is part of. It's a very well-equipped network, they have the latest technological tools related to hacking security systems and spying, and that's why we are almost certain that a big nation is behind their activities. We found very well-advanced equipment at Malho's house which I didn't need to check with the club about its location because I immediately assumed it must be located in the surroundings of the town's Catholic Church, for he used that church for most of his drugs' deals".